A MATTER OF TRUST

A MATTER OF TRUST

A novel about faith

Margot Vesel Rising

iUniverse, Inc.
New York   Bloomington

iUniverse books may be ordered through booksellers or by contacting:

iUniverse
1663 Liberty Drive
Bloomington, IN 47403
www.iuniverse.com
1-800-Authors (1-800-288-4677)

Because of the dynamic nature of the Internet, any Web addresses or links contained in this book may have changed since publication and may no longer be valid. The views expressed in this work are solely those of the author and do not necessarily reflect the views of the publisher, and the publisher hereby disclaims any responsibility for them.

ISBN: 978-1-4401-6430-9 (sc)
ISBN: 978-1-4401-6431-6 (ebook)

Printed in the United States of America

iUniverse rev. date: 8/17/2009

CHAPTER ONE

▼

Max woke up from a deep sleep with a start, his forehead beaded with perspiration. What happened? He was out of breath. He might as well have been running up a hill. He sat up and swung his feet over the edge of the bed, trying desperately to remember what he had been dreaming. Someone had spoken to him about something, but what? Forgiveness? *What did I do that needs to be forgiven*? If only he could be sure what he dreamed. Why couldn't he remember?

As he showered, dressed and ate his breakfast, he couldn't shake the dream. If only he could remember who was talking. He was troubled, but he would never get through this day if he didn't set his curiosity aside and go about being Max Madison, proprietor of Madison's Music. *Forget the dream*! He told himself firmly. He had a business to run.

Max parked his car in the lot behind the stores and went directly to the rear door. He put his key into the lock, turned it and pushed on the door. It didn't give. His hand flew up to his head, hitting it with disgust. Of course it wouldn't open. Force of habit had taken him to that door, but he had secured the back door with an iron bar last night. There had been attempts to break into the stores from the rear, so all owners agreed to bar the rear entrances. The street in front was patrolled frequently, and being well-lit at night, the chance for a break-in from the front was minimal.

As he walked around to the front, he glanced at his image in the window. He sighed. His wife used to tease him about his clean-cut jaw. He studied his image. He had a jaw, all right. He chuckled as he unlocked the door to the music store he had owned for almost twenty years. It didn't give him as much satisfaction as it had when his wife shared the joy of its success. His wise father, God rest his soul, knew exactly what Max needed to make his life complete. Granted, a man needed to feel useful, but he also had to feel that he was put on this earth to do what only he could do in his own way. That is not to say that others didn't own music stores, but Max ran his establishment with the creative talents and a sense of fairness that had been ingrained in him since his youth. *You are unique, Max*, his dad used to say. *There is no one just like you. Be proud of it. I am very proud of you, son.*

Max realized that he was standing in the doorway, lost in the past. He missed his dad, his friendship, his understanding and compassion. He had never known a man like Fred Madison, and he knew, if he lived to be a hundred, that he would never meet a man who could measure up to him. Could it have been his dad who spoke to him in the dream? But why would he? Max no longer shared his dad's love of God, and he never would again. He was once gullible, but not anymore. In a way, that thought was painful, but he had accepted it three years ago. He was glad that his dad's faith had been so strong, and was even more grateful that nothing had happened in his life to cause him to think otherwise. Not so for Max. He no longer had that blind faith that his dad had. He shook his head to rid himself of thoughts of the past.

He turned on the lights, walked through the length of the store to the back room. He hung up his coat and returned to the front to put money into the cash register, getting it ready for the day which he did out of force of habit. He was now ready for his normal daily routine.

The bell over the front door tinkled announcing that someone was entering.

"Maxwell Madison?" asked the stocky middle-aged man approaching the counter.

Max looked up from the invoice he'd been filing. "Yes. What can I do for you?"

The man had to reach up in order to shake Max's hand. "You're the proprietor of this *fine* music store, are you?"

Max could hardly miss the way he emphasized *fine*, and nodded to the little man who seemed dwarfed next to his own six-three height. The man was dressed in a cheap, but clean, neat brown suit. His gray streaked hair was cut short, not like so many of the young representatives who wore their hair long an unruly. He judged his age to be about that of his own forty-six years.

"My name is George Collins with Masterson Davis Instruments and Accessories."

Max had never heard of the company. "What can I do for you?" he repeated, aware that the man was a salesman. *I might as well nip this in the bud before the man makes his pitch.* "As you can see," he gestured to the many instruments lining the wall behind the counter, "I am fully stocked."

"I see that, but there's always room for more when you can make a better profit."

"I don't think so." His words were slow, but deliberate. "I do very well for my customers and they and I trust the quality. Is there anything else I can do for you?"

George said amicably. "It's what *I* can do for *you*. I have a superior line of accessories, far better than anything you stock from the manufacturers of these instruments." He designated the clarinets, saxophones and other instruments in the cases behind the counter. "Not only better, but we offer a larger discount than our competitors."

Right away, Max was suspicious, but didn't let on. If they offered a larger discount, in his opinion, it was for one of two reasons. Of course there were more, but sizing up the short stocky man with not much going for him, he couldn't think of any other possibilities. They either needed the business, since it was an unknown company; or their products were not as superior as he claimed and they needed to give the stores an incentive to stock their merchandise. Unfortunately, there were always a few of his competitors who would operate their business that way. "As you can see," he pointed to the glass counter, "I'm also well stocked with accessories. Besides, I have an understanding with my suppliers." He grinned. "They tell me using other accessories is like putting a Mustang engine into a Cadillac."

George was obviously trying to keep his outrage to himself. "I would hardly say that. You know as well as I do the companies you deal with thrive on their income from accessories. Of course, they wouldn't tell *you* that. They say you *have* to use their accessories because they are the only ones that work properly." He opened his case and took out some reeds for the various woodwind instruments and strings for the guitars and violins. "Now if you'll look at these," he shoved them closer to Max, "you can't tell the difference from the ones you stock."

Max frowned. "How does that make them superior?"

"The true test is in the use, and these babies will last as long as those from the so-called *reputable* companies." He shrugged. "It happens. The important difference is that the mark-up on these gives you a bigger cut. That's what every shop owner worth his salt is interested in, isn't it?" He pointed to the cash register. "Your customers won't know the difference." He punctuated his statement with a practiced laugh. "What they don't know won't hurt them."

Max was sure that this man was here to make a sale *now* and he had no intention of allowing the merchandise in his store. "Tell you what," said Max, "leave me your accessory list and I'll check it out."

"Gosh, I-uh-haven't a single list left. Stores have been dying to order; but I have a lot of supplies in the back of the van. Let me take your order and we can do business right now. No need to pay shipping and handling. Buy it outright and you get an extra five percent discount."

That did it. "Sorry, but I don't do business that way." He turned away from the man when he heard the bell over the front door tinkle, alerting him that someone had entered. "Glad you could make it, Sheila," he told his long-time employee. "We have a lot to do and Mr. Collins was just leaving."

George argued. "But I'm telling you--"

"Thank you for your offer, but I'm not interested. I'm well stocked and my merchandise is good quality. My customers are happy and so am I. Come back when you're with a reputable company. I'll be glad to talk to you then." His dismissal was so final that George had no choice but to leave.

"Well," Sheila chuckled, "he didn't even say goodbye."

Max chuckled. "I hated to do that to him, but there were too many signs that his products were not the *superior* products that he claimed they were. If I thought otherwise, I'd have at least bought a couple items from him, but I have no use for people who cheat their customers just to make an extra buck."

Sheila patted him on the back. "You're such a softie. You could have thrown him out on his ear, but you left him some dignity. Why?"

Max shrugged. "A man can always change."

"That's why I like working for you. You don't *condemn* a man. You give him a chance to change."

"I wish they *all* would, but in the end, it's their choice." He sighed as he closed the cash register and straightened some reeds in the showcase below it. "I think it's going to be a rather slow day. I'm going to work on a few of those repairs. Cindy Thompson needs new pads on her clarinet by Wednesday."

"The concert's on Friday."

He nodded. "She'll need a couple of days to get used the new feel. I don't understand how she could let it go so long. I'm surprised she didn't squeak her way through her solo in Gershwin's *Rhapsody in Blue.*"

"The University offered her a scholarship, you know."

Max nodded. "I just wish her dad didn't think girls don't need an education. He says girls end up getting married so why spend all that money on her?"

Sheila nodded. "My dad was the same way. That's why I work for you instead of teaching. He didn't let me go to college. He never thought about what would happen if a man died and left a widow helpless with no potential for earning a decent living."

Max smiled at her sympathetically. He remembered the day he hired her. Sheila Evans had been frantic to *secure employment,* as she put it. Her husband had died of a heart attack, totally unexpected. He left her alone with three teenagers to support. He'd had no life insurance and she could claim only the house and the car for which he had purchased a Death and Disability insurance policy. He knew Sheila was nearing sixty, but her slim figure made her look younger. She was a nice looking woman with smooth skin and very few wrinkles. Her dark blond hair had no gray showing, although he wasn't sure that the color didn't have some chemical help. It was none of his business. She was a bright woman, friendly and good to his customers. She had been eager to learn all aspects of the business, and she did. Sheila was definitely an asset to his music store.

"I saw your mother the other day," she commented on her way to the back room to hang up her coat. "She said she still enjoys working."

"Yes," Max practically growled. "She won't quit. Do you know that she'll be seventy this year?" He sighed, looking a little more pleased. "Well, she won't have a choice in a few months. Judd is retiring soon and Mom will be out of a job." He shook his head. "Since Dad died, I know she's been worried that she can't make ends meet, but she'll never let on." He watched Sheila carry her coat into the back room.

"Couldn't she work here, if she needs the money?"

He laughed. "You're dreaming if you think she would accept money from me."

"Even if she had a regular job here?"

"You must know my mother by now." His expression tightened. Max was concerned about his mother. "She's a dear sweet soul, always eager to help others; yet when it comes to helping herself, she seems oblivious to her own problems and what she has to do to solve them." He didn't think that she was in denial; she just hid her concern from others, especially her son.

Max had never been as close to his mother as a daughter might have been. His dad had been his best friend, his mentor, his hero. When he died, it left a big hole where his heart used to be. As hard as his mother tried to fill that empty space, it wasn't enough. He wondered at the time if she would survive her husband's death, but she did. It was probably her determination to heal Max that helped to heal her own grief.

His parents had been very much in love, even in their later years. Although they had intellectual *discussions*, he had never heard them bicker or argue. They respected each other and they taught that respect to Max. It was a family tradition which his daughter now shared. He smiled when he thought about Samantha. She was his life. He may go through the motions of living when it comes to work and social functions, but when it came to Samantha, he couldn't have asked for a better daughter. She was loving and kind like her mother had been.

Why was it that every time he thought about something beautiful, his thoughts went directly to the tragedy that took his wife from him? Would he ever get over her death?

Sheila returned and went to the cabinet to take out the dust cloth. "Doesn't your mother have an IRA or savings of any kind?"

"Yes, but she lost a lot of the retirement money they'd saved when that young John Hanson talked her into mutual funds. You know what happened."

She grunted. "How well I know. I lost five thousand myself."

"That's tough." He knew the only money Sheila had invested was the amount she could scrape together after she had taken care of expenses; and that was only since her boys were out of college and all three were gainfully employed. "I'm glad my money was tied up in the store at the time." He took the glass cleaner and went through his daily routine of making everything in sight sparkle.

The bell over the door tinkled. "Oh no," he whispered as he saw the woman who had entered the store. He was caught and wouldn't be able to duck into the back room.

"Mrs. Tillman," Sheila smiled and greeted her in a friendly tone. "What can I do for you?"

Mrs. Tillman had far too much makeup on; that along with her over-bleached hair gave an impression that Max didn't enjoy even thinking about. Her clothes were far too young for a woman in her late forties, and so colorful one would not be able to lose her in a crowd. The thought of losing her anywhere was a pleasant one, though not realistic, knowing the woman had a purpose . . . other than music.

"Please call me Veronica." She moved closer to Max, batting her eyelashes at him. "I really came to talk about the quality of the tone on Rachel's trumpet."

Max looked concerned. "Is there something wrong with it?"

"Well, no." Her voice was what *she* probably hoped was a sexy whisper. "I just wonder if you don't have something in a more professional line."

He frowned. "Do you think Rachel is that good?"

"Not now," she answered quickly, "but children need incentive, you know."

The lines across his forehead deepened. "But giving Rachel a professional quality instrument before she's ready would put a lot of pressure on her, and that doesn't always turn out the way you want."

"Are you saying that you *won't* sell me a better instrument?"

"Not at all, but I think you should think about it seriously before jumping into an expense like that."

"How wonderful of you to be so thoughtful." Her face lit up. "Maybe we could discuss it over a cup of coffee, my treat, of course."

Oh, oh. How did he manage to get himself into hot water like this? He was a widower with no intention of getting married again or even dating. Occasionally, a woman would come on to him in a subtle way, but Veronica Tillman was extremely forward and had no shame in saying exactly what she was thinking.

"I'm sorry, but I have an instrument to repair, a rush job, so I can't spare the time." He turned toward the back of the store and started walking. "Mrs. Evans will show you the instruments." He avoided using Sheila's first name so he wouldn't encourage Veronica's familiarity with her . . . or him. "Do some serious thinking before sinking that kind of money into a new trumpet." With the wave of a hand, he ducked through the door to the storeroom. He sighed with relief as he heard Veronica sputter her objection. He closed the door behind him, leaning against it as if it would keep the image of her out. "Whew!"

He picked up the clarinet and checked the pads under each key. They were badly worn. It's a wonder the girl put up with the instrument for so long. He pulled the pads out one by one, meticulously replacing them with new ones, making sure they were seated properly. He thought the work would keep his mind off the woman out front, but nothing could take away that grating, sugar-sweet voice that she thought was tempting him. How he hated to witness women behaving in that manner!

The phone rang. "Madison's Music."

"This is Peter Benson, Jefferson High. Is Lydia's French horn ready?"

The band director had brought the horn in last week, but it was so badly dented that he had to send it to an expert from a larger company. Max hadn't intended to do any repair work when he had first bought the store, but little by little, he took on some smaller repairs. "It should come back from Haroldson's this afternoon."

Peter sounded concerned. "We're having a program over at Grace Church tonight, but I'm going to be tied up all afternoon, Max." His voice was pleading. "Lydia *needs* her horn by six tonight. The program is right after the dinner."

Max held his breath. He was sure he knew what was coming.

"Surely you're going to the dinner. Could you bring it over to the church when you come?"

Max was silent. How could he tell Peter he wouldn't step foot into a church?

"I-uh-think Sheila will be there early enough to bring it. If not, I'll get a messenger service to bring it."

If the band director noticed Max's anxiety, he didn't acknowledge it. "Just so it gets there, Max. It would break Lydia's heart if she couldn't play tonight. I really appreciate this."

"No problem, Peter." He wiped the beads of perspiration off his brow as he hung up. He still felt the panic he always felt when someone mentioned church. Church left him cold, left him empty, unlike the way he felt before Bernice was killed. He hadn't stepped foot inside a church since her tragic death. He had no wish to even deliver an instrument because someone would challenge his renouncing a religion he'd held close to his heart for so many years.

Even his mother had tried to convince him to change his mind, but he refused. God no longer listened to him, so why should he waste any time on God? He clenched his jaw until it hurt. Like it or not, they'd all have to accept it because that's the way he felt, and he wasn't about to change his mind.

If you don't count on God, you won't be disappointed when God doesn't answer your prayers. He thought he had come to terms with this, but he was still bitter whenever the subject came up. He knew he was being paranoid. He shouldn't care what Peter thinks. Peter didn't attend Grace church, so he wouldn't know if Max went regularly or not. His mother attended, and everyone knew that. As far as the members knew, they probably thought he went to a different church.

He finished inserting the last pad and put the clarinet on the workbench, wiping his hands on a towel. The adhesive would be set shortly and he could polish it and test it out before putting it in the case ready for delivery. The next step was to convince Sheila to deliver the French horn. He listened at the door before going out front, thankful that Mrs. Tillman had left.

"I suppose I should have let you know she was gone." There was humor in her voice. "I don't think I've ever seen you looking so *trapped*."

He gritted his teeth. "It wasn't fear I felt. It was pure unadulterated disgust."

"In a way, I feel sorry for her, Max. She's been so lonely since her divorce that she resorts to throwing herself at you and who knows how many other men."

"You mean I'm not the only lucky one?"

She chuckled. "Who knows? Veronica married late in life and she had Rachel when she was in her late thirties."

Max figured on his fingers. "The woman must be close to *fifty*."

She nodded. "At least that."

"Why pick on me?"

"Because you're available."

"I am *not* available," he snapped.

Sheila studied him. "Do you mean that you are *never* going marry again?"

His jaw tightened. "That's right."

"Was your marriage that unhappy?" she asked, knowing that his wife had been a beautiful and loving woman.

"You know better than that." He looked out the window into space. "Bernice was a wonderful wife."

"Then why wouldn't you try to find someone who can make you feel that life is worth living?"

"Do I give the impression that my life isn't worth living? Samantha is enough to make my life worthwhile."

"She's a wonderful daughter, Max, but you have to have more in your life than just your daughter."

"Look who's talking. As far as I know, you haven't dated since your husband died."

"No, I haven't, but that isn't by choice. Jimmy's been gone nine years. I still miss him but I'm not opposed to meeting someone with whom I can have a relationship."

"Then why don't you do something about it?" he challenged.

She shrugged. "What can a woman do? Do you want me to follow Veronica's method of finding a man?"

He laughed. "Hardly, but there must be a way for you to meet men." He settled on a stool by the counter. "Don't any of our customers meet with your approval?"

"Oh, yes." Her voice dripped with sarcasm. "I like my men younger, like the teenagers coming in for guitars, or the first-year band directors who have to be younger than my sons."

"I suppose you're right. Very few of our customers are over forty."

"Except for Veronica Tillman." She laughed. "Now tell me to look at church. Most of the single men there are divorced or widowers old enough to be my father."

"Speaking of church," he was proud of himself for working this in so smoothly, "could you take Lydia's French horn to her when you go to the church dinner? She needs it by six."

She narrowed her eyes. "Max, I know you've had a problem with God, but won't you even go to a church dinner with your mother?"

He shrugged with a scowl on his face. "She knows better than to ask me."

Her face showed concern. "Do you want to talk about it?"

"No." He avoided looking at her by dusting the instruments in the case over the counter. "You *are* going to the dinner, aren't you?"

She didn't answer right away. It would serve him right if she were busy, but he knew better. "Your mother would have my hide if I didn't."

"Then you'll do it? You can even take off early, with pay, of course."

Her eyes opened wide. "*You're* closing up tonight?"

"Sure." His eyes spoke of his sincerity. "I appreciate your willingness to help."

"Is Samantha going to the dinner?"

"No. She's still working nights this week."

"She's w*orking*? I thought she was still in college."

"She is," he answered. "She's in training at the hospital, but their work *is* the training. They're evaluated on everything they do. It's sort of hands-on training."

"Like an intern?"

"I guess." He looked at his watch. "I have a few instruments to repair before this afternoon, so I'd better get at it."

"Is your mother ever going to remarry, Max?"

He laughed. "Mom? Why on earth would she want to?"

"Isn't that obvious? Women get lonely, as you well know, and don't tell me that widowers aren't lonely."

His jaw tightened again. "My life is fine the way it is, Sheila. I'm a forty-six year old man who has learned to fend for himself. I cook my own meals and I've even sewn on a button from time to time. I don't need a woman around to make me happy."

Her eyes pierced his. "Yes, I can see how ecstatic you are," she said dryly. "Life is just great."

He stiffened, looking past her at the cases holding the instruments. "Why are you so sarcastic?"

Sheila wondered how she dared to talk to her boss this way, but she felt she had to say something. "Because you've just been existing. I see you going through life as if it's a struggle, and I know it was; but Max, there comes a time when we have to accept the past. We can't change it, but we have to deal with it."

"I've dealt with it, Sheila. I've come a long way since the--" he hesitated, "since Bernice's death."

She put her hand on his shoulder. "I know how you feel, Max."

"No," he snapped, shaking her off. "Nobody knows who hasn't experienced it."

"And I haven't experienced my husband's death?"

"He died of a heart attack. Bernice was killed senselessly by that punk."

It was still a loss. She looked at him with pity. "What gives you joy, Max?"

"Samantha," he said simply.

She nodded. "What happens when she finds a young man and gets married? What happens if she moves out of town?"

He hadn't really considered that, not that the thought hadn't crossed his mind; but he couldn't visualize it actually happening. He sighed. "I'll survive."

"God didn't intend for us to just survive." The words had slipped out before she realized what she had said. "I'm sorry. I shouldn't have said that." If only he realized that he was doing God's work every day of his life, even dealing with sleazy salesmen. He couldn't unlearn all the things he was taught. He was a decent man with an admirable code of ethics.

Max stared at her. Why did everyone think they knew better what was good for him? They couldn't possibly know what he was going through. Sure, Sheila had lost her husband after he'd had a heart attack, but that wasn't the same. Bernice was killed, senselessly and violently shot. He took a deep breath and lowered his voice. "I appreciate your concern, but let me live my life the way I need to live it." He turned his back to her. "I have work to do." With that he walked into the back room and closed the door a little louder than he had intended.

It was two o'clock when Sheila went to the back room to inform Max that his daughter was on the phone.

He picked up the extension by the workbench. "Hi, Sam," he said in a cheerful voice. "What's up?"

"I just wanted to tell you I put a casserole in the fridge for you. Just heat it up in the microwave." She was silent for a moment. "I don't suppose you were planning on going to the church supper."

"You know better than to ask me," he said dryly. "Are you off to work?"

She sighed. "Shortly. I'm sorry I'm away so many evenings on this shift, but that's the life of a nurse."

"I keep telling Sheila you're working the night shift. I guess it isn't exactly the night shift when you're home by midnight, is it?"

"I haven't had the honor of being blessed with that shift yet, but for your information, the night shift is eleven to seven. I'll start that in a few weeks."

"What ungodly hours to work. I don't think I'd like that. What ever happened to nine to five?"

She laughed. "Not many people are thoughtful enough to be sick only during the day." She chuckled. "Only a few get that shift in my line of work and we have to take turns to get it."

His voice showed his concern. "What kind of a life can you have by changing shifts at the drop of a hat? You won't know how to tell day from night. How restful can your sleep be?"

"A lot of nurses do it, Dad. That's the life we choose."

"That doesn't make it healthy. You could have been a teacher."

She laughed. "Sure. Just like you."

"Okay, so teaching wasn't for me."

"I need to help people, Dad. God gave us each a talent, and mine evidently is helping sick people. Anyway, after today I change to days."

"Good." He sighed. Did *everyone* have to talk about God? "Well, have a good day-uh-night-uh-evening." He loved the sound of her laughter. "I'll get it straight yet. Thanks for thinking of me."

"Enjoy the casserole, Dad. See you tomorrow."

He hung up the phone. No matter what she said, even if she upset him, she made him happy. She was the light that reached his soul. She was the reason he was living.

He glanced at his reflection in the window. What did Veronica see in him? He never led her on, and he was, at best, nice looking if he stretched the truth a little. He was tall. Women liked tall men; but his hair was getting gray at the temples and it seemed like his eyes were a little too blue. He'd always wished he had inherited his dad's brown eyes. There was something warm and loving about brown eyes, or maybe it was because they belonged to his dad. He shook his head and looked away.

Was there nothing he could do to make himself repulsive to Veronica and all the other unattached women? Well, nothing that he was willing to do. He refused to be what he wasn't, and as far as he knew, he was still a gentleman. His conscience told him that a gentleman didn't always behave like he had at times. He would deliberately forget Veronica's name or act like he didn't remember her. He always shoved her off on Sheila who never seemed to have any trouble handling her. If he wanted to be honest about it, Sheila really didn't have to *handle* Veronica at all because once Veronica knew he wasn't going to help her, she quickly left. Perhaps he could grow a beard. No, with his luck she would probably run her fingers through it. He shivered at the thought.

Was it only Veronica who turned him off? No. He had to be honest. Since Bernice was killed, he wanted nothing to do with any woman. Never again would he give his heart to a woman and go through the heartbreak of losing her. He wasn't man enough to try again. He wasn't exactly a coward, or was he?

Max finished repairing the last instrument just before four. He enjoyed examining the finished instruments, knowing they were as good as new. It was time to go out front and relieve Sheila so she could leave. He wondered why he felt guilty. Was it because of the dream? Why couldn't he just forget the blasted dream?

The next day, Sheila opened the store for Max. She got the cash register ready, made sure the glass was sparkling so it would meet with Max's approval and dusted the instruments.

She looked up when the bell tinkled. She was almost startled to see an older man approaching. Hadn't she and Max just talked about never having any customers his age come into the store? And he was nice looking. He was tall with almost white hair and a face that said he was friendly to everyone. A man who reminded her of her late father. When she was able to get her tongue to work, she said, "May I help you?"

His brown eyes searched hers. "Am I correct that Maxwell Madison is the proprietor of this establishment?"

"He is."

"And you are *Mrs.* Madison?"

"Oh, no, no." She blushed. More like his mother, she thought. "I'm an employee."

"Oh. I understood that Mr. and Mrs. Madison both run this store together."

She looked at him skeptically. "At one time, Mrs. Madison helped out with the books, but that was some time ago."

"She no longer helps out?"

Sheila shook her head. "Mrs. Madison is no longer living."

He was obviously shaken by the news. "What happened? Was she ill?"

Sheila wasn't sure she should volunteer the information, but then, the man could ask it of anyone in the area and find out what he wanted to know. "She was shot by a youngster robbing a convenience store."

"How dreadful," he said.

"What was it you wanted?"

Still shaken, he moved down to the next section of counter space and sat down in one of the two chairs.

Sheila watched the man's face turn pale. "I'm sorry. Did you know Mrs. Madison?"

"Many years ago. My name is Jacob Tyler. Mrs. Madison was my daughter's best friend. I saw her name and address in my daughter's address book. I could have written her, but I came to tell her that my daughter died of cancer three months ago." He seemed to be staring into space.

Sheila touched his arm gently. "I'm so sorry."

He closed his eyes for a minute. When he opened them, he looked determined to shake his distress. "I only met her once or twice, but Janice often spoke of her. I'm sorry." He stood up to leave.

"Are you all right?"

He nodded, but not too convincingly. "I just thought . . ." He sighed. "It was just a lonely old man's desire to bring something back from the past." He shook his head. "I guess it doesn't work."

"Would you like a cup of coffee? I have some made in the back."

"I don't want to be a bother."

"You're no bother at all. I often wait for an hour or two before a customer finally comes in. It would be nice to have someone to talk to."

He studied her eyes. "Are you sure?"

She nodded with a warm smile. "Very sure." Sheila didn't like the look of defeat on the man's face. It was almost as if he had exhausted every possibility to do whatever it was he had hoped to accomplish.

"Very well then, if you don't mind."

"It would be my pleasure." She went into the back to get two cups of coffee.

During the next hour, she learned that he had been at his daughter's home in Fargo for the past six months. After she died, he took care of her affairs. She had been divorced for ten years, and had never had children so there was nobody else to take care of things. He was a widower with no living relatives, so the burden fell squarely on him and him alone. "Unpleasant as it was," he said, "it had to be done before I could return to my home in Minnetonka."

Before he left, Sheila promised to go out to dinner with him. He was nice enough, but she usually didn't accept an invitation on such short notice, especially with someone she had just met. She didn't, however, have the heart to leave him alone when he'd gone through so much and was just back in town after being gone so long. She had a feeling that his coming in when he did was somehow God's plan. She had no idea why she felt that way, but the feeling was so strong that she couldn't help but accept his invitation.

Two hours later, Max came in. Sheila greeted him happily. "You missed a wonderful dinner last night and a great program."

"Oh, I don't know. I had a wonderful casserole that my daughter lovingly made for me and I listened to Handel's *Water Music Suite.*"

"Uh-huh, and you chose that particular music because of the French horn solo you were missing."

Ouch! He wanted to deny it, but he had to admit she was right. Had Lydia played anyplace but the church, Max would have been there. "Guilty as charged," he admitted.

"Anyway, Edna and I had a nice time. She's such an elegant lady, Max. You are so lucky to have such a lovely mother."

"Yes, I'm very thankful."

She was thoughtful. "I'm not so sure she wouldn't like a man in her life."

"Mom?" He laughed. "No way. She likes her life the way it is right now."

"I asked what she was going to do when Judd retires. She looked sort of lost. I wish I hadn't asked her."

Max frowned. "What do you mean? What did she say?"

Sheila was thoughtful. "It wasn't what she said; it was more what she *didn't* say."

"I see. Woman's intuition?" He didn't take much stock in that kind of insight.

"Not exactly, but don't minimize the existence of it. Intuition has saved many a disaster." She might have saved a life if her intuition was working properly when Jacob Tyler came in a while ago. She wasn't sure she should say anything to Max about him, not yet, anyway.

He laughed. "Like what?"

"Like knowing when to interfere when Veronica Tillman comes in. Of course," she said innocently, "if you don't believe in intuition, I'll just keep my thoughts to myself next time and go about my own business." She grinned. "By the way, she's coming in tomorrow to pick out some music. She wondered if you could help her since you taught music in the past."

"And you said--?" He waited, daring her to answer.

Her eyes danced with amusement. "I told her you'd be happy to help her." She laughed. When she saw the expression on his face, she added, "You know I wouldn't do that to you. I said that you wouldn't be here Saturday. She wasn't pleased, I can tell you." She chuckled. "Look on the bright side. She might come back today instead."

He groaned and started sorting his invoices from yesterday. "I was pretty busy after you left yesterday."

She looked at the pile of receipts. "I can see that."

They worked in silence until their first customer came in. Two customers later, Max announced that he was going next door for coffee.

It was as if Sheila didn't hear him. She had thoughts of her own. "Are you so sure about your mother's perfect life?"

"Absolutely. I assure you that Edna Madison is quite comfortable with her life the way it is."

CHAPTER TWO

▼

It was Friday afternoon and Edna could think of nothing but going home to her cozy apartment. It was miserably cold outside, and she wanted the workday to be over so she could go home and stay in her apartment all weekend. She was chilled to the bone, but she should be used to it. This was a typical Minnesota winter, and she had lived here most of her sixty-nine years. What could she expect? Well, for one thing, she could expect the office to be heated to a comfortable level, but there were no thermostats in the front offices. Instead, the law offices in the rear of the building were so warm that the employees threatened to wear summer clothes to work. So why was the front office where Edna worked cold enough to almost freeze her coffee when placed next to the window beside her desk? Not even the heater under her desk provided much relief. Maybe it was just her age. Didn't they say your circulation decreased as you got older? Sixty-nine wasn't *that* old, was it?

There was a knock on the door frame.

Her boss insisted that the door remain open, but some of the clients coughed or knocked to draw attention to the fact that someone was there, waiting to be invited in. Edna looked up from her desk to see a very striking, tall, white haired man standing just inside the doorway. There was something about white hair that drew her attention. She liked it. It made almost any man look distinguished. He was rubbing his hands as if to increase his circulation. Edna suppressed a smile. She was about to ask if she could do something for him when he spoke.

"I haven't seen you before." His deep voice was so rich and warm that she was suddenly unaware of the cold. "Are you new here?"

The deep baritone sound of his words sent ripples down her spine. She shook her head half dazed. "I've been here for almost three years."

"Well,"" he said with a hint of a smile on his lips, "I'm sorry that I missed seeing you for almost three years. I don't come in often, but I do make it two or three times a year. How is it that I've missed you?"

She shrugged. "I never leave for lunch, so you must have come in on a Tuesday or Thursday. I only work part time." Why did she bother to say that?

He nodded. "That's very likely." He extended his hand to her. "My name is Michael Richards."

She put her hand into his, noticing that the hand she had always thought of as way too large, was small compared to his. The man must have been well over six feet tall. *Where were you,* she thought, *when I was younger and prettier and in the market for just such a man?* "Edna Madison," she replied.

Michael had been quite taken with her and realized that he was still holding her hand. He noticed she was wearing a ring as he let her hand go. He tried not to be obvious as he looked at it closer. Was it a wedding ring? If so, he would have to stop flirting with her, even if it was fun. He hadn't had much of that in his life in the last three years. To be honest, he never was much of a flirt, not even in his younger days.

Edna was aware of his eyes looking at her hand. Was he looking at the ring her daughters had given her almost thirty years ago? Self-consciously, she put her hand on her chest just over her breast. His eyes followed the movement. She became even more self-conscious as he kept staring. "They may be small," she said shyly, "but they're real."

Suddenly the corners of his mouth twitched, his expression changed and his face flushed. She was horrified. Had he not noticed the ring after all, and now he thought she was talking about her .

. . breast size? If only the floor had opened up and swallowed her. "I–uh–the ring." She held up her hand and showed him the gold band with the rubies which couldn't have possibly been a deeper shade of red than her face. "My daughters gave it to me when they were young, and the stones are very small, I know, but they assured me that they're genuine rubies." She laughed nervously. "As far as they were concerned, you'd think they were huge diamonds, they were so proud." She knew she was babbling but her embarrassment didn't allow her to remain silent. That would be even worse.

Michael couldn't control himself any longer and burst out laughing, but apologized at the same time. "I'm sorry. I had no business staring and making you feel uncomfortable. I was, in fact, looking at your *ring*." He nodded his head toward her hand which now nervously covered her mouth. "Your daughters have good taste."

Not true, she thought, but she didn't say it. She hadn't particularly thought the ring was beautiful, but she wouldn't hurt their feelings by not wearing it. They had given it to her out of love and she cherished it for that reason. Besides, since her husband was no longer living, she decided over a year ago to take off her wedding rings. She wore them when she felt like it, or when they complemented the other jewelry she was wearing. Although other women said they wore them to keep their husbands in their hearts, it somehow felt dishonest. Her husband was dead, gone for a very long time. A ring couldn't keep him in her heart any more than the memories she held there. She could feel that she was blushing. "No, I'm sorry. I--"

"So we're both sorry. Let's forget it." He strained to hold back a snicker. It would have been funny if they'd known each other for a while before something like this happened. "And where might the famous insurance agent Arneson be?"

Edna smiled. "Has everyone heard about Judd's award?"

He looked puzzled. "What award is that?"

"The Life for Life Award that the company presented him with last month." She studied him for a moment and determined that he was genuinely bewildered. "Aren't you a friend of his?"

There was a glint in his eye. "What makes you ask?"

"Just the way you talk about him. You sound so familiar with him."

He sighed. "I should be. He's my--"

He was interrupted by a man who stood almost as tall as Michael, but had a little more weight and slightly thinning hair. Her boss's eyebrows were raised. "Judd is your what?" he asked from behind Michael.

Michael smiled as he wheeled around to give Judd a bear hug. "Judd," he said to Edna, "is my--"

"Worst enemy," Judd finished Michael's sentence with a grin as he patted him on the shoulder and backed away from him. He took off his coat and hung it in the closet. "I see you two have met."

"Just," said Michael. "Every time I meet a pretty girl, you somehow end up spoiling it." He glanced at Edna whose face had started to turn pink. He liked that. He had met too many conceited, self-centered women who were so consumed with their looks that they were convinced their beauty could mesmerize any man. "You've been keeping this lady a secret. Does Mary know about her?"

Judd laughed. "Don't be an idiot. Mary *insisted* I hire her."

"Can't say I blame her." He turned to Edna and noticed that she was still embarrassed. Her white hair contrasted the flushed face, making it look almost beet-red. He was sorry that he had put her in such a position. "Don't mind me, I like to tease this old goat once in a while."

"Look who the kettle is calling black." Judd was really a good looking man, and in no way resembled an *old goat*. He was slightly less than six feet tall and had a nice build for a man his age. He wasn't exactly handsome, but he looked wholesome, friendly and trustworthy, all traits advantageous in dealing with his insurance clients. His hair was just starting to turn gray at the temples, and his eyes sparkled with the enthusiasm of a man who enjoyed life. Judd motioned Michael to follow him into his office, which he did after glancing over at Edna, giving a slight wave of his hand. Judd seated himself behind his desk and waited for Michael to be seated. "What brings you to Minneapolis?"

With a glint in his eye, he grinned at Judd and chuckled. "I really don't know. Whatever it was, I'm glad it brought me here." He glanced at Edna through the window separating their offices and winked at her.

Edna quickly looked away. What was going on here? Not five minutes ago she was so cold she was ready to go out to the trunk of her car and get her emergency wool blanket to wrap around herself; but now, her face was so warm, it almost felt like she had a fever. She didn't even notice when one of their clients walked past her desk and into Judd's office.

"What is this?" the man asked from Judd's doorway. "Senior citizen day?"

Judd turned toward him. "Gerald, come on in." He laughed. "You could be right, but you're no spring chicken yourself."

Gerald chuckled. "I'd say I have a few years on any one of you."

Judd introduced them.

Edna had glanced at her calendar before going into Judd's office. "Gerald has an appointment at three o'clock." She watched the well-endowed stomach on the short man jiggle with laughter.

"Then we'd better hurry," said Judd appearing overly concerned. "We don't want you to be late."

Edna sighed showing her frustration, her eyes going to the ceiling and back down. "The appointment is with *you*, Judd."

"Is that so?" He tried to look completely ignorant of the fact. "Well, come in and sit down."

"Nice meeting you, Gerald. See you in a while, Judd." Michael got up and followed Edna to the outer office. After Judd had closed the door, Michael glanced back at Judd with concern in his eyes. "Does he forget appointments often?"

Edna laughed. "Obviously you don't know him as well as you'd like me to believe."

Michael laughed. "I'm kidding. Of course I know him. We're like brothers."

She looked at him skeptically. "Really." She didn't believe him.

He studied her. "To be honest, he's my brother-in-law."

She tried not to show her disappointment. *Wouldn't you know?* The first attractive and interesting man she had seen in a long time had to be married, and to Mary's sister at that. What was he doing flirting with her or with anyone for that matter? She thought about that for a moment. "But if you're married to Mary's--"

"No. I was married to Judd's sister, Carol."

"Oh." She hoped she wasn't blushing. It was beginning to make sense. Judd had a sister by that name. Carol had died of cancer a few months before Judd hired Edna. "Oh," she repeated, a little more enlightened. "I'm sorry. I didn't know."

"I've been alone for almost four years now." He liked her soft voice. She was no raving beauty, but there were few women her age who were. Her hair was fairly short and combed back away from her face in soft folds and the silver-white color made her eyes look as blue as sapphires. Her nose was a classic nose that went along with her high cheekbones. She reminded him of Loretta Young, one of his favorite movie actresses from years ago. "So you've been here three years. Do you like working for Judd?"

"Very much. He and Mary have been wonderful to me. I don't know what I would have done without them." After seeing his puzzled expression, she thought she'd better explain. "When my husband died, I was a lost soul. I had no reason to go on living." She smiled affectionately. "They gave me back the will to live."

He stared at her. He knew exactly how she'd felt. He had felt the same way when Carol died. It's a blow, one from which you don't recover for a long time. "Was his death sudden?"

She shook her head. "I knew his illness was serious, but I didn't really expect him to die. He had pneumonia and they were trying to get that under control when he had a heart attack." She sighed and shook her head. "His heart was just too weak."

"I'm sorry for your loss."

She nodded as her eyes met his. "As I am for *yours*."

"So," he said, trying to leave the heavy subject, "life goes on. So what do you say we spring you from this place and have lunch?"

She looked at her watch and chuckled. It was almost four. "I ate my soup and salad hours ago."

"Soup and salad? What kind of a lunch is that?"

"A healthy one."

"You should at least come with me and keep me company with a piece of cake."

She shook her head. She was flattered, but she couldn't leave Judd to take care of the office. He had his own work. "I don't think I'd better, but thank you for inviting me."

"You're too conscientious."

"I suppose." She put a folder on top of the filing cabinet. She'd file it later when she didn't have an audience to watch her bend over to file it in the bottom drawer.

"Then would you come to dinner with me after work?" His eyes were pleading.

To refuse him suddenly seemed cruel. There was really no reason she shouldn't. She knew what it was like to be alone, but they hadn't established that neither one of them had remarried or were dating anyone. Well, what was the difference? People didn't have to be romantically involved in order to be friends, and she could always use a friend.

"Please?"

The corners of her mouth suggested a smile. "We close at five."

He nodded, pleased with the answer. He glanced toward Judd's office. "I suppose he'll be busy for a while."

"It's hard to tell. I don't know what his appointment concerns. It could be just a quick question about his coverage in which case he'd be done in a minute, or it could take an hour or more if he's in for a life policy." She shrugged. "On the other hand, he's a good friend, so they could talk who knows how long." She couldn't keep from laughing when she heard his stomach growl. "You haven't eaten, have you?"

"Actually, there was a detour and I got lost on my way here to ask Judd to lunch, but I'm glad now that my plan never worked out."

Edna got up and went into the storeroom. She returned with a cup of steaming coffee and three cookies. "This won't spoil your appetite, will it?"

"Hardly." He accepted them graciously. "That was very thoughtful of you."

"Not at all." She kept a straight face. "We wouldn't want people to think we were having a thunderstorm the beginning of February."

His eyebrows shot up. "It was that loud, huh?"

She laughed. "Not really." He didn't seem in the least embarrassed. She liked that. She studied his handsome features, his dark brown eyes and full lips. No man his age had a right to look that good. And he was wearing glasses. At their age, who *didn't* wear them? Didn't he know he made women's hearts flutter, even at her age? She felt like a woman again and she wished she had worn something a little nicer to the office. A simple skirt and sweater outfit was nothing to brag about.

He finished the cookies and took the last sip of his coffee. "So are we on?" He waited for an answer, but she only looked up at him. "For dinner, I mean."

"I uh--"

"Ask Judd for my references. If he doesn't think I'm trustworthy," he shrugged, "we'll forget I asked you."

Edna blushed as she heard Judd's office door open. Judd ushered Gerald out. "I wouldn't worry about it, Gerald. I'll suspend the coverage, but we'll keep comp on the car." He saw Gerald's confused expression. "Trust me. It will protect the car from theft, vandalism, damaging storms, and things like that."

"Sure." He sounded indecisive. "Six months?"

"We do it all the time for people who go south for the winter. It must be for a minimum of thirty days, but for no more than six months. You'd be back by that time, wouldn't you?"

Gerald sighed, his face unusually pale. "I should hope so." He turned to Edna. "Did you have a nice Christmas?"

Edna smiled. "Very nice. And you?"

He shrugged. "Could have been better, but I'll hope for a better one next year. Have a good year."

"You too." Edna was concerned at his tone of voice and the sadness in his eyes. The last time she noticed that much misery in his eyes was after his wife died two years ago. "Take care."

Gerald turned to Michael. "Nice meeting you, Michael. Maybe we'll meet again."

Michael smiled. "That would be nice."

Gerald left Judd standing in the doorway watching him leave. When he was out of sight, he came back into the office. "Gerald has prostate cancer. His condition is pretty iffy right now. He'll be going to the Mayo hospital next week."

"Oh dear," uttered Edna. "That sounds serious."

Judd nodded. "He's thinking the worst, of course. You know how he is."

"I know how a lot of people are. The *word* scares most people more than the illness." She gasped. "Oh I'm so sorry." She looked at Judd and Michael. "I shouldn't have said that."

"It's okay," said Michael. "Some kinds of cancer can be cured, or at least made manageable."

Judd nodded. "We just happened to be far too familiar with the kind that kills." He shook his head slightly as if shaking off the memories.

Michael cleared his throat. "Judd," he said changing the subject, "I believe your assistant needs a reference from you."

Judd frowned. "A reference?"

"A character reference. I invited her to dinner, but I'm afraid she's a little skeptical. Can you put her mind at ease?"

"Can I?" He studied his brother-in-law. "I'm not sure I can." His forefinger and thumb rubbed his hairless chin. "Let's see." He was thoughtful. "When we were in college, he was pretty wild. He often stayed up all night."

Michael defended himself. "Studying."

Judd nodded. "True. Then there was the time he was seen carrying a girl out of the Student Center."

Michael blushed. "I won't even comment on that."

"Oh," Judd snapped his fingers, "that's right. He was rescuing her from a fire that started in the coffee shop. She sprained her ankle when she tried to flee the building."

Edna laughed. "That's enough."

"Then you'll go?" Michael's eyes were pleading.

"All right, but I have to be home early. My granddaughter is coming at eight."

Michael nodded. "I'll have you home in plenty of time, that is, unless you live in Duluth."

She laughed. "No. I live in an apartment two blocks from Judd and Mary's."

"Good. That will make it convenient."

She looked at the smug look on his face. Should she be angry? If so, why? All he did was show an interest in her, but did she want to get involved with a man who lived someplace other than Minneapolis? Did she want to get involved with a man at all? The excitement she felt running through her body should have told her the answer. She was flattered. She was touched. But she was also being silly. All he wanted was a friend. She could understand that.

She tried to look puzzled. "Convenient for what?"

"I'll be staying with Judd."

"Oh," she said in a teasing tone. "I didn't hear him invite you."

"I'm family, Edna. They always expect me to stay with them. Mary would drive toothpicks under his fingernails if he didn't ask me to stay."

Judd stepped forward, grinning that neither of them seemed aware he was still in the room. "He's right, you know. Mary gets very emotional when it comes to family."

Michael laughed. "Well, not *that* emotional, but she wouldn't be pleased if she knew I was in town and staying at a motel."

Judd sighed. "I take it you'll be in late."

"Didn't you hear the lady? Her granddaughter is coming at eight o'clock. If she'll allow me to stay until I've met the girl, I should see you shortly after that."

"Good. I'll tell her to get the guest room ready."

"You know very well the guest room is always ready."

Judd nodded. "That's her wishful thinking. Most of the relatives have moved out of state so we don't use it often."

"Well, this one didn't. You can tell Mary I look forward to seeing her again. How long has it been?"

Judd walked over to the computer and punched in Michael's name. After hitting a few other keys, he looked up. "September tenth. You came in with the information on your new car."

"That's right. It's been that long, huh?"

Judd nodded.

Edna was a little indignant. "Do you mean to say he's a client and I didn't even know it? I don't remember even filing a paper under that name."

Judd laughed. "I believe Michael always asks for me. His folder is in my desk drawer. According to him, I'm the only one who knows anything about insurance."

"I see," she said thoughtfully. "One of those."

"That's not true, Edna. I swear. I ask for Judd because he's my brother-in -law. Besides, he never said his assistant was so--"

Judd laughed. "That's enough. Why don't you two get out of here and quit disrupting the business day?"

"Oh, I'm sorry, Judd. I wasn't thinking." She got up and placed some more papers on top of the filing cabinet. "I'll pay attention to my work."

"Edna," he said sharply and yet with affection, "I was letting you off early." He looked at his watch. "Twenty minutes early. Can you just graciously accept the favor?"

"But I shouldn't--"

"But you *should*. Besides, if you don't, Michael will be grumpy by the time he gets home, and we'll have to put up with him for the rest of the evening."

Michael just nodded as if to say *don't knock it.*

She looked from Judd to Michael and back and sighed. "All right, but I'll be in early tomorrow to catch up on the work I'm leaving tonight."

"Give yourself some slack, Edna. Max agrees with me that you work too hard already. You don't give yourself time to enjoy life." He probably shouldn't have made that comment. He couldn't remember the last time he heard Edna laugh a genuine laugh. Oh, she had her standard smiles and laughter for the clients, but her eyes were always sad. Was it the loss of her husband so many years ago, or was it Max? He knew she was concerned about him

"You know very well that you never leave the office for lunch and it isn't because you *have* to be here. Just go. Shoo." Judd waved his fingers toward the door, motioning her to get out. "I'll see you in the morning." He turned to Michael. "And I'll see you later tonight. Treat her right, Mike, or you'll answer to me."

Michael looked up. There was no humor in Judd's expression. He wondered what that was all about. Was there a reason for Judd's concern? He nodded, acknowledging that he'd do so, and vowed to himself that he would speak with Judd later tonight. There was just enough seriousness about his expression to make Michael a little uneasy.

Edna preceded Michael out the door. She turned back to him once they were outside of the building. "Which restaurant did you have in mind?"

"I thought you'd like to suggest one."

"Me?"

"Well, you're more familiar with this area. The places I'm familiar with are on the other side of town, and if you want to be home early, I suggest we don't stray too far."

"Thank you," she said quietly. He was certainly a thoughtful man. "What kind of food do you like?"

He patted his stomach, the size of which showed that he had a good appetite. "I'm afraid I like them all, Chinese, German, Italian..."

"How about American?" She was more teasing than serious.

"Definitely. Do you have a favorite place? Expense is no problem."

She nodded. "But you may not like it."

"I'm hungry, Edna." Patting his stomach, he feigned severe suffering.

She laughed. "All right, but don't say I didn't warn you." She walked to her car and stopped. "Do you want to follow me?"

"Why don't we go together and come back to pick up the other car later. I'll drive, or you can drive. Your choice."

"Hmmm." That was different, at least for her. Most men insisted on driving, some even insisted on driving *her* car, which she did not appreciate. "I'll drive." She realized she was testing him, but she didn't know why. He'll probably stay in town a day or two and then go back to Madison. Even so, it was refreshing that he didn't insist on driving.

He opened the door for her and she got behind the wheel, a little surprised and, she realized, very pleased. When he was seated in the passenger seat, she started the car and backed out of the parking space. Even when she pulled out into traffic, he didn't move a muscle. Either he was uneasy and didn't dare let on, or he was completely at ease. She hoped it was the latter.

Max looked at the clock. It was 4:55, five minutes before he'd close the store for the day. He wanted to check to see if his mother was all right. He dialed her number, but there was no answer. She should have been home by now unless she stopped for groceries. He should pay more attention to her. If he were any kind of a son, he'd offer to get her groceries for her. At the very least, he could go shopping with her so he could carry the groceries. She was too old to have to lift heavy sacks.

His mom was one special lady. He knew that his father's death was painful for her, but she had managed to pull herself out of the heavy grieving she had done. That was partly thanks to Judd for giving her a job. It gave her something to think about besides losing the man she loved so deeply. She seemed to have adjusted to life nicely. Sheila was wrong that his mom would like to marry again.

"Is it far?" asked Michael as she drove down the highway.

She glanced over at him. "Why? Does my driving make you nervous?"

"Not at all. You're a good driver." He looked relaxed.

She tried not to sound surprised. "Then you're at ease?"

"Completely." His lips curved up ever so slightly with a smile. "I trust you with my life."

"Good." She turned off the freeway after three miles and drove a short distance before she looked around, more than a little disappointed. "The place I had in mind is gone. I wonder what happened to it. She saw a sign that intrigued her. Then she spotted a building that looked interesting so she turned onto a side street and almost immediately into a parking lot. "I have to admit," she said studying the chalet-type building in front of her, "that I didn't know this was here. It must be new since I was in this area."

He was impressed. "So you've never been here before." What a lucky coincidence; or was it part of God's plan? This would be a first for both of them. Everything about the evening felt so right.

"This wasn't my original destination but I'm curious."

The sign on the building said *Adam's Haven.* He smiled. "What better way to get to know each other? It will be a new experience for us, one we'll be sharing." He released the seat belt. "I like the idea. For better or for worse, we'll do it together."

She wouldn't admit it, but he wasn't the only one who liked the idea. She did, too. When Fred wanted to do something special, he would take her to new places, restaurants, plays and musicals. She couldn't think of a better way to enjoy an evening. Her theory was that even if she didn't like a place, it was a new experience.

"Do you want me to scout out the place first?"

"I don't think that's necessary. There are enough Minnesota cars parked here to tell us local people like it. She opened her door and stepped out of the car.

When they reached the massive double doors of the building, Michael opened the one on the right and held it for her to enter.

"Oh, my!" exclaimed Edna, gasping as she looked around at the huge dining room. It was like walking into a different world. There were heavy burgundy window treatments draped elegantly over snow-white delicate curtains that covered the floor-to-ceiling windows which almost entirely surrounded three sides of the room. The only area that wasn't draped was an archway that probably led to the kitchen. Some tables had burgundy tablecloths with white dinnerware and sparkling crystal glassware; the others had white tablecloths set with burgundy dinnerware and crystal water goblets and salt and pepper shakers. "It's beautiful," she whispered to Michael, "but I'm afraid the prices will shock us. Please let me take care of my own."

"I told you that money is no object. I've spent the last three years accumulating, not spending.'

"But--"

He put his hand on her arm. "Please. Let's just enjoy the evening."

The hostess seated them by a window overlooking a pond that was surrounded on three sides by beautiful evergreens. An area close to the building had room for several tables for outdoor dining. Of course, that was for summer weather.

The handsome waiter's nametag read *Kevin*. His tall, slim figure was impressive in the black slacks, a black vest topping the long sleeved red shirt. The young waiter was friendly and efficient. After he took their beverage order for iced tea now and coffee later, he left them to study the extensive menu.

Edna grimaced. Maybe this wasn't such a good idea. "I'll never be able to make up my mind, eat and still get home on time."

"That's right," he remembered, "your granddaughter is coming."

She looked at her watch. "Oh, there's still time, but there are so many things on this menu."

"We could ask the waiter for suggestions, but," his eyes settled on a selection, "I think I've found what I want."

"Which one?"

"Pheasant. I have such fond memories of pheasant frying on the stove when I was young. I don't believe I've had pheasant for thirty five years or more."

She looked to see which page he was on and found the selection. "Oh, that does sound good. I didn't think Minnesota was known for pheasant."

"We lived in South Dakota during those years. South Dakota was, and I believe, still is well known for pheasant. Dad used to take us hunting. When we went home with our limit, Mother would can some of them." He sighed, remembering those fond days.

"I haven't had it that often, but I remember liking it."

"I see they also have Beef Wellington." He noted.

"Oh, don't do that to me," she scolded. "How am I ever going to decide which one I want?"

"I have an idea. We could order one of each and split them."

She smiled. "What a wonderful suggestion. Are you sure you wouldn't mind?"

He laughed. "I wouldn't have suggested it if I did."

"Let's do it." She was as giddy as a child. She couldn't remember how long it had been since she felt this way. She liked it. She didn't know how it was possible, but she felt young again.

Kevin brought their iced tea. When they had finished ordering their salads and side dishes, they sat quietly, looking around.

He tipped his head toward the far end of the room. "Did you see the baby grand piano on the platform?"

She smiled. "How could I miss it? I wonder if they'll have dinner music."

"We'll ask the waiter when he comes back." As if on cue, he brought their salads.

Michael asked about the music. "I'm sorry," the waiter responded, genuinely sympathetic, "but the woman who plays was just taken to the hospital. I'm afraid there wasn't time to get another artist. It's too bad. There's a large group coming in for the first time shortly and they're counting on entertainment." He couldn't hide the fact that he was worried. "They won't be happy, and the manager isn't coming in until eight tonight."

Edna was thoughtful, and finally made a decision. She looked at Michael. "Would you mind terribly sitting alone for part of the meal? I hate to have people disappointed."

He was puzzled. "What are you saying?"

"I play the piano. I'd be happy to help out a little, working around the time that we're eating." She studied his eyes and shook her head. "Forget it. It was a dumb idea."

"I'd love to hear you play, but won't you be nervous playing in front of a crowd?"

She smiled. "It's nothing I haven't done hundreds of times."

"Then, by all means, do it." He looked up at the waiter. "What do you think? Would you like some music between courses?"

He looked a little reluctant. "Can you *really* play?" he asked, remembering how many would-be musicians claimed to be good.

She sympathized with him. "Let me audition for you before your group gets here." She walked up to the piano, opened the keyboard cover and sat down. She played the familiar stains of *Autumn Leaves*. When she finished she returned to the table. "I didn't ask what kind of music the woman plays. If it's rock, I withdraw my offer."

"You're *really* good." Kevin's broad smile attested to his comment. "Sally plays classical and show tunes and some old stuff I've never heard before."

Edna grinned as she glanced at Michael. "Old stuff is right up my alley."

"Kevin," said Michael, "if she's going to be the entertainment, do you suppose we can move to the table next to the piano?"

"Certainly, sir." Kevin carried their glasses to the table beside the piano.

"Perfect." Michael followed Kevin. At the same moment, the hostess led a group of about ten people to a long table that had been set up in the middle of the room.

"I'm on," Edna said as she stood up to go to the piano. "I'll stop to eat when the food comes and then I'll play a little more afterwards. I hope you don't mind."

"Outside of missing out on some conversation with you, I'm being entertained in a very nice way." He grinned. "It will, however, cost you another dinner. I still intend to get to know you."

Edna smiled. He was nice, intelligent, considerate, and very stubborn. She wouldn't blame him if he walked out on her before the evening was over. When she stopped to think about it, how could she be so inconsiderate accepting his dinner invitation, then playing the piano leaving him sitting by himself? She'd have to apologize. "See you shortly," she said as she left the table.

During the next fifteen minutes, she played a little Beethoven, Chopin and two show tunes. While some of the people generally kept talking during the music, she could tell the guests enjoyed her playing because they stopped talking immediately to listen. When she saw the food being served to her table, she played a quick *Love Me Tender*, and returned to the table.

Kevin explained that the chef had divided the two meals, half of each meal on each plate. It was the most wonderful pheasant she'd ever had, and the Beef Wellington was so tender, she could cut it with her fork. Everything was delicious, even the twice baked potatoes, which usually didn't thrill her. Michael was equally pleased. "You sure know how to pick a good restaurant, Edna. Thank you."

She smiled shyly. "It was purely accidental, and you know it."

She was halfway through her meal when Kevin told her that the people at the long table asked her name, wondering if they might have heard of her.

Edna laughed. "My name is Edna Madison, and I'm afraid they haven't heard of me. I taught piano in Moorhead and Fergus Falls, and I had a few students in the cities; however, I'm sure that they wouldn't have heard of me through that."

"There's one gentleman who says he knows you. He'll come and talk to you when you're back at the piano. He doesn't want to disturb your meal." Kevin poured coffee for them before returning to the kitchen.

Edna looked at the people seated at the table, but not one of them looked familiar.

"I don't see anyone I know."

"Maybe it's an admirer from the past."

She laughed. "Oh, right. An admirer."

Michael frowned and looked at her over his glasses. "I don't like the way that sounds. Don't you like to be admired?"

"Of course, but," she looked down at her own image, "there's nothing to admire."

"I beg your pardon, but I find a great deal to admire." He shooed her off with his hands. "Go play for your public. I'll be right here, listening to every beautiful note."

Max had tried to call his mother for the last two hours. Where could she be? She usually went right home from work. It wasn't like her to be so late. She could have stopped at the grocery store on the way home, but that wasn't likely when she was tired after working all day. He knew she liked to go home, eat and enjoy the evening quietly. Did she get sick? Could she have had an accident? Maybe she had a flat tire and had to get a service station to come and attend her car? Why was he so concerned about her? She had taken care of herself for almost seventy years. He was just borrowing trouble. Still, when things weren't as they should be, he always got a sick feeling in his stomach, remembering that awful night when his wife was taken from him.

CHAPTER THREE

▼

Edna closed the keyboard cover and stepped away from the piano.

"Edna Carlson." A man stood directly behind her. She turned around and looked right into the eyes of a man almost her own height. His hair was just starting to gray at the sides, and his round face showed that he eagerly awaited her recognition. "Do you remember me?"

"I'm afraid I don't. Should I know you?"

"We were both students of Mrs. Van Patterson. We played in the same contest in Wadena."

Edna couldn't hide her shock. She mentally figured how many years it had been. "Do you realize that was over fifty years ago?"

His wide smile was friendly, but also teasing. He reached out his hand. "Peter Bradford. Don't feel bad. I wasn't very memorable then or now."

She ignored his comment. "You knew my maiden name. That was a surprise."

"It was a surprise to see you."

"But how could you recognize me after all these years?"

"Not you. It was the music. You have a style all your own. Mrs. Van Patterson often talked about it."

"She did? She looked down her nose at anything but classical music. To her, nothing else existed. I'm sure she didn't approve of my playing show tunes and popular pieces. She wanted only classical, and where that was concerned, I never was able to get it a hundred percent right. I'm sure you remember how she expected perfection from all of her students."

The man shook his head. "Not true. She often talked about your uniqueness."

"Are we talking about the same Mrs. Van Patterson?"

He laughed. "One and the same."

Michael came up to her and pointed to his watch. "I hate to interrupt, but we'll have to get going if you're going to make it home before your granddaughter gets there."

"Oh, that's right. Michael, this is Peter Bradford. Peter, Michael Richards. Peter and I studied under the same teacher fifty-some years ago."

Michael nodded his head with a smile and shook Peter's hand. "So you're the one who recognized her."

"Not her. Her style of playing. She's great."

"Peter, I'm afraid I have to run. I'm expecting company shortly. It was nice seeing you."

"Yes, but--but--" he sputtered, "where can I find you? Are you in the book?"

Edna wasn't sure she wanted to give him her number. "I work for Judd Arneson, an insurance agent with an office just off West Broadway on Fifty-Seventh. You'll find me there every other day. I have to run." She felt that by telling him that, she was being friendly, yet maintaining her privacy. Later, she could decide if she didn't want him in her private life, and would never need to give him her address.

"Arneson? Great. Nice seeing you again and nice meeting you, Richards."

Michael acknowledged, held Edna's coat and rushed her out the door, waving to Kevin as they passed by him.

"But my manager wants to talk to you," he called after her.

"We'll have to make it another day. We're running short on time," said Edna.

"Don't worry, we'll be back," Michael assured him. "You've got great food and even better service." He had left a twenty dollar tip for Kevin.

"Did you already take care of the bill?"

Michael shrugged and shook his head. "You might say that *you* took care of the bill. Kevin said the manager refused to take my money. He said you saved him *big time*, as he put it."

"Oh, dear."

He took her arm and led her to the car. "Don't feel bad. He had first-time guests who are sure to come back because of you. You did them a favor, and did me one, too."

"You? How is that?"

He opened the door, helped her into the car and went around to the other side. "I get to take you out to dinner again, this time on me."

Edna just looked at him. He was persistent, that was for sure. She couldn't make up her mind if she should be amused or irritated. Actually, she sort of liked it.

She dropped him at the office where he had left his car. As he got out, Edna felt uncomfortable about the way Michael had sat alone most of the evening just listening to her play. He was certainly good natured about it, but it wasn't really a nice thing to do. She looked up at him. "Why don't you follow me home and come in for coffee?"

"Are you sure? Your granddaughter is coming."

"I thought you wanted to meet her."

He smiled. "I'd like that very much. Which way to your place?"

"I'm two blocks west of Judd's house. Follow me."

"Great." He nodded happily and got into his car.

Ten minutes later, he pulled up beside Edna's car. They met on the walk in front of the three story building. "Nice building. It looks neat and substantial."

She nodded as she put her key into the security lock. "That's why I chose this place. I really hate tornadoes and I feel quite safe here."

"They're nothing to sneeze at." He studied the walls. "Is it concrete block construction throughout the building?"

She nodded. "And," she pointed down the short flight of steps, "I live on the lower level."

He frowned. "Don't you miss daylight? It's usually so dark and dreary."

"It's not a basement apartment. It's simply the lower level."

He followed her to the door that was numbered 120.

She unlocked the door. "Come in." She reached around the door frame, turned on the light and preceded him inside.

"Nice place," he commented, admiring the hominess of the living room. There were tasteful pictures on the wall, along with brass silhouettes of flowers interspersed around the room. The entire room was done in gold and brown. Impressive.

"Let me take your coat." He put his coat in her hands. "Sit down. I'll put the coffee on."

"You don't have to bother, Edna." He looked around. "I really like this. Are there any vacancies in this building?"

Her head snapped over in his direction. "Vacancies? Don't you live in Madison?"

"Not anymore. That is, my trip to the cities wasn't for just a day or two. I sold my house and decided to move a little closer to Judd and a couple distant cousins. They're all that's left of my family."

"You never had children?"

"Two boys, but they have families of their own and," he shrugged, "their lives are still unsettled. They haven't settled on any one place to spend the rest of their lives."

"And just where do these boys live?"

"Nathan lives in Seattle right now, but he's contemplating purchasing a business in Chicago. Albert headed right for New York, and he's not sure that's where he wants to be. He's scouting out a job in Miami."

Edna nodded. "And you don't want to live in any of those places."

He smiled. "Would you?"

She shook her head. The phone rang. "That will be Samantha." She picked up the phone. "Hello." She frowned. "Samantha? Honey, are you all right? --- I'll come right away. Stay there." Her face had turned as white as the walls as she hung up the phone. "Michael, can you help me. Something is wrong with Samantha."

Without asking what, he jumped up and followed her out the door and up the steps. He looked through the security door to see a young woman with long blond hair and delicate features. She was doubled over, obviously in pain.

"Gram," she managed to say as she teetered by the door.

Edna opened the door and Michael rushed out to help the young woman down the steps, silently berating himself for not being young enough to carry her. He knew that as much as he wanted to, it would not help for him to collapse with her.

He got her inside and lowered her to the sofa.

"What is it, honey? What's the matter?"

Pain was unmistakable with the deep lines on Samantha's face. "I don't know. I was on my way over and the pain in my side was like a knife . . . her words trailed off.

Michael noticed the moisture on her face. "Did this just happen?"

"No," she looked at him curiously. "My side hurt all afternoon, but not like this. Who are you? Are you a doctor?"

Michael laughed. "No. I was a medic in the Navy, but that was many years ago. Still, I think your grandmother should call an ambulance."

"Oh, no," she managed just as another severe pain hit her.

Edna put her hand on Samantha's forehead. "I think he's right, honey. You need to be seen at the hospital."

She shook her head, her eyes pleading with Edna. "Can't you take me?"

Michael took her hand and turned it over so he could take her pulse. "I think the paramedics should have a chance to give their opinions. It could be something very simple or something a little more serious."

Samantha looked at her grandmother, but knew instantly that she wouldn't be getting out of this so easily. "I'm going to be a registered nurse in a few weeks. Shouldn't I be able to tell . . ."

Edna smiled. "Medical students are the worst patients, Samantha. Don't you remember when Cindy Thomas needed surgery?" She turned to Michael. "Cindy was a registered nurse who needed surgery and they had to chase her all over the hospital to give her a shot. She insisted she didn't need surgery."

"That was different," muttered Samantha.

Edna nodded. "Maybe, but humor an old lady. Let me call."

"Call the hospital and see if you can talk to someone in the ER. Ask them what I should dooooo." The pain seemed to be excruciating.

Edna called the hospital, told the nurse Samantha's symptoms and was told that they were sending an ambulance immediately.

"I don't like this." Samantha grabbed her side.

"This is Samantha Madison, Michael. Samantha, this is Michael Richards."

Michael took Samantha's hand in his. "I'm very pleased to meet you, Samantha, but I hope we meet under better circumstances later. Tell me just exactly where it hurts."

Samantha moved her fingers to the area, but almost screamed when her fingers touched her side.

"Ever had your appendix out?"

Samantha shook her head. "Appendicitis doesn't hurt *this* bad."

Michael looked up at Edna and winked. He didn't want to alarm anyone, but unless he was mistaken, the girl was well on her way to a ruptured appendix, and it was crucial that she get to the hospital immediately. "I wonder if we shouldn't get her into the car and take her there ourselves." He heard the sirens just then and breathed a sigh of relief. "I'll let them in."

Less than two minutes later, two men and a woman walked into the room with a gurney. One of the men was dressed in scrubs, while the other man and the young woman wore ambulance uniforms.

The man in green scrubs bent down to Samantha. "I'm Doug Daily, an intern from Center City Hospital. Tell me what happened?"

"What do you mean *what happened*?" Samantha sounded outraged. Everyone looked at each other. "I hurrrrrrt," she cried out.

The young intern nodded. "Yes, I got that idea. Specifically where does it hurt?"

"My side." He took her pulse and asked the paramedic to take her blood pressure. "How long have the pains been this severe?"

""A couple hours."

"A couple hours and you just called us *now*?" he snapped.

She looked sheepish. "I thought it would go away."

"Well, it didn't." He placed his hand on her side. "Does this hurt?"

"Owwwwww." She swatted his hand away.

He nodded and looked up at the paramedics. "Well, guys, we need to get her to the hospital, stat."

Her eyes shot up to the young doctor. "Stat? Is that intern talk for let's pretend I'm a doctor?"

"Samantha!" Edna was shocked.

The intern shook his head quietly, getting the point across that this was not unusual behavior for someone in such pain. He turned back to Samantha. "I *am* a doctor."

She didn't believe him. "Then what are you doing with the ambulance?"

"It's my last week as an intern. I'm just riding along this week. And just why is it necessary for you to know this?"

"Oh," she said defensively in spite of her pain, "I'm just supposed to go along with whatever you have to say?" She tried to shove him aside and spoke to the others, raising her chin stubbornly. "I think not. I'd like a second opinion."

The surprised female paramedic stepped forward. "B-but he's a doctor, ma'am."

"And does that make *your* opinion obsolete?"

"Well, no, but--"

"Fine." Samantha grated her teeth. She wasn't sure why she was being so uncooperative, but she couldn't seem to help herself. The man was gorgeous, if you like the tall dark and handsome type. His almost black hair and eyebrows made him look like a movie star, and no man had a right to those long eyelashes that any woman would kill for. His unreadable, obsidian eyes made him seem completely in control. He didn't even react to her insults. "Owwwww."

"Let's get her on the gurney, guys. Now!"

They nodded and lowered the gurney next to the sofa.

"Don't you have to start an IV?"

"Later. Come on, guys. Let's go."

Samantha's face drew together with pain. "Do you know what you're doing?"

"I'm *trying* to get you to the hospital if you'll cooperate," he said with clenched teeth. She was starting to get on his nerves. He had to get her to the hospital, because unless he missed his diagnosis, they'd take her right into surgery.

She was obviously scared. "Gram," she cried, "don't leave me."

"I'll meet you at the hospital, honey." She went to her granddaughter's side and patted her hand. "Don't worry."

Michael smiled at her convincingly as they started to wheel her out of the room. "I'll drive her. You'll be fine." Outwardly, he was as calm as the intern, but inwardly, he hoped that they weren't too late. She could have a tough time of it if peritonitis set in. He got his coat from the closet and reached in to get the coat Edna had worn earlier. They followed the gurney out to the ambulance.

"I'll have to call Max." Edna touched her forehead. "Do you think it's serious?"

He wasn't about to lie to her. "I think it could be. She's feverish but she doesn't seem to be burning up. The need to get her to the hospital right away." They watched as they lifted the gurney into the ambulance.

The intern turned away from his patient to put her grandmother more at ease. He didn't want to mislead her, but it would do no good for her to worry. "We'll see you at the hospital," he said. "Don't worry." Edna could see the intern sitting beside Samantha before the paramedic closed the ambulance doors.

Michael and Edna watched the red lights come on as the ambulance drove off. "He said *don't worry*? How can I *not* worry?" she asked.

Michael took her hand in his and led her to his car. "Are you all right?"

"I can't relax," she admitted.

"Of course." He nodded. "Just don't get into such a state that you end up a patient as well. That won't do her any good."

"I know." She got into the car and nervously waited for him to come around the other side.

As he drove, he had to do something to calm her down. "Tell me about Samantha, Edna. She seems like a nice girl."

She laughed hoarsely. "You can say that after she treated that young man so horribly?"

Michael laughed. "Patients get that way sometimes."

"Not Samantha. She's such a sweet girl and she's going to graduate with her degree soon. She worked very hard for that."

He covered her hand with his as he turned onto the highway on their way to the hospital. "You take care of yourself and let them take care of her, okay?"

She nodded. "I know what you're thinking."

His eyebrows raised. "You do?"

"That I'm just an overprotective grandmother."

"You're a *loving* grandmother. I can see that." He wanted to keep her talking. "Is she getting her degree in town?"

Edna nodded. "She wanted to stay close to her dad. Her mother died three years ago. She was going to quit college, but she transferred to Minneapolis instead. She had started college in Duluth, so the transfer was relatively easy."

Michael knew that if he could keep her talking, she would have less time to worry. Worry wasn't good for anyone, but at their age, it was best if it could be diffused.

"So she's going to be a registered nurse?"

"Yes. She wants to work in the ER. She loves not only helping people, but she craves the excitement that she says she can't find any other place."

Michael tried to absorb the thought. "It seems to me that the help she can give to patients is so much more crucial than nursing in general. I would think she'd want to follow up on her cases. Can she do that in the ER?"

"I don't know. I never thought of that. I wonder if *she* has."

Michael was thankful when he saw the hospital ahead. "I see they have valet parking."

"It's a service they started only recently. It's very much appreciated."

"I'm sure it is," he said as he pulled up beside the door. He got out, handed the valet his keys and waited for the stub of the parking ticket.

They entered the hospital just as Samantha was being wheeled through the door. Edna spoke with a nurse. "That's my granddaughter. Am I able to go in with her?"

The intern nodded to the nurse. "Let her come with us."

Michael was glad that Edna was able to stay with Samantha. "I'll wait out here."

"Thank you. As soon as I find out anything, I'll come out here. I'll have to call my son." Edna followed behind the gurney.

"Do you want me to call him for you?"

Edna hesitated for a moment. She shook her head. "Let's wait until we know what's wrong. I don't want to alarm him needlessly."

"I'm pretty sure it's her appendix."

"Her *appendix*?"

Michael gave her a little shove. "Go on in and find out. I'll be here."

Michael took advantage of his time alone and called Judd. He explained about Samantha and what had happened.

"Is she going to be all right?"

"I don't know, Judd. I certainly hope so. Edna's in there with her now."

"Where are you staying, brother-in-law?"

Judd knew very well where he would end up, but he'd go along with his teasing. "I'll have to get a motel, I guess." He sighed heavily for a dramatic effect. "But it will have to wait. I have no idea how long we'll be here."

Judd chuckled. "You'll stay with us, Michael."

"Thanks, Judd, but I'm afraid it could be long after your bedtime."

"You know where the spare key is, and you know where the guest room is. Let yourself in, and we'll talk in the morning."

"I wanted to talk to you about relocating."

"You want to move?"

Michael shook his head as he grinned at his brother-in-law's reaction. "Is it so bad to want to be closer to my relatives?"

"Of course not, Mike, but what brought this on?"

Michael sighed. "I don't really know. All I know is that I woke up one day last week and realized I was totally alone and I didn't like it."

Judd sympathized with him. When Carol died, she left him alone. One son had moved out to Seattle five years before, and he wasn't about to come back to Minnesota. He hated sub-zero weather and blizzards. The other son moved to New York, but was looking into a warmer climate. "I think it's a great idea. Are you looking for a house?"

"No. I'm looking for a place like Edna has. It's neat, convenient and just what I need. I don't relish the thought of mowing the lawn and shoveling snow anymore."

"I suppose you have to be careful after your heart attack."

"I don't want to tempt fate. I need exercise, but I think that's a little more extreme than the doctor was thinking. Anyway, are you sure you won't mind having me in the same town?"

"Do you need to ask me that, Mike? Mary and I would love to have you closer."

"Tell me about Edna."

There was silence at the other end. Judd wasn't certain what he should say. He was pleased that Michael took an interest in Edna. She needed someone in her life. She had been alone since her husband died, and she kept pretty well to herself. "She's a nice lady, Mike. The only thing I ask of you is that you don't hurt her. She hasn't had an easy time of it, and I'm afraid when I retire, she'll be thrown into a life she won't enjoy. She not only needs the money, but she needs to be around people. She's good with people."

"I can tell, but don't worry. I won't hurt her if I can help it."

Judd chuckled. "You are a fast worker, brother-in-law of mine, but I like that. More power to you. Go for it."

"Are you sure you don't mind about my staying with you tonight?"

"Not at all, but I hope for your sake that you won't be at the hospital all night."

"I rather doubt it. I think they'll take her into surgery for an emergency appendectomy."

"You think that's what it is?"

"I'd bet on it. I only hope they don't wait until it ruptures."

"I should hope not. There are excellent doctors at Center City Hospital. They'll figure it out unless you already told them."

"Me?" He snorted. "No way. I'm not about to stick my neck out. It was just an observation on my part."

"An educated one. Hang on, Mike." Michael could hear Judd talking to Mary, telling her about Samantha and about Michael staying with them. Then he spoke to Michael again. "Mary says the guest room is ready for you. You'd better not get a motel if you know what's good for you."

Michael laughed. "Okay. I'll take her up on that."

"Mike," Judd started cautiously, "you usually let us know ahead of time when you're coming. Why not this time?"

Michael was silent for a moment. "I don't know. I sold the house, but I didn't have a clue where I wanted to go. All I know is that I had to get away from Madison. By the time I got here, I'd decided what I wanted to do. You know, I'm always able to think more clearly when I'm behind the wheel."

"So you're saying that *Edna* wasn't responsible for your decision."

"She wasn't. Actually, when I came into the office, I wanted to feel you out, see what you thought about my moving here. Before I got a chance to bring it up, that friend of yours, Gerald, showed up. Would it have made a difference – about Edna, I mean?"

"Not really. It's just better this way. You knew what you wanted before you met her. If there's going to be a relationship there--"

"What do you mean *if*?"

"It's that bad already, huh? Be careful, my friend. Don't act hastily. Take your time and get to know her, and let her get to know you."

"Are you insinuating that my pleasing personality wouldn't please her?"

Judd laughed. "Not at all. I don't know her that well, but I firmly believe that two people have to tear down their defenses, be themselves before they can truly consider a relationship. It has to be based on honesty or it's no good."

"Gee, Judd," his voice dripped with sarcasm, "I never would have known that."

Judd laughed. "I know you *know* it, but sometimes you have to be reminded. Too many couples don't relax and show their true selves until after they're married, and then it's too late. Just think about Mary's nephew. Cal was such a phony, but Chris didn't see it. She didn't find out until a few months after the wedding that she never really knew the man she married."

"They were divorced, weren't they?"

Judd sighed. "Yes. Now Chris is single and missing Cal. They found out that they weren't compatible, but she misses him when they're apart. Funny, how you can miss someone you don't really know. It's worse yet when you miss someone you know isn't good for you."

"Hmmm." Michael's eyes followed the noise he heard in the hallway past the nurse's desk. "I'd better hang up. There's a bit of activity down the hall. I'll go see if it involves Edna."

"I hope everything goes well, Mike."

"So do I. See you later." He hung up the phone went over to the ER door to look through the glass of the door that Edna had gone through, but he saw no sign of her in the long hallway.

The intern had brought in a chair so Edna could sit in the corner of the cubicle where Samantha had been hooked up to the usual machines. A young doctor came in and examined Samantha's chart. "I'm Dr. Erickson." He extended his hand, but Samantha was too busy dealing with her pain to shake it. "When did all this start?"

She spoke harshly through gritted teeth. "I already told him," she said pointing to Doug.

He turned his attention to Doug.

Doug nodded and gave him the vital information. "She has severe pains in her abdomen, lower right. She had them for about two hours before they called for the ambulance."

"Your diagnosis?"

"Appendix," Doug replied, "ready to perforate."

"What?" screamed Samantha. "You didn't tell me that."

He shrugged. "You didn't give me a chance to ask you much of anything, let alone tell you anything."

The doctor's gaze went from Doug to Samantha and back. "Is there a problem here?" he asked with narrowed eyes. He waited for an answer. "Miss Madison?"

"No problem," she said grabbing her side with another pain. "It's just," she pouted, "that he didn't do things properly."

Although the attending physician didn't feel he had the time to delve into this matter, he felt he had to. He saw the beads of perspiration on her forehead. "Hold on just a moment." He stepped out of the cubicle and went over to the desk to call for an orderly to take her to the OR; then returned to her side. "What do you think Dr. Daily should have done?"

"A lot of things."

"And why are you so certain that he was acting improperly?" He unhooked her from the monitor and hooked her up to an auxiliary, battery operated monitor and laid it beside her on the gurney.

"It – wasn't exactly –owwww" She looked around. "What are you doing?"

"I'm sending you up to surgery, Samantha. Your appendix has to come out."

She started to get up, but Doug gently pushed her back down. "Listen to the man."

"But you think I have a burst appendix."

Doug nodded. "I said it was ready to burst. What makes you think it isn't?"

Her chin again was raised up in defiance. "I know what the symptoms are, and I don't have a fever."

"Whatever you thought you had or didn't have before," interjected Doug, "I think you'll find you have one now."

Samantha looked over at Edna who had been sitting helplessly in the corner, afraid to interfere. "Listen to them, Samantha." Her smile was warm and sympathetic. "I think a medical degree carries a little more weight than that of an RN. You're the patient this time. Let them take care of you, honey."

Doug looked up at Dr. Erickson who nodded to him. "Dr. Daily and an orderly will take you up to the OR. Please, cooperate with them. I don't want to frighten you, but it's important that we get you into surgery immediately."

"Gram?" There was fear in her eyes. She held out her hand and Doug nodded his approval to Edna.

She took her hand in hers. "I'll be in the waiting room. I'll call your dad and let him know." She kissed her cheek. "Be good, honey. It's not that bad."

"H-how do you know?"

"I was in the same situation over fifty years ago. Now go get your appendix out."

What else could she do? "I love you, Gram."

"I love you too, honey. I'll come and see you as soon as they let me."

"Does Dad know?" she asked.

Edna smiled gently. "I'll call him right now."

Samantha nodded. At least she wasn't so bad that they felt her father should be here right away, but she was still scared. She turned to Doug. "I suppose they're going to let you practice on me." Her tone was filled with pain.

"Surgery isn't my specialty, Samantha," Doug said kindly, "but I hope they'll let me observe." The orderly had come down to get her and together, he and the orderly wheeled the gurney out of the ER.

For some reason, his being there made Samantha feel better.

Before she knew it, she was transferred from the gurney to the operating table. She stared at the ceiling. She had been in an OR many times to observe various procedures, but this was different. She had occasionally given a thought to the patient, but thinking more in terms of the surgery being necessary to help the patient, possibly even saving the patient's life. Never had she thought of what the patient might be *feeling*. Suddenly she didn't feel very qualified to get her degree. How could she have been so obsessed with herself that she gave no thought to the patient's fear or mental well-being?

"There," said the nurse who finished prepping the area of the incision. Another nurse was putting a clear fluid into the IV port that they had put into her arm while she was in the ER. She explained that they would put the anesthetic into the IV.

"I know," she said weakly. She searched the room for any sight of Doug. When she saw him, she held out her other hand. "Stay with me?" she begged.

He took her hand and nodded. "It'll be over before you know it."

She tried to chuckle. "That's comforting?" She squeezed his hand. "Tell my grandmother and my Dad that I loved them very much."

He looked at her, his eyes narrow slits. "What's this? You love them now, and you'll love them when you wake up. Right now, you're going to go to sleep."

"You don't understand. It would really hurt my dad if anything happened to me. Since my mom died, I'm all he has."

Doug patted her arm. "He'll have you for a long time to come."

The anesthetist started to explain what she was doing, but Samantha didn't hear very much of the explanation as her body relaxed and she sank into a restful sleep.

CHAPTER FOUR

▼

Edna went to the waiting room where Michael sat reading a magazine. When she approached, he looked up at her worried face.

He stood up and motioned her over to an empty seat beside his. "How is she?"

"They're taking her to surgery right now for an emergency appendectomy, but you knew that." She looked at him with admiration. "I have to call Maxwell, but first I need to go to the reception desk where they'll give me a pager."

"A pager?" he asked as he got up and followed her down the hall.

She nodded. "Rather than announce the names of the family members over the loudspeaker system, you register and they give you the pager. That allows you to leave the waiting room if you want to. They can reach you anywhere in the hospital."

"That's very efficient," he said. "Now tell me, how are *you*?"

She shook her head. "I'm more than a little worried, although I have the utmost confidence in the medical staff." The receptionist was on the phone, so Edna leaned against the desk and took a deep breath to calm herself. "I can't help wondering what will happen if it already ruptured."

"I'm pretty sure it's close to that, but that doesn't mean it has already ruptured. Don't worry. They got her into the OR fast. It isn't as if it's always fatal, you know. If they catch it quickly, it just takes a little longer for them to recover." Edna registered her name and received the pager. She found the phones and dialed Max's number. "Max, it's Mom. You weren't in bed, were you?"

"Just getting ready to turn in, Mom. Where the devil have you been?"

She was surprised at his tone. "I'm at the hospital."

Max wanted to jump to his feet, but he froze. So he was right to be worried. "What's the matter? Is it your heart? Was there an accident?"

"No, Max, it's not for me. Samantha had some pain--"

"Pain?" he almost shouted. "Where? What's wrong with her?"

"Maxwell, settle down. Take a deep breath." She waited for a moment. "They have to remove her appendix."

"When did this happen?"

"Just now. Please, Maxwell, don't get upset."

"She's my little girl – uh, my daughter. How can I not be upset?" He thought about how his mother must feel and decided he had better get hold of himself. "I'm sorry. This can't be good for you, Mom."

"I'm fine. I'm with Michael Richards, Judd's brother-in-law."

Max let that fact slip by him. "Which hospital?" The cordless phone was cradled in the crook of his neck as he spoke. He was trying to put his pants on so he could leave.

"Central City Hospital. Please calm down, Maxwell. It's really a very simple surgery."

"Are you sure? There is no such thing as a simple surgery. Things can always happen. Can't there be complications?" He went on before she could answer. "Of course," he said on a sigh. "There can be complications in any surgery. I'll be there as soon as I can. Don't worry. Everything's going to be all right."

"Yes, of course. I'll see you when you get here."

Max pushed the button that disconnected the phone and flopped down on a chair and stared straight ahead. What if he lost Sam? When he noticed that his hands were shaking, he stood up resolving to get hold of himself. "Snap out of it, Madison," he said out loud. "You're not helping anyone this way." He finished dressing and returned the phone to its cradle. Who was his mother with?

What was his name? Something like Richard Michaels. That wasn't important now. He had to get to the hospital.

Edna hung up the phone and joined Michael. "He was ready for bed. He's upset, of course. I didn't know how I could tell him without upsetting him."

"Will it take him long to get here?"

"I imagine that he'll have to get dressed if he was ready for bed. I'd say about half an hour. Oh, Michael, I didn't even consider you. Please, feel free to leave. I'm so sorry to have imposed on you."

Michael took her hand in his. "You didn't impose on me. I'm glad I could be here for you."

"But you should leave. It's getting late."

"Edna," he said with a smile, "if you think that I'm going to leave before I know that Samantha is safely settled in her room, you're slightly mistaken."

She sighed and put her hand on his arm. "Thank you. I can't tell you what a comfort you've been to me, Michael."

"How do you know I'm not being selfish? After all, this allows us time to get to know each other a little better." They sat down.

She made a humphing sound. "How to get to know a frantic old lady?"

"I'll ignore that. Coffee?" he asked. "The coffee shop is open and with the pager, they'll be able to reach you there. Besides, she's going to be in surgery a while."

Edna looked at her watch. It was ten o'clock, and it would take Maxwell at least half an hour to get here. "I guess we could," she said not quite convinced that she should leave, "but I want to be back here when Maxwell gets here."

He nodded. "Of course." He held out his hand to help her up and they walked down the long hall to the main area of the hospital.

"Stop worrying, Edna. I'm sure these doctors have done appendectomies thousands of times."

"I know." She laughed with embarrassment. "My appendix ruptured over fifty years ago. They saved me, but I guess it was nip and tuck for quite a while."

"But you survived. Just think of all the strides they've made in medicine since then. The variety of new antibiotics is a miracle in itself. Back then, penicillin was the miracle drug, and the only antibiotic we were aware of when I went into the service." He put his hand on hers. "Relax. Coffee, tea or a soft drink?"

"Some herbal tea sounds nice."

Max took a deep breath. He wasn't going to borrow trouble. He'd done too much of that during his life, especially during the years since Bernice died. Life just seemed to have lost all meaning for him, except for Samantha and he couldn't think what life would be like without her. She had saved him from his dark thoughts thousands of times. She had been at college in Duluth for a while, and at that time, he knew that surviving was his only purpose in life, and that was only for Samantha's sake. How did other men go on living after they lost their wives? Most of them managed to move on. Why couldn't he?

He shook his thoughts off. They weren't doing him any good right now. If he went any farther with them, he might consider that God would take his daughter the way He took Bernice. He didn't even want to consider the possibility. He pulled himself together, put on his coat, grabbed his hat and left for the hospital.

Why did life have to get so complicated? Why couldn't life be what you made of it instead of taking unexpected sidetracks? What kind of God allowed a wonderful woman to be taken from her family? A loving woman in the prime of life should be allowed to live to a ripe old age instead of having her life snuffed out when she was barely into her role as a wife and mother. Tears slid down his cheeks as he drove. He didn't want to feel so morbid, didn't want to feel so helpless. His fist pounded the steering wheel. A man should be able to control his future and the future of his family.

He gave a thought to the God he had trusted so naively as a child. He had blindly accepted the faith his family had instilled in him. How often had he prayed for his parents, for other aging relatives, only to have them die and fade out of his life? Even then, he accepted that there was a time to live and a time to die, but Bernice-- God didn't have to take her. He didn't have to let her die. Everyone said she was in the wrong place at the wrong time. Why had God let her go to the store just then? Couldn't God have stopped the kid with the gun from even attempting to rob the place? At the very least, couldn't He have prevented the kid from killing Bernice? He frowned as a word invaded his thoughts. *Forgive.* He shook his head to shake away the thought. That wasn't what his dream referred to, was it? *Move on.* That's enough, he thought. His fist pounded the steering wheel. Nobody spoke to him. It was his conscience talking in his dream and now. He groaned. He didn't feel guilty. God was the one who should be ashamed.

Max sighed as he wiped the moisture from his cheeks. He had to stop thinking like this. It had been far too long. He had become accustomed to living without Bernice, without her cheerful face across the table from him, without his loving wife next to him in bed. He parked the car in a space near the end of the parking ramp and walked to the elevator. By the time he got there, he realized that he had accepted Bernice's death, accepted his loss. He was still bitter about her death, of course, but he was more bitter about the injustice of the circumstances. Would he remain bitter for the rest of his life?

As he approached the entrance, he admitted that he hated himself for his moods, for what he had put everyone through, even Samantha. If only her life would be spared. His mother hadn't sounded like Sam's life was in danger, but then, his mother wouldn't want to upset him when he was going to be driving to the hospital. She had always said one shouldn't drive when one is upset.

He went into the building and asked directions to the waiting room where his mother would probably be patiently sitting. On his way, he wondered if he still looked to God for help. What a strange thought. He vowed right then that he was going to do all he could to make Samantha's life more pleasant. He would do whatever was necessary to keep his dark thoughts to himself and not burden her with them. She was the light of his life, the breath of air that sustained him. It was about time he showed her how special she was to him. No more grumpy remarks, no more black moods that surely influenced his daughter's every minute.

"Maxwell." His mother's voice was gentle, but he could see the worry in her eyes. He walked over to where she sat next to a man who must be about her age. He must be that man . . . Richards?

Michaels? Something like that. He had a strange feeling but couldn't explain why. His father had been gone long enough so it shouldn't bother him if his mother was seeing a man. Anyway, he could be just a friend.

"Mother," he said as he kissed her cheek. "Have you heard anything?"

Edna shook her head. "It shouldn't be too long now. Maxwell, this is Michael Richards, Judd's brother-in-law. He was nice enough to drive me here."

Max warmly shook the hand Michael extended. "I appreciate you helping mother." He looked around. "Isn't there anyone I can ask about what's going on?"

Edna reached out and touched his arm. "Patience, Maxwell."

He shook his head in protest. "She's my daughter, Mom."

"I know."

Michael pointed down the hall at the nurse's desk. "You might ask one of the nurses, but they may not know any more than we do."

"Thanks." Max left them to talk to a nurse.

"You know they're not going to tell him anything, Michael," she whispered.

He nodded. "I know, but he has to feel like he's trying."

She smiled and nodded. "Of course." What a wise man he was. "Thank you for thinking of it."

"He's a nice looking man, Edna. I can see he's your son. He has the same blue eyes, the aristocratic nose and that special look that says *I care about my mom.*"

Edna laughed. "If you're trying to take my mind off Samantha, it won't work, but I thank you for trying."

"I was telling the truth. He's a striking looking man, and you're a beautiful woman."

"Hmmph. I've never been beautiful." The look she gave him was like saying she knew he was pulling her leg.

"Beauty," he said as he reached over and put his forefinger under her chin, "is in the eye of the beholder, and I'm convinced that you have very bad eyesight."

She was glad she didn't have to comment because Maxwell returned and sat next to her. "It shouldn't be too long."

She looked at him hopefully. "Is that what they said?"

He nodded and chuckled. "I'm sure that's what they tell all the families. Even the nurses don't always know what's happening in the OR."

"What line of work are you in, Max? May I call you Max?"

"By all means," he answered. "I own a little music store in the suburbs."

Michael looked at Edna and nodded. "Your mother's talent no doubt inspired you to choose that line of work."

Max smiled at her warmly. "It didn't hurt. She insisted I had musical talent and she cultivated it."

"So you play too?"

"Not like she does, but I get by. At least I know the instruments."

"And he can play each one of them too," she said proudly.

Michael looked at Edna. "*All* the instruments? Isn't that going a bit overboard?"

Edna laughed. "That wasn't *my* idea. He started college with the intention of becoming a band director like his father. Naturally, to do that, he had to study each instrument. He's proficient at each of them."

Michael turned to Max. "So you were a band director. That's interesting."

"Not as interesting as I originally thought. Oh, it's a great profession for some, but not for me. I found that I absolutely loved directing a band, but I wasn't so eager to teach a variety of students, some of whom had absolutely no talent."

"I see. So you bought the store."

"Dad suggested it. He even loaned me the money for the down payment." He looked down at the floor. "I'm just sorry that he didn't live to see how successful it's become."

Michael nodded, knowing well how it felt to be cheated out of the life he had planned. "We never know what's ahead of us, do we?" He noticed that Max looked sad, yet at the same time, there was anger in his eyes. He wondered why. Hadn't Edna told him that

Samantha moved back in with her dad after her mother died? It was probably best to leave that subject alone, at least for now.

"Maxwell Madison?" said a woman who approached them. "Is that you?"

Maxwell's chin stiffened. He looked at his arms and down at his legs, and dryly said, "I think so. I don't know who else it would be." He recognized the caked on make-up of the over-bleached blond wiggling her more than ample hips. "You look familiar." He didn't want her to think she was unforgettable, which she was, but not for the reason she would like to think.

"Of course, silly." She batted her false eyelashes at him. "I just saw you in the store the other day. I'm Veronica Tillman, Rachel's mother." She waited for a look of enlightenment on his face, but there was none. She was more than a bit irritated. "Rachel plays the trumpet. You spent a great deal of time helping her choose her instrument." She squelched her irritation, knowing that men didn't enjoy being the object of criticism.

"I trust she's happy with it," he said in a cool manner.

Edna couldn't believe her ears. Was that rude man her son? She looked at Michael and shrugged her shoulders, implying that she didn't have a clue why he was behaving that way.

A voice came over the intercom. "Mrs. Tillman. Please report to the fifth floor nurse's station." The message was repeated.

"I have to run. My son broke his arm and they must have the cast on. Maybe we'll see each other again." She started toward the elevator. "It was really nice seeing you."

Maxwell did no more than nod in her direction.

Edna waited until the woman was out of earshot. "Maxwell Madison," she scolded. "I can't believe you can be so rude and to a customer, no less."

Michael winked at Max. He couldn't hold back a chuckle. "Edna, before you say too much, you might consider the woman's motive."

Max nodded at Michael in gratitude. "He's right, Mom, unless you'd like to have that over-painted barracuda as a daughter-in-law. That seems to be the only thing on her mind when she comes into the store, which has been far too often lately."

She shook her head. "So you recognized her all along?" She still couldn't believe her son's rude behavior.

"Of course. She comes into the store with the flimsiest of excuses."

"Oh dear. I didn't realize." She shook her head in disbelief. "Granted she's not your type, but--"

"You're too innocent to recognize a woman like that, Mom."

"I beg your pardon," she objected, but before she could say any more, the pager she held made a sharp, yet subdued noise. As if on cue, they all jumped up and went to the reception desk. Edna gave her name and handed the woman the pager.

The woman looked at her clipboard. "Dr. Coleman will see you in the conference room shortly." She pointed to the room just down the hall. "The door is open. You can wait in there."

Maxwell anxiously rubbed one hand with the other. "Is there any news you can tell us about the surgery?"

The receptionist smiled kindly, but deliberately ignored his question. "The doctor will be in shortly."

Max took a deep breath and nodded, resigned that he would have to wait, but he didn't have to like it. "Thank you." The words came out more sarcastically then he had intended.

Michael could sympathize with him. He turned to Edna. "Do you want me to wait out here?"

"Oh, please, come in with us."

"Are you sure?" He looked at Max and noticed he nodded his approval.

"Yes." She took his hand and led him to the small conference room where Max had already taken a seat.

She sat next to him. "Maxwell, you have to relax."

"But what if--?"

"We won't borrow trouble," she said sternly. "Worrying is not helping you or your daughter and you know it."

He nodded. "I know, Mom." He sighed and stood up looking down at her before he started to pace.

"This room is too small for pacing, Maxwell. Come and sit down."

He shook his head. "I can't sit down."

Edna sighed and looked at Michael as if he could do something to persuade her son to relax and keep an open mind.

Dr. Coleman entered the room just then. He extended his hand to Edna, taking her hand in both of his. "She's doing fine right now," he said, "but since the appendix ruptured, I want to keep her here a few days. We have to make sure that there's no systemic infection."

Max wanted to shout questions, but he clamped his mouth shut.

The doctor looked from one man to the other.

"This is my son. Maxwell Madison, Samantha's father and," she gestured with a nod of her head, "Michael Richards."

They exchanged greetings.

Max frowned. "Then it wasn't just a simple appendectomy."

"You're right, not that we haven't seen a great many like your daughter. I'd say she was a very lucky young lady. Her appendix had ruptured just prior to the surgery, but we got everything. Still, she's running a fever, and I'll want to make certain she's truly rid of that before we send her home. I may be overly cautious, but I'd rather be convinced that she won't have a problem."

"Of course." Max couldn't help worrying. "When will you know?"

"I'll discharger her twenty-four hours after her fever goes down to normal."

Edna touched her son's hand. "That sounds wise, doesn't it, Max?"

"Yes, of course, but you say she'll be all right?"

"I have no reason to think she won't be." He spoke with confidence, but he glanced toward Michael who had a questioning expression. "You're into medicine?"

"I was years ago."

"You're aware, of course, that sometimes there are complications, but I don't anticipate any and I expect her recovery to be complete."

"No concern about peritonitis?"

The doctor shook his head. "I don't foresee that problem. I cleaned her out good, but remember that even then, we're able to deal with it. Years ago," he shrugged, "that wasn't the case." He added confidently, "We've come a long way."

Michael nodded, more to reassure Edna and Max. He had known the answer, but they had to hear the doctor make the statement and relieve their anxiety.

"She's in recovery now. They'll notify you when they take her to her room. I'd advise limiting your visit to five or ten minutes tonight. She'll be tired and she'll need her rest, and you will, too."

"Of course." Max shook the doctor's hand. "Thank you, doctor."

He nodded. "If you have any questions, ask one of the nurses to get hold of me."

Edna stepped forward. "Should we wait here?"

"Ask the receptionist if they've assigned a room yet. If so, you can go to the waiting room on that floor. If not, you can get the pager and wait in the coffee shop until they have the room number. It's going to be a while. It generally takes an hour or so. People seem to pass the time easier with different surroundings." He nodded and left.

They asked the receptionist about the room. Since one had not yet been assigned, she gave the pager back to them and said she would page them as soon as she knew the room number.

"Let's wait in the coffee shop."

Max shook his head. "You go ahead. I'll wait here by the desk."

Michael nodded. "Can we bring you anything, Max?"

"No thanks. I'll just wait here."

Edna smiled sadly. "You could go to the chapel."

Max's blue eyes were as cold as steel. They met hers. "Yeah, right."

Edna shrugged. She didn't want to leave him, but she didn't see how she could stay without making him feel like her *little boy*. He hated being treated like that and she couldn't blame him. Once a mother, always a mother, they say, but she had no intention of minimizing his concern for his daughter. It was natural. She only wished she could help him get through the next hour until he could see Samantha for himself.

Max didn't know what to do with himself. Maybe he should have gone to the coffee shop with them. Instead, he chose to stay near the desk, hoping the receptionist would tell him he could see his daughter.

He was getting more anxious by the minute, so he started to pace the hall, making sure that he was always within the receptionist's view. He sighed, partly from frustration, and partly from exhaustion. He shook his head and headed for the coffee shop.

"Max? Max Madison?"

He was about to join his mother when he heard the voice. He turned back to see a nurse approaching him. She must be here with news about Samantha. "Yes?"

"You don't recognize me, do you?" Her voice was soft, as soft as the beauty of her face. There was something familiar about her, but he couldn't connect a name to the face. She was taller than most women, having to look up only slightly for her eyes to meet his. He frowned. "Should I?" And yet, there was something familiar about her.

Seeing the frown on his face she thought that he was starting to remember her, but he didn't say anything. She blushed ever so slightly. "Not really. We went to college together our first two years."

"That was a lifetime ago," he said with a chuckle. "I have to admit there is something familiar about you, but my memory fails me."

"You're right. It *was* a long time ago. You went on with your music studies, didn't you?"

He nodded. "And you?"

She stretched out her hands indicating her nurse's uniform. "I went into nursing. What are you doing here this time of night?"

"My daughter had an emergency appendectomy. I'm waiting to see her."

As she nodded, her golden curls fanned her shoulders. Something about her hair was ringing a bell. His whole body stiffened. Could it be the girl, now obviously a woman, who taught him his first lesson in rejection? Of course. College. Band. Why should he feel that old hurt from so many years ago? "Peggy?" He couldn't seem to control those feelings. That was a lifetime ago. "Peggy Swenson."

Her smile rewarded him. "What brought your memory back?"

"The hair." He had never gotten the chance to run his fingers through those golden strands. "It's shorter than it was back then, but I remember sitting behind you in band, fascinated by those long, golden curls bobbing up and down as you played the clarinet."

She laughed. "So how has life treated you?"

His expression turned dark for a fleeting moment, but he managed to derail the unpleasant memories. "There have been . . . unexpected tragedies, but," he shrugged, "life goes on."

He noticed a flicker of sadness in her eyes. "So it does."

He studied her for a moment. "It sounds like we've both had a kick in the teeth."

She took a deep breath. "That's what it feels like, doesn't it?"

"Are you on duty?"

"I'm on break for the next," she looked at her watch, "fourteen minutes."

"Want something to drink?"

She peeked into the coffee shop. "I'd like that."

He put his hand on her back as they walked down the hall and into the coffee shop. "Coffee?"

"Yes, please. I'll get a booth over there."

He returned with the coffee and after setting the cups on the table, he sat across from her. "So tell me. Are you married? Do you have a family?"

"I was married," she answered curtly, "but my husband ran off with his partner in his dental office."

"I'm sorry."

"Don't be. It was good it happened before we had children." She couldn't hide her sadness. "How about you? You have a daughter, so you're obviously married," she blushed, "or not, in this day and age. Single parents are nothing unusual nowadays."

He nodded. "I was married," he said on a sigh. "We had a daughter and life was great. After two years, I decided I didn't like teaching, so I opened my own music store. Everything was going fine until my wife--" he took a deep breath, "until my wife was killed . . . three years ago."

She put her hand on his. "I'm so sorry. A car accident?"

His whole body stiffened. Why did they always ask? "She was shot."

Peggy's hand flew up to her mouth as she gasped. "Oh, Max. How awful."

He shrugged. "She just went to the store." He frowned, remembering that unbelievable night. "He was just a kid with a gun, wanting money that he didn't have to earn." He shook his head. "I'm sorry. I still have difficulty accepting the circumstances."

"I understand. It must be hard to get past that, but you said life goes on. Did you find someone else?"

"A woman? No. I haven't looked for anyone, and no woman has just walked into my life." Until now, he thought. Life was strange. He'd had a crush on Peggy in college. In fact, he had asked her on a date once, a date that never happened. "Didn't we date at one time?" It wasn't as if he didn't remember.

She blushed. "You asked me to the Spring Party, but I got the flu."

"That was it." He was quiet for a moment, frowning because she sounded so sincere. Could it be true? "You *really* had the flu?" He didn't believe her at the time.

"Yes." She blinked with confusion. Did he not remember? "Why do you ask?"

"I–I thought you didn't want to go out with me, that you'd changed your mind, and it was just an excuse to save my feelings."

Her expression was one of shock. "Is that why you never asked me out again?"

He studied her, puzzled. "You really *did* have the flu?"

She nodded. She wasn't sure if she should be irritated or amused.

"Oh, Peggy, I'm sorry." He shook his head back and forth miserably. "It really hurt when you cancelled out. When the guys teased me, I told them I was mad and that I wouldn't touch you with a ten foot pole; but it was hurt, not anger. I refused to put myself into a situation like that again. I wasn't going to give you another chance to let me know I wasn't good enough for you."

"Not good enough for me?" She glared at him, overcome with disbelief. "Is *that* what you thought? Oh, Max, how wrong you were."

He shrugged. "Well, it didn't matter anyway. You left college at the end of the semester."

She looked down and nodded. "I– uh, I couldn't stay there. I transferred to Duluth. I couldn't see you in band everyday, knowing that you didn't return my feelings."

"Excuse me, Maxwell." His mother stood by the booth expectantly. "Is there news about Samantha?" She smiled at Peggy.

"I haven't had any word." Max nodded at Peggy. "Mom, this is Peggy Swenson. Peg, this is my mother."

"Yes. I'd know her anywhere." She smiled courteously. "How are you, Mrs. Madison?"

Edna studied the nurse. "You know me?"

"Max and I went to college together. I saw you at every band concert. I don't think you missed one."

Edna smiled. "We certainly tried not to. So you became a nurse."

Her smile was proud. "Yes."

"And I take it you like nursing."

Peg smiled warmly. "I wouldn't want to do anything else."

"That's nice." She looked back to where Michael was sitting waiting for her. "I'm sorry I interrupted, but I thought you had news for us. I'll get back to my table and let you two to talk. It was nice seeing you."

"Nice seeing you, too." Peggy checked her watch and started to get up. "I'm out of time. I have to get back to the floor."

Max stood up. "Will I see you around?"

"I hope so." She started to walk off.

"Wait." Max went after her. "What is your last name now?"

"Swenson. I took my maiden name back when Jack left me."

"How can I reach you?"

Peggy smiled. "I'm in the book, under Margaret Swenson. She started to walk away and turned back. "By the way, I only work nights one week out of each month. This is my last night shift."

He smiled and nodded. "Thanks, Peggy. Can I call you?"

"Sure, unless I get the flu." She winked at him and left.

He smiled as he watched her shapely figure leave the coffee shop. He scratched his head and broke out in a hearty laugh. Suddenly aware of where he was, he glanced back and saw that knowing grin only a mother could pull off.

She nodded. "Would you like to sit with us, dear?"

His eyes were still on Peggy. How could he have forgotten her? He knew why, of course. He had deliberately blocked her out of his mind. It took months before he wasn't thinking of her day and night. It was a year before he met Bernice and transferred his affection to her. By the time they were engaged, Max thought he had it made.

He remembered back to those college days. Peggy was the most beautiful girl in college. At least, he thought so, and she hadn't changed all that much. She still had that cute little nose, almost turned up, but not quite. And her blue eyes sparkled when she talked, except when she talked about her husband leaving her. That would be almost harder than accepting the death of a spouse. At least he knew that Bernice loved him and didn't leave him willingly. Poor Peggy. He had been sure he was in love with her before he even asked her for a date. It wasn't only her beauty, it was her bubbly personality. She always looked on the bright side of things. She never complained, not even when the band director asked her to play second chair clarinet, when she was clearly better than the others. He would have to make it a point to see her again.

"Maxwell?"

His mother's voice brought him back to the present. "What?"

Edna narrowed her eyes at his curt answer.

Max forced himself to move his eyes away from where Peggy had been.

"I asked," she said trying not to chuckle, "if you wanted to sit with us until Samantha is in her room."

"Uh, no thanks. I think I'll go back up to the desk."

Edna watched as he left the coffee shop. She turned back to Michael and sat down. "I think my son has finally turned a corner in his life." When he looked puzzled, she explained about Bernice's death and how it had affected Max.

"What a tragedy," he said.

"Yes, it was so senseless."

"And what happened to the youngster who shot her?"

"He'll spend the next twenty years behind bars."

Michael shook his head. "I will never understand how a man can kill another human and get out of prison after a few years to live out the rest of his life. There's no justice in that."

She put her head down and closed her eyes momentarily. "I know."

Michael could see that she hadn't gotten past that part of her life. "Does one ever get over something like that? I mean, I had a hard time getting over Carol's death. I've accepted it, and I think I've moved on, but part of me will always miss her."

"I know what you mean. I miss Fred, but life is for the living. We can't dwell on the past."

"Are we as sensible as we sound?"

"I'd like to think we are. Simply paying lip service to a belief isn't enough. We have to make an honest effort to get past tragedies because nobody can predict or prevent them." Wasn't that strange? She had spent the past few years merely existing, and suddenly, she knew she was living, experiencing and enjoying life. "If we give up on our own lives, we've done our Creator a huge disservice."

"You are one wise woman, Edna Madison."

If Michael only knew how he had opened a door for her. One thing remained the same. Her son hadn't enjoyed the same revelation; at least he hadn't in the past. If only the nurse Max had just met could have some influence on his life. It was interesting that they knew each other long ago. She didn't like to borrow trouble, but she also didn't want to count on what they call a *long shot*. She sighed. "I haven't known how to help Maxwell. I'm sure he still has nightmares about the shooting, about seeing her in a pool of blood. That's a little different than what we went through losing our mates."

Michael's eyed opened wide. "He actually *saw* her?"

"When the police called him, he insisted on going right down to the store. They tried to stop him, but he wouldn't listen. Once he was there, he went right over to her. He had to see for himself that there was nothing anyone could do. It was a neighborhood convenience store just a few blocks from his house."

"I can well see how he would have nightmares." Michael took the last sip of his coffee. "More coffee?"

"No, thank you." She looked at her watch. "Wouldn't you think she'd be in a room by now?"

"It's been less than half an hour, Edna. Sometimes it takes longer to come out of the anesthetic."

"You said you were a medic in the service."

His head bowed in acknowledgement. "I was."

"Wasn't dealing with the wounded and the dead depressing?"

Michael hesitated for a moment. "It was downright brutal at times, but it was also interesting. Besides, we saved a lot of lives. You value life a little more after seeing that side of war." He took a deep breath. "Anyway, I'm glad I didn't opt for medical school."

"What profession did you choose?"

"I kept my foot in the door, so to speak. I was a hospital administrator in a small town for a few years, but I wanted to live in the city, so I accepted the same position at a treatment center for alcoholism. Of course, I've been retired for almost five years now."

"Do you miss it?"

"Hmmmm," he was thoughtful. "I miss having a purpose in life. Maybe that's why I put my house up for sale and decided to move closer to Judd."

She was surprised. "So you're really moving to Minneapolis?"

He raised his eyebrows. "Any objections?"

"Heavens, no." She laughed. "I thought you were just joking."

"Until last week, I might have been. I, too, have turned a corner in my life." He shook his head, looking a bit puzzled. "At least, I think I did. I don't seem to be able to remember how useless I felt last week. Coming down here has been good for me. Being with you has given me a whole new attitude."

She smiled. "And how does it feel?"

"Pretty good. It's--" he searched for the right word, "it's liberating. I only hope it lasts and that I didn't act hastily. I feel like I've burned my bridges behind me. Before I left, the real estate agent told me that someone was interested in my house already. That means I have to find a place to live. Maybe you'd like to--"

The pager interrupted him. Without a word, they got up and left the coffee shop.

Max paced the floor in the waiting room. There were only two people on the other side of the room, so he didn't think he was bothering anyone. He supposed that there wasn't much going on this time of night, except for emergency surgeries.

He wasn't as stressed as he'd been when he first got to the hospital. He would soon be able to see Sam, see for himself that she would be all right. It wasn't that he didn't trust the doctors; he didn't trust God. His track record made him skeptical about anything in life.

His thoughts went back to Peg. Imagine meeting her again after all these years. She had changed, of course. She wasn't a girl anymore; he could tell from the way her figure had filled out in just the right places. She was a woman, a very attractive and interesting woman. He sighed. So what? Something would probably prevent their reestablishing their friendship after all these years. They both had baggage, if you want to call it that. They each had a life during which they had become different people, even cynical, although he couldn't exactly pin that term on Peg. He wouldn't blame her if she were. Imagine your spouse having an affair and asking for a divorce. It seemed downright cruel. All he knew was that *he* had certainly become cynical, whether from just growing up or from the tragedy in his life. He imagined that her unhappy marriage had changed her way of thinking.

No, as much as he wanted it to be so, they weren't the same people they'd been so many years ago. They couldn't just pick up where they left off, could they? And just where had they left off back then? After the date that never happened, there'd been no communication, no friendship, no nothing. He saw to that, and when she left college, that was the end of it.

CHAPTER FIVE

▼

Doug watched as the nurse tried to bring Samantha out of the anesthetic. She was flushed because her fever was still elevated, but even now, she was cute. He could admire her peaches and cream complexion, even if the color was off. He'd be worried about her if her color were normal. Her little nose was cute when she didn't stick it up in the air stubbornly. He chuckled to himself and wondered if she would be so feisty once her health was under control. Her eyelids fluttered, but she didn't respond to the nurse's voice saying her name.

"She's not coming out of it, huh?" he commented. "Maybe I should try." He stepped forward.

"Do you know the patient, doctor?" That voice sounded familiar.

He looked at the nurse as she turned around. His heart sank. Of all people to be here with Samantha, why did it have to be Jean? "Let's just say we became acquainted recently."

She stepped away from the bed and gestured toward the patient with her hands.

"Be my guest." Her words were sharp and cutting to the point that his stomach revolted, but he wasn't going to let it get to him. He wanted to try to revive Sam. "Maybe a man's voice will bring her out of it."

She looked around the room. "Where, oh where can we find a man?" Her words were cold and biting.

Doug shot a glaring look at her. "No need to let personal differences enter the workplace, Jean."

"Personal differences?" Her voice was harsh. "Is that what you call it when--"

He kept his voice as calm and impersonal as he could. "That's exactly what I call it when a man isn't interested in a relationship and the woman won't quit trying." He stepped up to Samantha and took her hand, rubbing it between his hands. He glanced back at Jean who stood at the foot of the bed sneering. "No matter what you're planning to say, this is not the place to discuss your feelings on the matter." He turned back to Samantha. "Wake up, Samantha. You have visitors waiting to see you. Your grandmother is here and your dad was on his way last I heard. Come on, open your eyes."

Jean stepped forward, ignoring Doug's attempts to revive the patient. "Are you saying that you're willing to discuss our relationship?"

"Jean, there isn't any relationship. Can't you accept that?" He was disgusted that he had once again let her goad him into arguing with her. "We have to put our differences aside if we're going to work together from time to time, or--"

She narrowed her eyes, waiting for him to finish what he had started to say. "Or what?" she challenged.

"Or one of us will have to work elsewhere. Since I start my residency Monday, it would be impossible for me to change hospitals." He turned back to his patient. "Samantha, wake up. Open your eyes." He watched them flutter. "That's it. Open them wide. No, don't close them again. You want to wake up. You want to see your grandmother and your dad."

"Well, *I'm* not about to leave," snapped Jean.

"If you can't behave like an adult about this, I'll have to report you."

"You wouldn't!"

He kept his voice as calm as he could. They should never been having this conversation, and certainly not at the bedside of a patient. "Don't test me, Jean. We have nothing in common. I'm simply not attracted to you. I'm sorry, but that's the way it is. Now let's drop it."

"But you never gave me a chance," she whined.

"That's quite enough. Please leave the room. We have a patient who needs medical attention, not insight into the private lives of the medical staff."

"We'll see about that." She stormed out of the room.

He shook his head and went back to reviving Samantha. He had noticed that her eyelids responded to the harshness of Jean's voice and he didn't like it at all. Whether he wanted to or not, he would have to report this incident. He had no choice.

Jean had flirted with him for the past year. When he didn't react to her forceful come-ons, she'd out and out asked him for a date. He was gentle when he explained that he wasn't interested in dating, but she wouldn't listen. She started to make it a point to schedule her shift when she knew he would be there. She checked his assignments and went to the charge nurse to request the same assignments. It didn't always work, but she got her way often enough to make his life miserable. But now this was too much. The girl was nice looking enough; she just wasn't his type, if he even had a type after the grueling time he had spent as an intern. He had given up dating when he first started medical school. He was serious about becoming a doctor, and nothing was going to stand in his way. Well, he finally made it.

Doug glanced toward the door Jean had left through. Couldn't she understand? He simply wasn't attracted to Jean, and nobody would tolerate her explosive reaction when she didn't get her way. End of story.

"Samantha, hon, open your eyes." He rubbed her hand again not only to increase her circulation, but to comfort her with the physical contact. "Samantha."

"Hmmm." Her response was groggy, but it was a response.

"That's it. Open your eyes."

"Nooo," she groaned.

He laughed. "Come on. You can do it."

Her eyes opened and she worked hard to focus them before she looked around. Everything was blurred. She was tired and couldn't keep her eyes open. She tried several times, but failed. Her voice didn't want to work "Where--"

"You're in the recovery room. Your surgery went well." He was smiling. "Dr. Coleman successfully removed your appendix."

She moved her head ever so slightly as her eyes fluttered again, this time staying open. "Appendix? Oh, yeah, I remember." She became agitated. "Gram. Where's Gram?"

He quieted her by touching her arm. "She's in the waiting room. We have to get you awake and into a room before she can come in."

She nodded. "Okay." She took some deep breaths and again looked around.

Although she could see a little better, it still left a lot to be desired. Everything looked fuzzy and off kilter. Her mind was sluggish, but she was talking and thinking; that had to be good.

After a while, she was alert enough to look around the room. "Was someone else in the room?" Her speech was a little slurred. "I thought I heard voices."

Doug grimaced. He knew Jean's outburst would bother Samantha. "A nurse was here a little while ago." He stroked the back of her hand.

Her speech was still a little slurred. "She was mad."

He chuckled. "Well, she wasn't a happy camper, but let's concentrate on getting you ready for company. Your family wants to see you before they go home.

"What time is it?"

"It's almost twelve o'clock."

"Good. It's almost lunchtime."

He chuckled again. Oh, she was a cute one. "That's twelve o'clock *midnight*."

"Oh?" She tried to clear her head. "Night? Oh. Oh, now I remember. You came with the ambulance."

"Yep. I'm the klutz that did everything wrong."

She spoke in the middle of her yawn. "I am . . . so sorry."

"What's that?" He cupped his ear as if eager to make sure he heard her correctly. "You mean you didn't mean all those things?"

She shook her head. "I wasn't very nice, was I?"

"Well, I'll forgive you this time." He realized that he was still rubbing the silky smooth skin of her very feminine hand. As much as he'd rather go right on holding it, he placed it carefully on the bed beside her. He checked her vitals and recorded the information on her chart. "Don't beat yourself up over it. You were in a lot of pain."

"Still," she yawned, "that was no excuse."

Doug grinned at her.

"What?"

"Nothing."

A rather stocky, older nurse came into the room with a troubled look on her face. "Have you seen Jean?"

Doug nodded. "I was about to request another nurse to take her place."

"Really?" Her tone teased. She knew that Jean had been chasing him.

"Really," he said matter-of-factly.

Her grin disappeared. "I wondered when you were going to wise up."

He glanced at Samantha. "We'll discuss this later. I'll be at the nurse's station." He turned back to Samantha. "I'll see you later in your room."

Samantha barely nodded.

The nurse acknowledged his departure and she moved to Samantha's side. "I'm Ellen. I'll be your nurse for the rest of your stay in Recovery, which shouldn't be too long." She had a pleasant face and her manner was kind, efficient and friendly. "Let's get your vitals and make sure the meds have worn off so we can get you into a room. Your family is anxiously waiting to see you."

Still groggy, she had trouble trying to sit up. Ellen helped her. "I feel like I've been drugged."

The nurse chuckled. "You have. The anesthetic does that. It will wear off in a little while. By morning, you won't even remember what you're feeling now."

"Promise? I don't like this feeling."

"Really. A lot of patients tell me it's like floating on a cloud."

"No," Samantha said emphatically. "It's nothing like that. I'm dizzy, my mind is fuzzy and I don't have control of myself. I don't like that. Besides, my stomach doesn't feel too good."

"You see? You're thinking rationally. That's a good sign. You'll improve pretty fast from now on. By the time we get you to your room, you should almost be yourself."

Samantha chuckled. "What if I want to be someone else?"

Ellen laughed. "You're definitely coming out of it. I like your sense of humor, young lady. It's important to keep that."

Samantha nodded and sighed. "Why don't I hurt?"

Ellen laughed. "Don't knock it. The pain will come soon enough, but it won't be nearly as bad as the pain you had before your grandmother called the ambulance."

Lorna, her nurse for the night, settled her into the room. She explained that her roommate was a little girl, Katie Jordan, who had been in an accident that jeopardized the lives of both of her parents. They were both in ICU, fighting for their lives, but Katie hadn't been told just how serious the accident was. She was led to believe that her parents would be all right if some unforeseen complication didn't crop up. Katie had been in surgery to set her broken arm. They checked for any internal injuries, but so far, they had found none. The child had been sleeping in the back seat at the time of the accident and seemed to have been spared more serious injuries.

Samantha was transferred to a bed by the window in room 512. She looked over at the slim figure of the little girl. Her heart went out to the sleeping Katie.

Lorna was in her mid fifties. She was friendly and caring as she checked the girl's pulse. "If she has nightmares, please call for us right away." She moved back to check Samantha's pulse. "I hope you don't mind being in the room with her. Poor thing. She's frightened and hurting, and she needs someone, someone like you."

"Like me? What can I do to help?"

The nurse smiled. "What you do comes naturally."

"I don't understand."

"You're younger than most of the patients on this floor. Katie needs to be around someone cheerful."

"And you think I'm cheerful? You should have seen me with the intern who came with the ambulance."

Lorna was rather on the heavy side, so her whole body jiggled as she chuckled. "I heard about that."

"You did?" What had the intern told her?

She patted Samantha's hand. "Now don't fret. Doug simply told me about your pain and your reaction to it."

"Doug? Is that his name?"

"Didn't he tell you?

"Oh, I suppose." She grimaced. "I wasn't really interested in listening to anyone at the time."

Lorna finished covering Samantha. She was totally sympathetic. Samantha liked that. It made her feel less guilty and less like an outcast of society. She really did know she shouldn't have behaved that way, but she couldn't help herself. She looked at the nurse's kind face. It exuded caring and understanding. "It's time we let your family in to see you so they can go home and get some sleep."

A minute later, Max and Edna entered the room quietly, worry showed on both of their faces.

"How are you, dear?" asked Edna from one side of the bed.

"I'm okay. Tired, I guess."

Max moved to the other side of her bed and kissed her on the cheek. "We've been told to keep our visit short. You need your rest. Is there anything we can get for you?"

Samantha shook her head lazily. "I sort of think I'll be sleeping late."

"In a hospital?" He shook his head. "Don't count on it. I guess this is your first experience as a *patient*."

She understood what he meant. She had seen enough in her training to know that they wake you up early. "It was wishful thinking, I guess." She looked over at Katie and motioned them closer so her whispers couldn't be heard. She told them about Katie's injuries and the injuries of her parents. "Maybe you could get her a little something before you come back tomorrow." She looked at them hopefully. "You *are* coming back to see me tomorrow, aren't you?"

Max squeezed her hand. "Wild horses couldn't keep me away."

Samantha frowned. "But your work."

"It's Saturday, honey. Sheila will be there."

Edna smiled and brushed a strand of hair behind Samantha's ear. "And you know I'll be here, Samantha. What do you think Katie would enjoy?"

She glanced over at the sleeping girl. "I don't know what girls her age enjoy."

Edna laughed. "If *you* can't remember when you were that age, how on earth do you expect me to remember?"

Lorna came back into the room. "Time to say goodnight," she announced quietly.

"Of course," said Max, again kissing his daughter's cheek.

Edna did the same. "We'll be back in the morning."

Samantha tugged on Edna's hand. "I'm sorry I was so awful before."

"Don't give it a second thought." She patted her hand before she turned to leave. She and Max looked back at her and waved as they left the room.

Michael had waited for them just outside the room. "I take it the patient is okay?"

"According to the nurse, she's still running a little fever, but they hope the medication will take care of that." Edna searched Michael's eyes. "You do think the medication will take care of it, don't you?"

He nodded reassuringly. "There's no reason to believe it won't."

"On your way home?" Doug had just come down the hall.

Edna shook his hand. "Thank you for all your understanding and help with my granddaughter, doctor. You've been more than kind and very forgiving."

Doug wasn't used to gratitude and he was embarrassed. He dug the toe of one foot into the floor. "Shucks, ma'am, it weren't nothin'."

They all laughed. Max shook Doug's hand. "Thank you, young man." He couldn't understand how a man so young could be a doctor, but he deserved the title, so he corrected himself with a nod of his head, "Doctor."

Max and Edna said goodnight and walked down the hall with Michael. Max dropped behind them when Michael took Edna's arm. He had waited patiently until now. "Tell me more about Samantha. Has the anesthetic completely worn off?"

Edna looked thoughtful. "I'm not sure. She acts a little groggy and she's tired, but she looks well under the circumstances."

"Let's go home," said Max, coming up behind them. "I'll take you home first."

Michael shook his head. "That's all right. You need to get some sleep. I'll take Edna home, and I can swing by and pick her up in the morning. I see that visiting hours start at eleven."

Max looked to his mother for her approval. He wanted to be the one to bring his mother back, but his mother was entitled to make up her own mind. "Whatever you want, Mom. You say the word."

Edna looked from Max to Michael. What should she do? Michael had been nice enough to sit through an evening far different from what he had planned. She couldn't just dismiss him. "Don't you have other things you'd rather do, Michael?"

He shook his head and grinned. "Not a thing."

"All right," she agreed, "if you're sure."

He spoke cautiously as if he wasn't sure if he should say it. "I was hoping we could have lunch after we visit your granddaughter."

"You don't have to do that."

"I know. I *want* to."

Edna nodded. "Let's go then." She turned back to Max and kissed his cheek. "I'll be fine, and you *do* need your rest."

Max shook Michael's hand. "I trust you'll be around for a while."

He smiled. "You can count on it."

"Michael is thinking about moving to Minneapolis."

"Really? You're related to Judd, aren't you?"

"Yes. I want to be a little closer to him in my old age."

"And your wife--?"

"My wife died a few years ago."

"I'm sorry. You'll be moving alone then." Suddenly Max looked at Michael in a completely different light. The thought crossed his mind that Michael was an intruder. He couldn't visualize his mother caring for a man other than his father, but his father had died long ago. His mother and Samantha were all he had left. Obviously, Michael had no one where he lived, wherever that was. Max sighed.

"I want to be close to what little family I have left."

He understood. "I know the feeling."

They took the elevator down to the main floor and exited the building together.

They said goodnight and he watched as Michael took his mother's arm and led her to the car. It was just a few hours ago that he had told Sheila that his mother liked her life just the way it was. How presumptuous of him! Still, the thought bothered him. *How can a man my age have this feeling of --- jealousy?*

What would be so bad if she and Michael became serious about each other? He was getting ahead of himself. His mother was probably just being kind to Michael because he was related to her boss. Judd probably asked Edna to help him out and spend the evening with him because he and his wife were otherwise occupied. He grinned with a certain satisfaction that he had figured everything out so quickly.

As he stood watching the car drive off, the grin changed to a frown. Since when was he so concerned about his mother's life? Why did he feel the need to explain it away as a favor to Judd? He was no better than the gossiping women who embellish a tidbit the size of a mushroom and transform it into the size of an exploding atomic bomb.

He reached his car, unlocked the door and slid behind the wheel. "I'll have to watch myself. God forbid if I turn into a busybody in my old age," he said out loud.

He looked up at the building as he started the car. He had been surprised to see Peg here. He'd been so shocked that he was unable to absorb everything she'd said. What were her words? *I couldn't see you in band everyday, knowing that you didn't return my feelings.* Could he have been so wrapped up in his own self-pity back then that he refused to let her know how *he* felt about her? He really had loved her, as much as he could love a girl he'd known only in classes and Bible study.

He turned off the ignition and went back into the hospital. When he got to the main desk, he asked where he could find Peggy Swenson. After telling her that he and Peg were old friends, the nurse told him to wait while she paged her. "I'm afraid I can't let you go up to her floor at this time of night." She waited for Peg to answer her page.

"I understand." What had he intended to say to her? How could he possibly talk her into— what? A date? Yes, a date. After all these years, he was going to ask Peggy Swenson for another date.

"She'll speak with you on the phone, sir," said the nurse as she handed him the receiver.

"Peggy?"

"Yes?"

"It's Max." He took a deep breath trying to slow down his pounding heartbeats. "Will you have dinner with me?"

There was momentary silence. "When?"

"I don't know. Maybe tomorrow?"

"You mean tonight?"

He laughed. "Yes, I guess it would be tonight. Samantha is going to be in the hospital a few days from the sounds of it."

"Your daughter?"

"Yes. Anyway, I know she's well taken care of for now. How late do you sleep?"

"Oh, probably until about four."

"How does six o'clock sound?" She didn't answer. "Peggy?"

"I–I can't believe this. After all these years." She took a deep breath. "Six o'clock would be fine. How shall I dress?"

"Not too casual. I want to take you to a nice place, but it won't require an evening gown."

"Of shucks, and I have so many."

He laughed. "Just be comfortable. What's your address?"

"It's 5612 Wentworth Ave. It's on the corner of Wentworth and Hobson."

"I'll find it, Peg." He cleared his throat. "Thanks for giving me a second chance."

"I'll see you at six." Her voice was soft and sweet. "Goodnight, Max."

He handed the phone to the nurse. "Thank you."

She smiled at him. "I couldn't help overhearing. Peggy's a nice lady. I'm glad you're taking her out to dinner. She needs someone in her life."

He wanted to ask why, but he didn't. Something must have happened in her life. Probably her idiot husband walking out on her. There would be time for questions later. He was going to have a date with Peggy Swenson after all. What was it she said? *Unless I get the flu.* He chuckled. She'd better not, but if she did, he wouldn't give up like he did last time. How could he have been so stupid? No, sir! If she told him she had the flu, he would go over to her place and take care of her and nurse her back to health.

He once again reached his car, only this time feeling like a teenager about to go out with the Homecoming Queen. He had used all his self-discipline to keep from skipping and jumping all the way to the parking lot. He didn't feel anything like a man a few years shy of fifty. He was smiling, and for the first time in years, his smile was genuine.

As he drove, he thought about his mother and Michael Richards. What kind of a man was he? He seemed nice enough, helpful, educated, and caring, but was that enough? If Michael and his mother did get involved, was he good enough for her? He laughed out loud. "Is *anyone* good enough for my mother?" He sighed. "Mind your own business, Madison," he reprimanded. He would go home and get some sleep so he could go back to see Samantha. After that, he was going to make plans for his date. His d*ate*.

Michael was quiet as he drove Edna back to her apartment. She was a nice woman, just as Judd had said; but Judd had implied something that Michael couldn't quite grasp. He didn't want to play guessing games. Perhaps he should just ask her, but how could he do that? *Hey, Edna, you got a problem?* Or perhaps, *Feel free to tell me anything. I'm a good listener.* Forget it! He would ask Judd first thing in the morning.

"You must be tired, Michael." Edna could tell that she had interrupted his thoughts. She tried to look at his face, but all she could see was his profile, and that was lost in the shadows. Only when they passed under a street light was she briefly able to see his features. How could she describe his expression? Anxiety? No, not even close. It was more like concern.

"No more tired than you. You worked all day."

"True, but I suppose you drove all day."

"Well, part of the day." He sighed. "All in all, I'd say it's been pretty exciting and wonderful if you can overlook Samantha's emergency."

She laughed. "We can all do without that kind of excitement."

"Oh, I don't know. I wouldn't have missed meeting you in Judd's office for anything." He smiled at her, briefly taking his eyes off the road. "Dinner and listening to you play was one of the highlights of my entire life."

She snickered. "That's a little extreme, don't you think?"

"No," he said seriously. "I can't remember when I enjoyed music that much. You're an excellent performer and you're not full of yourself the way a lot of musicians are. You're gracious and--"

"Oh, dear," she interrupted laughing softly. "You exaggerate when you're tired."

"I don't know if you believe me or not, Edna, but I'm not tired. It's like you gave me a new lease on life. It's exciting, exhilarating."

"Michael, you spent the last few hours sitting around in a hospital just waiting."

"Yes, and it was a great feeling. It gave me a purpose. It made me feel good to have someone to wait for."

She studied his face. "Has life been that bad for you?"

He didn't answer. "Will you think less of me if I tell you that I haven't felt needed for a very long time? I suppose after Carol died, I had nothing to occupy my time or my thoughts. I felt a loss, even if some of the chores were less than pleasant. Since then, I've been doing nothing but vegetating. That's not a good feeling."

She nodded. "I know that feeling all too well. Judd and Mary gave me a new lease on life. I hope you can experience that, too."

He pulled into the parking lot of her building and turned off the engine. "I already have. I can't tell you how grateful I am."

"Michael," she said softly as she touched his arm, "I learned long ago that if it isn't inside of you to feel significant in this world, someone else isn't going to create that feeling in you."

"I don't know if I agree with that, Edna. Because you are so warm and caring, you've made me feel like a man. I haven't experienced that feeling for so long."

Just a few short hours ago, she felt like a woman for the first time in years. It was he who made her feel that way. It was high time to get inside and get some rest. "I'm glad that you're pleased. Right now, I must go."

He got out of the car, came around and helped her out and walked her to her door. "When would you like me to pick you up?"

"Are you sure you want to?" She felt guilty monopolizing his time, even if he did say how important it was to him to feel useful. "You don't have to, you know."

"Didn't we just talk about this? I want to . . . no, I *need* to feel useful."

"Very well. Come at ten-thirty or so. We'll aim at getting to the hospital around eleven, give or take a few minutes. I'm sure you'll want to sleep later tomorrow."

"You, too."

"Oh, I'll probably be up before eight."

He looked at his watch. "That isn't even eight hours from now."

"I know." She took her key out of her purse and unlocked the security door. They walked to the elevator and waited for the door to open. They could have walked down the few steps to her floor, but they were both tired. As they got in and selected the lower level button, their eyes met and held. She was suddenly short of breath. What was the matter with her? Could one man affect her that much? Maybe, but maybe she was overly tired and mentally exhausted from the emotions of Samantha's ordeal.

The elevator dinged, took them down to her floor and dinged again as the doors closed ready for the next resident to call on it. They walked the few feet to her door. "Thank you so very much, Michael. What would I have done without you?"

"You would have managed," Michael said kindly, "but thank you for making me feel needed."

"Poor Michael. Whatever happened that you were so empty?"

"That's exactly the right word. Empty. My life was one big void."

"But it will never be that way again, because you know it's within you to rise above all that negativism. With God's help you can overcome anything."

"Would you mind if I kissed you on the cheek?"

She smiled. "I'd like that."

He bent down and kissed her cheek, keeping himself from sliding his lips over to meet hers. That would have to wait for another time, and God willing, it *would* happen. "Thank you," he said as he moved away from her. "Ten-thirty tomorrow?"

Her eyes held his, but she finally managed to tear her gaze away from him to unlock her door. "You mean ten-thirty *today*. It's after midnight." She smiled. "Thank you, Michael."

She stepped through the door and glanced toward the stairs that Michael had just climbed. She slowly closed the door and leaned against the door jam. She was definitely overtired. Why else would she feel so giddy? So Michael kissed her. So what? It was just a peck on the cheek. Well, maybe a little more than a peck, but it wasn't as if it were a romantic kiss on her lips. Had it really been *that* long since a man had even touched her, made her feel feminine? Even if she was almost seventy, she reacted with the emotions of a young woman. Imagine that.

She hung her coat in the closet and stopped to glance at the hall mirror as she passed it. The tired image she saw told her that she was definitely sixty-nine going on eighty. She had no business being disappointed. What made her think she would look any younger? Still, there was something about her eyes. They glowed. Why? Was that happiness? She began to realize that what Michael had said made sense. Yes, she stopped feeling sorry for herself when she started working. She had interests outside this apartment, but she hadn't truly felt alive until today, until Michael came into her life. She smiled to herself as she made her way to her bedroom. Her body was so very tired, but she hadn't felt so alive in years.

Michael found the key hidden on top of the doorframe of the back door. He unlocked it and went inside. They must have left a light on for him in the kitchen. He closed the door quietly and crept into the room.

"How are things at the hospital?"

Michael jumped, not expecting anyone to be up. "Judd! You sure know how to make a heart stop beating."

"Sorry." Judd sat at the kitchen table with a cup in his hand. "I couldn't sleep so I came down for some warm milk. Care for some?"

"No thanks. I hope I didn't keep you awake."

Judd shook his head. "I find that as I get older, I have sleepless nights." He shrugged. "I don't know if it's old age or--" He stopped speaking abruptly and looked down at his cup. "Or wondering if I'm doing the right thing by retiring."

Michael took off his coat and draped it over a chair as he sat down across from Judd. "Hey, you deserve retirement. You could have given up working five years ago."

"I know, but I wasn't ready then."

Michael studied Judd's bland expression. "And what makes you think you're not ready now?"

"I don't know. I know Edna is going to have a hard time with it. Her husband didn't leave her any retirement or insurance more than a couple thousand to take care of funeral expenses."

Michael shook his head. "That's rough, but she's such a fine musician. She's so good that she could play at any number of restaurants in the city."

Judd looked at him quizzically. "And you know this how?"

"I heard her. She's great." He told Judd about the last minute cancellation of music at the restaurant and how graciously Edna stepped in to help.

Judd shook his head with a smile. "That's Edna. She's a valuable employee, and a *lovely lady,* as Mary calls her." He looked into his cup, deep in thought. "So you think she could manage with no work?"

"I don't know about her finances, Judd, but she's one talented lady." He noticed a burden being lifted off Judd's shoulders. "Is that what this is all about? Worrying about what Edna will do?"

Judd shrugged. "I guess so."

"Don't give it a thought. Edna might not need to worry about her future."

Judd raised an eyebrow. "Oh?"

"Well, that's just a thought, one I hope becomes reality." Before Judd could come back at him for his premature thoughts, he changed the focus to Judd and Mary. "Are you planning anything special after you retire? Any trips abroad or cruises or anything?"

"I've been thinking that Mary would like to go out to see her sister in Manchester, New Hampshire."

"Nice country out there."

Judd finished his milk. "You've been there?"

"Just once. A bunch of us spent our furlough there. It was only three days, but we managed to see a lot of scenery. You know, those people really honor servicemen and veterans. I've never seen anything like it."

"Mary mentioned that. I wonder why that is."

Michael shrugged. He had another subject to discuss with him. "I need to know what you implied when you cautioned me about Edna. Is there something in her past that I should know about?"

Judd sighed. "There are a lot of things in her past, but aren't there things in everyone's past when we reach this age?"

"I can't help but think you had something specific in mind."

"Not really. Her husband died, of course. Then, there was the death of her daughter-in-law. She was shot." He shook his head sadly. "Such a shame."

"She told me about it." He studied Judd for a moment, waiting for another comment. "You're sure there isn't anything else?"

Judd tried to hold back a grin. "Are you trying to tell me that you are serious about her after having known her for what?" he checked his watch, "something like twelve hours?"

Michael chuckled. "It doesn't sound like me, does it? I can't explain it. Maybe I just got fed up living alone and just existing, but when I saw her, I knew she was someone special." His eyes met Judd's. "Does it bother you, my being with a woman other than Carol, I mean?"

"Not at all. You can't give up living because Carol is gone."

"But what if I fell in love? Would it be disloyal to love another woman?"

He looked at his brother-in-law sideways as if sizing him up. "Do you believe that there is only one woman put on earth just for you?"

Michael laughed. "No. I know better than that. It just seems strange."

"I'd say go for it, Michael." He got up, rinsed his glass and put in into the sink. "You deserve some happiness."

"Just like you do, Judd."

CHAPTER SIX

▼

Samantha woke up when the nurse came into the room to take her temperature, pulse and blood pressure. She looked at the clock on the wall in front of her. "Six o'clock?" she asked yawning.

"Right on the button," said the cheerful voice.

Samantha opened her eyes and studied the petite figure of the girl who couldn't have been much older than Samantha herself. She was sure that the nurse's pretty face was responsible for many a male patient falling in love with her. She had been warned about that in her training. She strained to see the name tag. "Muffy?"

"Yes?"

"Is that really your name?"

"Yes. Terrible, isn't it?"

"Not at all, but we were told in training that we'd have to go by our given names. They emphatically told us never to use nicknames."

"It's not a nickname." Her face turned slightly pink, but she busied herself with her duties so it wouldn't be noticed. "My mother had every intention of naming me Muffy. I really should change it, but it would break her heart." She picked up the clipboard, ready to record the numbers. "You said *training*. Training for what?"

Sam saw the confusion in her eyes. "I'm only a few months from my RN degree."

Muffy almost squealed. "That's great. You'll love being a nurse. I do."

"But I want to work in the ER. It's going to be so exciting."

Muffy shook her head. "Not to me. I'd hate it." She took Samantha's temp in her ear and wrote down the results. "I want to take care of patients and know that I'll see their progress and their recovery."

Samantha thought about that. "I guess that's one disadvantage of the ER, but I need the excitement." She held out her arm for the blood pressure cuff.

"Are you sure?"

"Oh, yes. I'm on ambulance duty in my spare time. I love it."

Muffy concentrated on her blood pressure for a moment and wrote it down, putting the chart back on the foot of the bed. "Are you a paramedic?"

"I'm an EMT. I opted for RN instead of paramedic. It was a tough call, though."

"I envy you in a way," she sighed, "but I'm more than happy where I am."

Samantha smiled. "That's good."

"Your breakfast will be here at about eight. Can I get you anything before then?"

"You can do that?"

"Why not? How about a cup of tea to tide you over? Unless you want to go back to sleep. I can close the door, but the doctors will be making their rounds soon."

"This early?" Of course she should know better. She worked with doctors who came in at six o'clock sharp.

"A few do, but most of them come in around eight." She adjusted the blinds on the window and started for the door. "I'll see you tomorrow. I'm in report in ten minutes, but I'll get your tea. I hope you have a good day."

"I'm sure I will." She watched Muffy leave. It was nice talking to her. She was so bubbly and cheerful. She wished her dad could meet someone like that, older, of course, but someone who could lift his spirits. He was so serious since her mother's death. It was almost like showing her that she shouldn't move on and get on with life, as if she should follow his example. She couldn't, of course, and in reality, she didn't think he meant for her to grieve this long. She would always miss her mother, particularly when she knew her dad wouldn't understand a girl's problem.

She had tried not to think about it, but sometimes the thought came uninvited that maybe she wasn't enough to make her dad feel like life was worth living. She had done everything she could to make his life more pleasant. At first she thought it was time he needed, but how much time did he need to diminish the sorrow of his grieving? She felt totally inadequate. She was sure that it wasn't his *intention* to make her feel that way, but that's the way she interpreted it. She prayed for him every night.

Muffy popped in and out with the tea she'd promised her. "Enjoy."

As if on cue, Doug came in. "Well, she's awake, and not too grumpy, I hope."

Samantha's face turned red as she nervously chuckled. "How could I sleep when they take my vitals every four hours?"

Doug looked at the chart. "Then you slept more soundly than you think. They took your temp every two hours during the night."

"I had a fever?"

"You're still running a slight one this morning, but it's nothing to worry about. And," he winked at her, "in case you'd like a second opinion, the paramedics are tied up, but Dr. Coleman will be in shortly."

Samantha wanted to duck under the covers. "I am so sorry."

He laughed. "We went through that last night, remember? I shouldn't have mentioned it, but it was sort of cute."

"Cute?" she yelped. "It was rude. My grandmother must have wanted to drop off the face of the earth."

"I have to admit she *was* a bit concerned about the sudden change in your personality, but I put her mind at ease." He looked at the chart and had a pleased expression.

She watched his face. "What? Is what you're reading good news for me?"

"It says your temp is down a bit, but we'll still have to watch you for a couple of days."

"A couple of days? Why?"

"Because, Samantha, your appendix ruptured." He had a smug grin on his lips. "Your grandmother implied that you're an RN."

"Not yet. I'll have my degree in May."

He nodded knowingly. "And so it is from your *education* that you know so much about ambulance protocol?"

"No," she said stubbornly, her chin lifted into the air as she stabbed him with a serious look. "I'm an EMT and I have ambulance duty every other weekend."

"Really?" He seemed surprised but his expression soon turned to one of concern. "So I really didn't follow the proper procedure?"

She laughed. "I thought we went through this last night, too."

He joined in her laughter. "We did. Are we friends?" He held out his hand.

She looked at the long, slender fingers skeptically for a moment before she reached out her hand. "Friends." He made her hand seem small and feminine and warm. In fact, she felt warm inside too. It must be the fever.

Katie yawned and mumbled. "Morning."

"Good morning, sunshine. I hope we didn't wake you." Doug stepped over to her bed. "How was your night?"

"It was sort of noisy sometime in the middle of the night, but I went right back to sleep. I guess I didn't care enough to stay awake." Her eyes opened wide with guarded enthusiasm as she looked over at Samantha. "Are you my new roommate?"

"It looks like you're stuck with me for a day or two."

"Or a few," said Doug. "Katie, this is Samantha. She just had an appendectomy."

"What is that?" she asked sleepily.

"We had to take her appendix out. It's a little thing in your side that sometimes causes problems. When it does, we take it out."

She nodded. "Sort of like tonsils," she said. She quickly changed the subject. "Is there any news about my mom and dad?"

He touched her arm affectionately. "Sorry, sweetie. I wish I had some news for you, but you know they're in good hands. Just have some faith."

Samantha wondered if Doug truly didn't have any news, or if it was so bad that he couldn't tell her. Surely, she would have to be physically able to handle bad news. Obviously, Doug needed help to change the subject. "So where do you go to school?"

"In Forest Lake. It's not very far from here."

"That's where you live?"

Katie nodded. "I'll be missing a lot of school." Tears formed in her eyes.

Doug smiled at the little girl. "Katie has no place to go when she leaves the hospital. Until her parents can leave, we get to keep her. Isn't that right, sweetie?"

Katie bit on her lower lip trying to keep from crying as she nodded.

"And she is known as the darling of the fifth floor."

Katie perked up a little. "I am not."

"You are, too. Everyone is waiting until you can be in a wheelchair and visit a room or two. Of course," he added, "we can't let you off the floor, but you have a lot of friends asking about you."

"Really?" She watched him nod. "But they don't even know me."

Doug shook his head. "It doesn't matter. They know *about* you. You're a pretty cute kid, you know."

Her lower lip trembled as her mouth slipped back into the almost crying pout. "I wish I could see my parents."

"I know, kiddo, but rules are rules. We can't take you off the floor, and even if we could, we can't let you go into the ICU."

"What's ICU?"

Samantha jumped in. "It's the Intensive Care Unit. It's a place where patients get the most special care in the whole hospital." She smiled at Katie warmly. "Your mom and dad must be pretty special people."

"Uh-huh. Do you have a mom and dad?"

Samantha turned a little pale. "I have a dad. He'll be visiting me soon. You'll get to meet him."

"Where is your mom?" Katie asked curiously.

Doug listened with interest as he checked out Katie's broken arm. Maybe he would get to know a little bit about this woman who intrigued him.

"She died a few years ago."

Katie got fidgety. "Was she in a car accident?"

Samantha knew right away that she shouldn't have mentioned it, but Katie asked. She didn't want to lie. "No, Katie. My mother was in a convenience store when a man came to rob it and he shot her."

Katie's eyes opened wide and tears started to slide down her cheek. "I shouldn't have asked you. I'm sorry."

"It's okay, Katie. It happened a long time ago."

Her cheeks glistened with the tears as she swiped the sleeve of her gown over them. "But don't you miss her?"

"Yes, but life has to go on. You get used to the loss. I'll never forget my mother, but she wouldn't have wanted me to be sad and miserable for the rest of my life." *The way Dad is,* she thought.

Doug patted her shoulder. "She's right, Katie. It looks like your arm is doing pretty well. How is the pain?"

"Not so bad anymore. They're still giving me pills."

"I know, and you're still chewing them." He made an unpleasant face at her.

She grinned. "Some of them taste pretty awful. Sometimes I'd rather feel the pain than taste the pills."

"Well, young lady, you'll just have to learn to swallow them."

"Don't let him bully you," said Samantha. "As one pill chewer to another, I have to tell you that I couldn't swallow pills for a long time."

"Yeah," teased Doug. "Some example *you* are. It says here," he picked up the chart, "that you had to open up the capsules at midnight."

"So?" she said defiantly. "I haven't learned to swallow *capsules* that big yet. I'm working on it." She turned toward the next bed. "Maybe Katie and I can learn together."

Doug laughed. "I don't know. If you two have your way, you'll teach the whole floor to *chew* pills instead of swallow them."

Katie giggled.

"What's all the noise in here?" An older and obviously good natured nurse came into the room. "Why, my goodness. Somebody is going to send the good humor police in here if you're not careful." She tried to look stern as she walked over to Katie's bedside. "Keep that giggling down, young lady," she scowled teasingly. She glanced over at Samantha. "I see you have a roommate."

"That's Samantha, Cassie."

"Hi, Samantha Cassie." She heard Katie laugh as she shook her head and acted like she was correcting a blunder. "No, *I'm* Cassie. I'll be your nurse for this shift. You can call me anytime for anything except--" she looked over to Katie.

"Except for room service," Katie finished the sentence. "She doesn't do room service unless you're *really, really* hungry."

Samantha laughed. "I see. I suppose you've been *really, really* hungry a few times since you've been here."

Cassie patted Katie's head. "This one's got no bottom to her tummy."

"Is that right?" Samantha played along. "And does that mean that I get room service if you have to make a trip here for Katie anyway?"

"Hmmm. I'll have to think about that." She checked Katie's vitals and recorded them.

"Maybe. but she can't get us any Black Cherry Chocolate ice cream."

"Really? Is that your favorite?" asked Sam.

Katie's tongue swiped across her lips and she nodded.

"Well, we'll just have to see if my dad will bring some in for us." She turned to Cassie. "Would anyone object?"

"Don't' know why. Neither one of you will be on a special diet; at least you probably won't be after this noon. If you are, we'll just hold it until you *can* have it."

Sam nodded. "I'll call him after breakfast."

Katie's eyes opened wide. "Honest?"

"Honest." She smiled when Cassie winked at her as she left the room.

Samantha waited until eight-thirty before calling her dad.

"How are you feeling, honey?" he asked, his voice filled with concern.

"In spite of my liquid breakfast, I feel fine. Dad, but I need a favor."

"You name it."

"I need a pint, no make that a quart of Black Cherry Chocolate ice cream."

"You need *ice cream*? Samantha, are you sure you feel all right? Do you still have a fever? Will the cold ice cream make you feel better?"

Samantha laughed. "Dad, I'm okay."

"But ice cream?"

"My roommate and I both like the Black Cherry ice cream."

"I see. So you want a quart of Black Cherry and a quart of Chocolate?"

"No, Dad." Her eyes went to the ceiling and back as she glanced at Katie who was laughing. "The chocolate pieces are in the same ice cream with the black cherries. It might even be called Burgundy Cherry and the chocolate might be called fudge. I'm sure you get the idea."

"Okay. I got it. The name of the ice cream is Black Cherry Chocolate or some words that mean the same thing that can be substituted for it."

She laughed and grabbed her side. "You got it. Clear as mud, huh?"

"How is your little roommate doing?"

"Well," she glanced over at Katie, and chose her words carefully, "it's hard to tell, but every little thing will help ease the pain."

"I know it's difficult for you to talk in front of her. You're doing a nice thing, honey, in spite of your own discomfort. That makes me proud to be your father. By the way, do you hurt very much?"

"A little, but the ice cream should take my mind off it."

He chuckled. "Anything else I can bring you?"

"Just what I mentioned last night."

"A gift for your roommate, but I don't have the slightest notion what to get."

"I'm sure you'll think of something."

"Do you need it today?"

She hesitated, hoping her dad would realize that it was important. She didn't want to put him on the spot, though. "Not necessarily. Are you getting any ideas?"

"I know where I can find out, but not until tonight. I'm—uh—seeing someone tonight."

Samantha was curious. "Someone?"

"A classmate from college."

She tried not to show her disappointment. "I suppose he's got grandchildren who can advise him."

"Hey, I'm not that old." He tried to sound insulted. "Anyway, it's a *she*, and she has no grandchildren. She works here at the hospital."

Did she dare hope that her dad was actually having a date with the woman, or was she just a friend, maybe even married? "Really?"

"If you're extra nice, maybe you'll meet her before they discharge you."

"I hope so. Dad, is she--" Dr. Coleman entered, interrupting her question. "Got to go, Dad. The doctor just came in. I'll talk to you later." She hung up.

"Good morning," he said as he picked up the chart and read the entries. "How are you feeling?"

"I feel fine. I think I can go home."

He laughed. "Oh, you do, do you?"

"Well, the pain isn't bad at all, and appendectomies are fairly simple procedures, aren't they?"

He grinned. "Ah, it's the RN talking."

She blushed. "Well, I might as well use what I learned."

"Well, don't be too hasty. You're still running a slight fever. Granted, it isn't much, but I want it down to normal for at least twenty-four hours before I dismiss you."

She sighed. "You're concerned about peritonitis, aren't you?"

He nodded nonchalantly. "It pays to cover all the bases."

She nodded. She didn't want to act like a spoiled brat. Besides, she wanted to be a good example for Katie. "Well, that's okay because my roommate and I are going to have ice cream after lunch."

He glanced over at Katie, remembering the family background the nurses had told him about. He had a daughter about her age, and as hard as he tried to imagine her in that situation, he couldn't.

The poor child must be scared out of her mind. "So you like ice cream?" he asked her.

Her eyes opened wide. "We can have it, can't we?" she asked almost fearfully.

He smiled. "I can't think of a single reason why you can't, unless of course, your doctor objects." He walked over to her bed and picked up her chart and read. "Now, let's see," he said as if studying the chart. "No, I see nothing here that would indicate that you shouldn't have it, unless--"

Katie squinted and frowned, questioning. "Unless what?" she almost squeaked.

"Well, it depends on which flavor. I'm afraid," he said thoughtfully, "you can't have any ice cream with . . . anchovies."

Samantha burst out laughing and grabbed at her incision. She didn't realize that she had that much pain.

Dr. Coleman noticed. "Sorry," he whispered.

She nodded and understood that it was for Katie's sake.

He looked around Katie's bed. "I don't see anything to keep you busy. Has no one brought you anything to keep you occupied?"

She shook her head. "Just a book."

Cassie came in to tend to Katie.

"Well, nurse," said the doctor, indicating to Cassie that she should listen to his request, "we'll see if we can't get you something you can handle with one hand." He ruffled her hair and went back to Samantha's bed.

Samantha watched as Cassie closed the curtain between the two beds. She motioned to the doctor to come closer. "Dad is going to pick something up for her, but we don't have any ideas."

"I have a daughter about her age. I'll ask her about it."

Samantha thanked him.

"Now, Miss Madison, how is the pain?"

"It only hurts when I laugh."

He studied her. "Did you know there's a movie by that title?"

She laughed and grabbed her side again. "I guess I have heard of it, but it's a very old movie." She wondered if she should have said that. He might think she was pinpointing his age, and not very nicely.

He made a point of snickering before becoming serious. "Back to business." He winked at her. "I have other patients, you know." Again he studied the chart and listened to her lungs and heart. "I don't think we'll have a problem."

"So when can I go home?"

"It's just a precaution, Samantha. It will all depend on when your fever goes down to normal, and I don't want you eating ice cream half an hour before taking your temperature."

She chuckled. Chuckling wasn't nearly as painful as out and out laughing. "Does that really work?"

He shrugged. "It can, but being an RN, I'll trust you not to try it."

She sighed. "I won't. I give you my word."

"Good enough." He replaced the chart at the foot of her bed. "I'll see you tomorrow unless something comes up." He bent down so he could speak softly into her ear. "Keep up the good work with your roommate. She has a rough time ahead of her."

"How are her parents?" she whispered.

He shrugged. "From what I hear, it can go either way."

Samantha nodded as she watched him give her a slight wave of his hand as he walked out the door.

Edna had just cleaned the kitchen when the phone rang. "Hello."

"Hi, Mom, it's Max."

"Is anything wrong?"

"Samantha's fine, if that's what you're thinking. She called earlier. I have to stop and get some ice cream for her."

"Ice cream? How strange. I'm sure thy have plenty at the hospital."

"Ah," he answered, "but not Black Cherry Chocolate. She wants it for Katie."

It was possible that Max was too busy to take the time. "Is that a problem? Do want us to stop and get it for you?"

"Not the ice cream. She asked me to get something to keep Katie occupied, but I won't see Peggy until tonight. I have no idea what an eleven year old would like."

Peggy? He was seeing her tonight? What did Peggy have to do with a gift for Katie? She wanted to ask, but she didn't want to discourage him in any way from an attempt to live a normal life. Just maybe Peggy was a start. "I've been stewing over that myself. I think I'll stop at the gift shop and get her a teddy bear or some stuffed animal. Even big girls like stuffed animals."

"Good. That will tide her over until tomorrow, don't you think?"

"I'm sure it will."

"And—uh—Mom, I'm going on a date tonight."

Edna couldn't help smiling, but it took some effort to keep her voice from reflecting the joy she felt. "That's wonderful, Max. She seems like a nice girl."

He laughed. "She's not a girl anymore. She's a nice *woman*, Mom." He cleared his throat. "Well, I'll be leaving shortly, so I'll see you at the hospital."

"We should be there sometime after eleven."

"Mom," Max spoke hesitantly, "about Michael, I just want you to know that-uh-that it's okay with me if you want to see more of him."

At first she was angry that he felt she needed his approval, but she softened when she figured out why he'd said it. "Are you thinking of your father, Max?"

Max was silent for a moment. "Don't mind me. It's just strange to think of your mom with anyone but your dad."

"I suppose, but your dad has been gone for many years now. I will never stop loving him, Max, but he's not here anymore. I finally learned to accept that. I'm not doing anything for *him* by not seeing other men, you know."

"I know. I guess I realized that today when I was talking to Peggy. Life really has to go on, doesn't it?"

Thank you, God she thought, but she tempered her elation and spoke quietly. "Yes, and you have to remember that humans have a great capacity for love. If you had had brothers and sisters, I would have loved them just as much as I love you."

Max feigned hurt feelings. "You always said I was special, that you couldn't love anyone more than you loved me."

"Max, didn't I tell you that I would love them all as much as you, but not more?"

He shouldn't tease her like that. "Oh, was that what you said?" He took a deep breath and laughed. "I love you, Mom. See you in a while."

"Good bye, son." She hung up the phone and stood motionless for a time. If Max had thought she was having a relationship with Michael, it could only work in her favor. She understood how devastated he was when Bernice had been shot, but nothing seemed to motivate him to do more than exist. Samantha, of course, was the center of his life, but Edna had often noticed that Max seldom smiled, even when he was with his daughter.

If only she could convince him without saying a word, that life after a spouse's death could be enjoyable. She would have to show him, be an example. He would see how normal it was for her to add other people to her life; hopefully, he would add others to his own life. He was such a special man. She was so proud of his many accomplishments, and he was such a caring son. She only hoped that Peggy was worthy of his friendship. Without consciously thinking about it, she hoped that Peggy would turn out to be more than just a friend. *Please, Lord, help Max to know You again.*

Katie almost said something to Sam as she looked over at her roommate, but Sam was napping, so she didn't want to disturb her by talking. Her roommate was nice. Everyone here was nice, but it wasn't like being with her mom and dad. She really missed them. She wanted to ask the nurses about them again, but maybe she didn't want to know the answer. They told her the other day that the accident was serious, and that neither of her parents had regained consciousness. She knew what that meant.

Jerry was a classmate, and his dad was killed in an accident last May. He was an undertaker who had gone to a neighboring town to get the body of a man who died at his daughter's house in that town. It was a rainy night, very dark and somehow, a semi driver didn't see the station wagon. Jerry's dad, they figured, didn't see the semi either, and when he was unable to stop, it went right under the trailer part of the truck, shaving off the top of the station wagon.

Jerry stayed home from school for several days, before his mother insisted he go back to his classes.

She remembered that Jerry had once told the class that his dad took care of dead bodies. He had told Jerry that when a person dies, their hair keeps growing. She shivered. What made her remember that? Her memories went back to Jerry's dad. He was unconscious for over a week before he died. She hadn't wanted to recall that fact. She turned in her bed, hoping to see Samantha awake, but she wasn't. She tried to hold back the tears, but she couldn't. She buried her head in her pillow so the sobs wouldn't wake Samantha.

It was then that Max walked into the room, instantly noticing Katie crying. His heart went out to her. He wondered if she had gotten bad news about her parents. Poor thing. What could he do to help? He saw that Samantha was sleeping, so he went to Katie's bed, sat down and put his hand on her shoulder. Katie looked up and threw herself in his arms.

Max immediately thought back to the night he held Samantha in his arms after he had told her that her mother was never coming home. Tears formed in his eyes, but he would have to fight them. This poor little girl would really fall apart if she saw him shedding tears.

Katie hung on to him for a long time. When she got her sobbing under control, her head ducked out from under his chin. She looked up. "Do you have bad news for me?"

Max smiled. He wondered who she thought he was. "I don't think so, unless you decided that you don't like Black Cherry Chocolate ice cream after all."

Samantha opened her eyes just in time to see her dad holding Katie. She didn't want to interrupt a moment like that, but she thought she had better let Katie know that he was no threat to her. "Katie, this is my dad, Max Madison."

"Oh, no." She covered her mouth with her hand. "I'm sorry."

Max shook his head. "It's been a long time since I held a little girl in my arms." His head nodded toward his daughter. "She's been grown up for some time."

"I thought you were the doctor who's taking care of my parents."

"I'm a doctor," he said, "but not that kind."

Katie scrunched up her nose, her forehead a mass of lines. "What other kind of doctor is there?"

"I have a PhD. Oh, well, it's unimportant," he said, but he was glad that he had diverted her attention.

Samantha was thankful that he had handled the situation so easily. She had noticed the tears in his eyes, and immediately realized that he'd been thinking about her mother's death. She raised her eyebrows. "Did you bring the ice cream?"

He grinned, ruffled Katie's hair and moved over to his daughter's bed. "Would I forget a thing like that?"

Samantha was puzzled, but pleased. She was seeing a side of her dad that she hadn't seen since her mother's death. He seemed more casual, friendlier, more easily able to handle a situation like this. The black mood that seemed to be part of him the last three years appeared to be lifting. Was it Katie who was responsible for it or was it something else? Did she dare hope it was his date?

"I gave it to the nurse," he assured them. "You two should be having ice cream after you finish your lunch."

"What if we don't eat our vegetables?" asked Samantha with a grin.

"You know the rules, Sam," cautioned Max.

She nodded and started to speak when Katie piped up. "No vegetables, no sweets."

Max nodded with a smile. "She's not only pretty, she's smart."

Sam liked her dad like this.

Lorna came into the room. "Well, what have we here?"

Sam frowned trying to place Lorna in their room at a specific time last night. "Were you here all night?"

Lorna nodded. "They're short handed, so I stayed on for the next shift."

"Lorna, this is my dad, Maxwell Madison. Dad, this is Lorna. She's one of the nicest nurses in the hospital."

Lorna acknowledged him. "I wouldn't go that far." She turned toward him and bowed her head slightly as a greeting. "I'm pleased to meet you, Mr. Madison."

"Lorna took care of me last night."

Katie perked up a little. "Are you going to be our nurse today?"

"You bet. You're stuck with me until three o'clock this afternoon."

Katie's voice was soft. "I'm glad you're here."

Lorna tweaked Katie's nose. "So am I, kiddo. Now, let me take your vitals so you can have your lunch."

Katie chuckled. "Where are you going to take them?" she asked.

Lorna frowned. "Take what, honey?"

Katie giggled. "Our vitals? Where are you going to take them?"

Lorna laughed. "To the kitchen, of course. Now, quiet down, or I'll have to remove the sweets from your diet."

Katie lifted her chin and pretended to get instantly serious and held out her arm for Lorna to take her pulse.

Lorna kept her smile to herself and feigned a strict attitude. "That's better." She went to close the curtain. "You'll excuse us for little while, won't you? I have to make sure Katie's full attention is on me."

Max played along. "By all means. We wouldn't want to be responsible for Katie missing her ice cream."

"Ice cream, huh?" Her hand was on the curtain, but she hadn't moved it yet. "Well, what is it going to be? Vanilla or strawberry?"

Katie answered. "Black Cherry Chocolate."

"Ohhhh, my favorite," Lorna squealed.

Max shrugged. "Guess I'll have to go back to the store."

She laughed and shook her head, rubbing her hands down her sides. "Oh, I think my hips can live without it."

"I want you to have some too, Lorna." Katie's eyes were pleading.

"That's sweet, honey, but right now, let me do my job so I can move on."

Katie nodded and watched Lorna finally pulling the curtain closed.

Max moved over to Samantha's side and took her hand. "How are you, Sam?"

"I'm fine, Dad. Thank you for bringing the ice cream. Did they have it at Carlson's?"

"No such luck. I found it at Hanson's ice cream store."

"I'm sorry, Dad."

"Hey, it was my pleasure." He leaned closer to her ear. "No word on her parents?"

Sam shook her head. "No change," she whispered. "Both still unconscious. Poor thing. Sometimes she tries to act like it isn't happening."

He nodded, knowing the feeling. During the few minutes it took to get to the store the night of the shooting, he had done the same thing. "It's called denial, honey."

"What's called denial?" Edna entered the room.

"Hi, Gram." She held her hand out to her.

"How are you feeling, dear?" She approached the bed and took Sam's hand.

"I'm okay."

Edna bent lower with sympathy in her eyes. "Do you hurt very much?"

"When I laugh, so don't make me laugh." She looked at the sack in her hand. "What did you bring for Katie?" she whispered.

Edna took the little white teddy bear out of the sack. It was about seven inches tall and had a red heart around its neck.

"Oh, it's darling." She hugged it to her chest.

Edna watched the pleasure in Samantha's eyes. "I see I should have brought two of them."

Michael entered with a sack.

"I wondered what happened to you. Did you get lost, Michael?" asked Edna.

"Since there are two young ladies in here, I thought we should bring something for each of them." He handed the sack to Samantha.

"How sweet of you to think of me." Samantha opened the sack and peeked in. "Ohhh," she squealed. She took the slightly larger teddy bear out of the sack and held it to her chest.

"What is it?" asked Katie from the other side of the curtain. "What's the matter?"

"Nothing, Katie," replied Samantha as she tucked the smaller bear back into the sack just as Lorna pulled the curtain back.

Katie looked at the stuffed animal and smiled. "Oh, he's so cute."

Edna picked up the first sack that held the smaller, identical bear, and gave it to Katie. "This one is for you, sweetheart."

"For me?" Katie took the sack and stared at it for a moment before she opened it to remove the small teddy bear. "Oh, it's just like yours," she told Samantha happily.

"So it is." Sam's grin was genuine. "Yours is just your size."

Katie's eyes went to Sam's bear, then back to her own. "And yours is just *your* size. Thank you," said Katie to Edna and the others. She hugged it to her chest.

Sam smiled at Michael. "Thank you so much." She studied him for a minute. She hadn't really had much time to think about him because of the pain and being so scared. "You're a very nice man."

"Because I brought you a gift?" He shook his head. "I thought you deserved something after your ordeal last night. I trust you're recovering."

"I am, and as soon as my fever is completely normal, I can go home."

"Don't expect it to go away so quickly. Your body was fighting an infection. It takes a little time."

She nodded. "I don't think I've seen you before. Have you known Gram long?"

"Not long at all. We had dinner last night, but. I'd like to get to know her a lot better." Michael glanced at Edna who was blushing. "She's a very interesting lady and I want to know more about her." He added, "I had the pleasure of listening to her play the piano last night. It was fantastic."

Lorna moved around the room and checked Sam's blood pressure and temperature, adding the figures to her chart. "I'll leave you to your visitors." She threw Katie a kiss and left the room.

"Mom's really a very accomplished pianist," commented Max. He couldn't help wondering what circumstances prompted her to play for him. "Where did you hear her?"

"At a romantic little restaurant," his hands flew upward and glanced in Edna's direction, "somewhere in the outskirts."

Edna told Max about finding the restaurant and about the group expecting to be entertained by a pianist who didn't show up.

He pursed his lips and nodded. "So naturally, you jumped in."

"I had to help that poor waiter out, Max. He was so distraught. You should have seen him."

"She's marvelous," said Michael.

"Yes, she is," he agreed.

Samantha had listened intently. "That must have been exciting, Gram."

Edna shrugged. "You like to help out when you can. That young waiter was so upset. His manager wasn't there at the time, and I think he felt responsible. I couldn't let him suffer."

Michael laughed. "Well, you now have a friend for life."

Max moved up a little closer. "So you say this is a really nice place?"

"It's lovely, Maxwell. It's called *Adam's Haven*. Why don't you go there tonight?" The words had popped out before she had a chance to remember that she hadn't intended to say anything.

Samantha eyes were focused on her dad. "You're going out tonight?"

"Uh--yes. I already told you I met an old friend in the coffee shop last night. We went to college together."

"So," teased Samantha, "you want to impress this guy with a *romantic* restaurant?" She knew very well that her dad was talking about the nurse he had met. She could only hope that this would put his life back on a normal track.

"Well, honey," started Max, his cheeks getting very red, "it's not a he. She's a nurse down on second floor." He frowned. "I told you about her." Maybe it was the fever or the traumatic trip to the ER that prevented her from remembering. He was getting a little concerned. Maybe he should call Peggy and call off the date.

Samantha acted like she just remembered. "Oh, yes. The one you met here."

"If you're not feeling well," he offered, "I can cancel the evening with Peg and stay with you."

Sam shook her head. "Don't be silly, Dad."

"Are you sure you don't mind?"

"Positive. Besides, they'd throw you out when visiting hours are over."

All this time, Edna had tried to get Sam's attention, lest the conversation would make him change his mind. She mentally threw up her hands and decided she couldn't control what was happening, nor did she have a right to try. What would happen would happen. She only hoped that Max wouldn't get cold feet.

"Dad, why on earth should I mind? I think it's wonderful. You haven't been out for dinner with anyone except your cousin Charlie, and the last time he came to town must have been at least two years ago."

"It's been that long, huh?"

"Yes, and it's about time you see what goes on outside the house. You said I might get to meet her?"

"I hope so, but it's just dinner with a friend, honey." He wanted to make her feel comfortable with his *date*. "We played in band together at the U."

Still, Sam hoped that this dinner was responsible for her father's new disposition. She liked seeing him this way. It seemed like he cared about life again, and his eyes had lost that emptiness. In spite of the fact that her dad didn't believe in God anymore, she prayed that this woman would be a meaningful influence in his life. He deserved it. He needed it. And wouldn't it be wonderful if she…. She wasn't going to let her imagination run away with her, but secretly, she hoped that her dad would find a woman he could love. Her mother had been gone for a long time, and he had to move on. She only hoped that he didn't think Sam would think any less of him if he decided he could love another woman. Many people lost their mates, and they didn't spend the rest of their lives alone; at least, most of them didn't. God didn't intend for us to be alone. She was sure of that.

Chapter Seven

▼

Peggy woke up at three-thirty, looked at the clock and tried to go back to sleep, but Max kept popping into her mind. What was she going to wear? What did she have that was nice but not too showy? She thought of her emerald green dress, but decided chiffon was too dressy. She could wear her royal blue suit, but that was too business-like. She sat up in bed and pictured herself in the slinky black, long sleeved dress she had never dared to wear. She got it because the clerk at the dress shop said it was "her." She had to admit it was elegance personified. She was going to wear the black dress, even though it had a fairly low neckline. It was modest enough. It just wasn't the sort of thing she usually wore, but then, she felt immodest in any dress that wasn't below her knees.

She got out of bed and went to the closet, removed the dress and hung it on the back of the door. What about shoes? Max was tall, unlike her ex-husband. She wore only flats when she was married to Dennis. Although she was three inches shorter than he was, he insisted that she not appear to be anywhere close to his size. In fact, he didn't want her equal to him in anything or in any way. Tonight, she would wear her new black heels. They weren't dressy, just elegant pumps; but they were high heels and they were perfect for the dress tonight. Another time, she might want something strappy.

She jumped into the shower. Why was she getting so excited? Thoughts of Max had occupied most of her two years at the U, but this was different. They were both adults now, and he probably wanted no more than to renew a friendship. She was sure he didn't have any romantic interest in her. How could he have? She wasn't the pretty young girl who played the clarinet now. She wasn't bubbly and silly the way she'd been at that age. Still, it didn't hurt to daydream a little, did it?

Secretly, she was hoping that God was smiling down at her, telling her that she *could* have a life filled with love and happiness and even the children she once dreamed of, even if it had to be through adoption. Yeah, right! She had loved God all her life, but she sometimes had the feeling that God had His own plans for her, and she knew that He didn't always answer her prayers the way she wanted Him to. All she had to do was have faith that God knew what He was planning for her. Secretly, she still hoped it was what she would plan for herself, but she trusted God. Whatever He chose, she knew it was in her best interest.

As she let the water run down her body, it was like washing away all the years of unhappiness. If only that time could just be flushed down the drain like the water.

She thought back to college and the night of the party. How could Max have thought she used the flu as an excuse not to go to the party? Come to think of it, how could she up and leave the U just because he didn't seem to care for her anymore? She really hadn't stuck around long enough to find out if he would ask her out again. Had she counted so heavily on his being a part of her future that she simply gave up? That's what she did. She gave up and moved away, and eventually married the wrong man.

She sighed as she turned off the shower and picked up the towel to dry herself. She glanced at her image in the full length mirror on the door and shook her head. How ugly. Age had taken its toll on her body. That was normal, she knew, but for most women, their husbands' bodies aged right along with theirs. What was it the poem said? *Grow old along with me*? Something like that. Well, not this lady. She had chosen the wrong husband. What man would *want* to look at her now? She opened the door to rid herself of the view and went into the bedroom.

She would settle for being his friend. She needed a friend and from what he had told her about his life, so did Max. She chose her black bra and panties and a black half slip. She might just as well go all the way and wear some jet black pantyhose. They were sheer, so it wouldn't look like she was poured into a black bag with an opening for her head. She laughed at the thought. She was getting silly. She must be nervous.

By the time she finished using the curling iron, it was five-forty. Did her hair look more like Max remembered? She let it fall into soft curls rather than tight ones the way she wore it to work. It resulted in her hair looking longer than he had seen it at the hospital. A little cologne on her wrists and behind her ears and she was finally ready. One last look at her make up proved just right. It hardly looked like she had any on, but she needed the mascara to darken her eyelashes. The older she got, the more she needed the contrast.

She popped a breath mint into her mouth and transferred the necessary things from her handbag into a smaller purse. She wouldn't need much more than a comb, lipstick, compact, and just a few dollars in case she had to take a cab home. What a stupid thought! Max wasn't like that; at least, he hadn't been. He couldn't have changed that drastically. He still seemed to be the sweet, lovable Max he was in college, but a little older. He was a lot more attractive with a body as fine a masculine physique she had noticed in a long time, even if she vowed not to notice men at all after she was served with the divorce papers.

She took her good black coat out of the closet and put it over the back of the easy chair. She was ready. All she had to do was sit and wait for Max to show up, but she found that she couldn't sit still. She paced and finally settled on rearranging the pictures and mementos on the entertainment center. Did she keep herself busy to avoid thinking that she was making a mistake? Should she have found some excuse not to go out to dinner? She took a deep breath. No. This didn't feel like a mistake, but if it was just wishful thinking, she would have to learn from yet another mistake in her life. *Please, dear God, don't let this be wrong like it was when I married the wrong man.*

Doug's day was finally over, but he wanted to check on Samantha. There was really no reason that he should, but he wanted to see how she was doing. It was no crime to take a special interest in a patient he tended with the ambulance. She was a pretty girl but there was something about her, a sadness, a melancholy look in her eyes. Maybe it was just a seriousness about her that told a story about her past. He wanted to know what it was that made her seem so fragile, so vulnerable; but if asked, he wouldn't be able to say why he felt the need to find out more about her.

He shrugged to himself. It was probably his way of reacting to the end of his internship. It had been a hard year of too much work, too little sleep and no time for a social life. Well that was all different now. He would do his residency here and then he'd be off to a small town, a community that desperately needed doctors. He wanted, needed to go where he wouldn't be just another doctor in a city of more doctors than people really needed. He was glad he felt that way because he really had no choice. That would be his life for the next three years.

He liked the idea of getting to know his patients, and seeing them socially. He didn't want to follow in his father's footsteps, practicing medicine in an elite part of the city, remaining aloof because he felt he was a step above ordinary people. He shook his head. He loved his dad, but he could be extremely narrow-minded. He probably would never forgive Doug for refusing his offer of a partnership in Omaha, but so be it. Doug intended to live his life, not his father's. Thank God his mother understood. She stood between them when they argued, and in the end, softened the blow for her husband when Doug announced his intentions. As it turned out, Doug managed on his own, determined to do whatever he had to in order to achieve his goal.

He entered Samantha's room and saw Katie and Samantha holding up white teddy bears, talking to each other as if they were the bears.

He laughed. "Am I intruding? I didn't bring *my* bear."

Katie giggled and held up her bear. "Look what Samantha's grandmother brought me."

"That's cute, Katie. Do you suppose if I get sick and end up in a bed, somebody will bring me a new teddy bear?"

"I would," she said sweetly.

He ruffled her hair. "I'll bet you would." He turned to Samantha. "And how is the older patient doing?" He picked up her chart. "Still a low grade fever, I see."

Samantha sighed. "It won't go down to normal."

"Give it time."

She was restless. "I have to get back to my training. I'll be missing too much."

"Even nurses get sick, Samantha. Whether you're here or at home, you still have to have time to recuperate."

"You're a nurse?" asked Katie.

"Just about. I'll be a full-fledged RN in May, if I ever get back to school."

"Wow." Katie had tears in her eyes. "Maybe I'll be a nurse when I grow up, or maybe a doctor who takes care of people who have accidents."

"Hey, don't cry," said Doug. "I stopped up at ICU and there are some encouraging little signs with your mom."

Her eyes opened wide. "Really?"

"Now, don't get too excited. It's way too soon to tell, but she doesn't have a fever, and they say there's some brain activity."

Her eyes looked so hopeful. "Is that good?"

He smiled warmly. "That's *very* good."

"And my dad?"

Doug didn't want to give her false hope, but there hadn't been any more negative reports on him. "He's holding his own, honey."

She hung her head. "That's not so good."

"Hey, it's better than bad news. It means he's fighting." He squeezed her shoulder. "Hang in there, Katie. Give it time. It may not be easy, but sometimes that's all we can do besides pray."

She nodded. "I pray all the time. Do you think God hears me?"

"I'm sure He does." He was going to say that God might have his own plan for her parents, but why plant a thought like that before it actually became necessary? Miracles do happen. He had seen a couple of them himself during his training.

"You have to have faith, Katie," said Samantha, but she heard how empty her own words sounded. She wished right now that she really believed what she was saying.

Three years ago, she didn't have time to pray or have someone tell her to have faith. Her dad had sat her down and told her that her mother was gone, dead. It was the worst moment of her life. She remembered feeling paralyzed, not able to talk or move. She couldn't even cry. When the words finally made sense, she felt like the bottom dropped out of the earth she stood on and she was falling into a blackness she never knew existed. Then, she couldn't stop crying. Her mother was gone. She would never see her again. Never hug her or talk to her about all the little things that happened during her day. Her mother would never help her pick out a dress or give her advice on growing up. She would never again teach her to cook or bake extra special recipes.

Doug's comments on having faith in God jolted her out of her unwelcome memories. Still, she couldn't help wondering about God. She knew that her dad lost his faith in God that day, but she wasn't sure how she felt. She couldn't renounce God. Maybe she would wait and see if Katie's parents survived the accident. She had prayed right along with everyone else. Surely God would listen– unless He had other plans. Isn't that what ministers always said? God answers your prayers, but not always the way you want. Religion was confusing to her.

"Samantha?"

Sam again snapped out of her thoughts, realizing that she hadn't heard a word of the conversation that evidently hadn't been finished. What had they been saying? How could she not let on? "Hmmm?"

"Are you okay?" Doug was at her side, hand on her forehead.

She nodded. "I'm fine." She might as well confess. "I was miles away for just a minute."

Katie giggled. "Where did you go? I didn't see you leave."

Sam laughed. "I guess I took a mental journey." But she wasn't going to tell Katie or Doug any more than that.

"Well, girls, I'm off duty, so I'm going to go home and get some sleep, something I've lacked for the last year."

"You're all done with your internship?" asked Sam.

His hands flew up. "All done."

"Congratulations," she said and reached out her hand.

He took it in both of his. "I hope I'm around to congratulate you." He held her hand longer, liking the feel of the softness. He realized it was inappropriate, and as much as he wanted to keep the connection, he squeezed her hand before releasing it. "Maybe I'll run in tomorrow and check on you two."

Sam sighed. "I suppose I'll still be here, but isn't it your day off?"

He nodded. "I start my residency Monday," he winked at Katie, "but I can still come in and visit my friends." He walked to the door and turned back. "Behave yourselves, girls."

Max was all dressed and had an hour to spare. Maybe he should stop at the store and make sure Sheila had everything under control. She always did, but he needed something to do to pass the time until he went to Peg's. He just couldn't sit at home and twiddle his thumbs until it was time to leave.

Sheila was waiting on a customer, an older man. He chuckled to himself. Hadn't they just spoken about the young age of the people who came into the store? Sheila seemed intent on what he was saying.

They both looked when the bell over the door tinkled.

"Max," said Sheila, motioning him over. "Come over here. I want you to meet Jacob Tyler."

Jacob stood up and extended his hand. "I'm happy to meet you, Mr. Madison."

"What can I do for you, Mr. Tyler?"

"Not a thing. I had a mission when I came to the store, but it turned out to be futile." Max looked at Sheila to clarify what the man had said, but before she could speak, Jacob went on. "My daughter and your wife were best friends at one time. I simply came to inform her that my daughter died three months ago." He sighed.

"I'm sorry. Sheila told you, of course, that Bernice was killed three years ago. I'm sorry for your loss." He frowned. "Tyler?" He frowned as he tried to recall if Bernice had ever mentioned the woman, but the name wasn't familiar to him. He shook his head.

"Her married name was Duncan, Janice Duncan."

"Of course. Bernice wrote to her about once a month, if I remember correctly."

"I suppose it was about that often, at least when I was around. I used to visit her as much as I could. When Janice's husband divorced her, she slumped into a deep depression. I imagine she stopped writing at that point."

Max was thoughtful. "It's possible that after our tragedy, some of the letters, if she still wrote, were returned unopened. My daughter or my mother, or possibly I sent them back myself. We all had a hard time dealing with her death."

They talked for a few minutes about Sam and her surgery before Max looked at the clock. "It's time to close up. I have to run. I have a–uh, I'm going out to dinner."

Sheila smiled. "I happen to be going to dinner myself," she said sounding a little like she was boasting.

"Is that right?" He glanced over at Jacob.

She nodded. "Jacob is just recently back in town and he asked me to share a meal with him."

Max nodded his approval. "Then why don't you two get going? I'll lock up."

"I've taken care of the cash. We can stop by the bank on our way."

"That's great." Max extended his hand to Jacob. "I'm glad we met. I hope I see you again."

Jacob glanced at Sheila. "That's entirely possible."

They left and Max locked up with a smile on his lips. First, Michael walks into Judd's office and meets his mom. Max himself finds Peggy at the hospital, and now, Jacob Tyler pops up out of nowhere. There must be something in the water.

When the doorbell rang, Peggy's excitement doubled and she wanted to run to the door, but she deliberately walked slowly. It seemed like it took forever, but she was finally there. She stopped and ran her hands down her skirt before slowly opening the door. She froze for a moment. He looked so handsome in his charcoal wool suit. It was hard to believe how much more attractive he was now than when they were in college. Realizing the awkwardness of the moment, she cleared her throat. "Come in."

Max smiled. "You look beautiful, Peg." His eyes swept over her.

"Thank you. You look nice, too. I just need to get my coat." Why did her legs feel like rubber? She turned to go over to the chair where she had left the coat, but Max already had it in his hands, holding it for her.

Max had wanted to look around to see how she decorated her home, but he was too excited about going out with her. He wanted very much to put his arms around her and just hold her. How stupid could he be? Where had that thought come from? He felt like he was back in college, watching . . . wishing . . .

"Thank you." She smiled. "I don't remember you being so polite in college."

He never thought he could blush, but he did. Back then, he had been a typical overconfident teenager. He wondered if he even knew what the word *etiquette* meant back then. "I've learned a thing or two during the last twenty years." He shook his head. "I wonder how my mother could tolerate me when I was younger. It was as if she never taught me any manners."

"Mothers have unconditional love."

He laughed. "That must be it." He opened the door and extended his arm ushering her out.

She locked the door behind them. "Where did you decide to go?"

"Mother stumbled onto a nice place. She suggested we try it. The food is excellent and she assured me that it isn't filled with teenagers. It's called Adam's Haven and looks like a chalet. Have you been there?"

"I've never heard of it. I thought I knew about most of the places around here."

"Then it will be a first for both of us." He chuckled to himself. His mother had told him that Michael had said much the same thing to her. He hoped the place would live up to their recommendation.

"So you live by yourself?" he asked.

She chuckled in a cynical way. "I certainly hope so."

He flinched. "I didn't mean you might live with a man."

"I know." She grimaced. "It's just that Dennis told me I'd never make it on my own. I'll die before I prove him right."

Max frowned. "Didn't you say that *he* left you?" She nodded. "Why would he say a thing like that?"

Peg took a deep breath. "I don't know. At first I refused to talk about a divorce and he was angry. He accused me of staying married because I couldn't make it on my own. He said I needed his money."

"You'd get alimony anyway, wouldn't you?"

She shook her head. "Money wasn't the issue. He came home one day which, by the way, happened to be my birthday and asked me for a divorce. He said he loved his secretary and wanted to marry her." She cleared her throat. "Actually, he said he *had* to marry her. She was pregnant."

"Ouch. You must have gone bananas. You had no clue?" He was working up an intense dislike for the man.

"Not a one." She sighed. "Actually, I learned that I'm better off without him. I'm happier without him. I didn't realize what a cheat he was. All those nights he said he was out of town, I learned later that he was in a hotel with her. And most of the time, they were top line hotels with room service and the works. I understood then why he made me chip in so much for the household expenses. I only wish I had taken an active part in the finances." She sighed again. "Well, that's my story. You are sitting beside the most naïve, stupid woman you have ever known."

"You had every reason to trust him, Peg. He was your husband."

"Why didn't I know what was going on? How could I be so trusting to never question his behavior? Other wives would have been suspicious from the start."

"I'd say that Dennis was a rat. You really are better off without him. So have you started dating again?"

"No. Well, except for tonight."

He put his hand over hers. "It's a start."

"How about you?"

He shrugged. "Ditto."

She was surprised. "This is your first time?"

He nodded. "I haven't found anyone I wanted to be with until now. I'm glad you were in the coffee shop last night."

She had that smile that turned his chest to mush. "So am I."

He turned into the parking lot of the chalet style building. He parked, turned off the ignition and got out, walking around the car to help her out. "I hope it's not a bad experience."

"If your mother said it was nice, I'm sure it is."

The hostess seated them near the front of the room, explaining that there would be music for their entertainment shortly. Max had reserved a table near the piano. It was a good thing he had called when he did because the dining room was almost filled to capacity. She handed them both menus and lit the candle on the table. "Kevin will be your waiter tonight."

A tall, nice looking young man stepped forward when the hostess left. "Hi. I'm Kevin and I'll be your server. Can I bring you something from the bar?"

Max looked at Peg. "Something from the bar?"

She shook her head. "Whatever you're having."

Max moved his attention to Kevin. "Do you have lemonade?"

"Yes, sir. How about a pitcher?"

Peg laughed. "How about just a glass," she suggested to Max. "I'm not into liquids when there's such interesting food."

Max laughed. "A glass it is."

"We have a nice raspberry lemonade."

"That's fine." Max waited until Kevin left the table. "I'm sure I wouldn't know raspberry from strawberry, but it sounds good."

"It's very good." She opened her menu and looked over the items. "How interesting. They have pheasant."

Max perused the dinner items. "I see that. I also see Beef Stroganoff, Walleye Pike and Orange Roughy. They all interest me."

"It's too bad they don't have a sampler platter." She kept looking at the menu.

Max looked up from his menu. "What looks good to you, Peg?"

"Everything." She studied his face and smiled. "You mean I get to order for myself?"

He laughed. "What did you think? That I was going to impose my preference on you? I wouldn't make your decision for you."

She sighed. "Dennis always insisted on doing just that. He never asked what I had in mind. The trouble was that he always ordered what *he* liked and he didn't care if I liked it or not. He thought a good wife would like what he did. At least, he didn't order me the cheapest thing on the menu. Come to think of it, the way things turned out, I wonder why he didn't."

"Along with his many charms, I see he was a bully as well."

"Absolutely. He felt he was superior to anyone else. He claimed he had excellent upbringing and commented on how few people actually gained from it as much as he did." Her eyes had been staring into space. She didn't like to think of Dennis under any circumstances. Why did the subject keep coming up?

Kevin waited for them to close their menus before stepping forward. "Have you made a selection?"

Max nodded and bent his head toward Peg.

"I'll have the pheasant with the house salad, red potatoes and the vegetable medley."

Kevin looked to Max. "And for you, sir?"

"I'll have the Orange Roughy with--"

"Sir, I would suggest another entree. The roughy we have today is inferior, and the chef prefers not to serve it."

"I appreciate your telling me. In that case, I'll have the Beef Stroganoff, Caesar salad, vegetable medley and . . . mashed potatoes instead of rice, if I could."

Kevin nodded. "Of course." He took the menus from the table and left.

Peggy watched him go to the kitchen. "He seems like such a nice young man."

"Mom said he has to be her favorite waiter of all times." He told her about his mother's experience with Michael.

Peg's eyes were filled with admiration. "I can't believe she actually got up there and played the piano."

If only she'd look at him like that. "She's good, Peg."

"Oh, I don't doubt that, but to get up and play in front of all the people." She waved her hand around the room.

"I doubt that she cares about that. She loves music and," he shrugged his shoulders, "she's a true artist."

"And as I remember," she recalled, "so are you." Now she showed her admiration for him.

His head moved shyly to the side. "Well, perhaps at one time--"

"Don't be modest, Max. You were in every music class and you learned every instrument; you were in choir, band, and ensembles. You accompanied the choir and you even played in the piano quartet."

He laughed. "But I can't hold a candle to Mom. I don't do those things anymore."

"That's a shame." She had always enjoyed going to the monthly college programs so she could listen to Max perform. She felt so proud that she knew him. The other girls envied her – at least they did until the date they never had.

After Kevin brought their salads, he a told them to enjoy them and left. Max was uncomfortable as Peggy bowed her head for a brief prayer. It was as if he weren't there. He didn't feel slighted exactly, but praying was something he didn't share with her. Not anymore. There was an emptiness in him, but not a wish to feel as passionate as she did about prayer. He ignored the feeling.

An hour later, after they had enjoyed their meals, a middle-aged woman dressed in a long purple gown stepped up to the piano. In spite of being rather heavy and wearing far too much makeup, Max thought she presented herself quite well. Her face was neither pretty nor plain. It was unremarkable. Doctors often used it to say there was nothing out of the ordinary; in other words, nothing to remark about. He chuckled to himself at that term. He'd heard that some patients felt slighted when they read or heard that word, as if they were nothing special.

The woman's very blond hair probably came out of a bottle, but he would listen to her play and not judge her on her appearance. Secretly, he would like to have suggested a more natural presentation, but it was really none of his business.

Kevin removed their empty plates and asked if there was anything else he could get for them.

"It was a wonderful meal," said Max. "I have to tell you that my mother recommended Adam's Haven. She came in last night and played the piano for you."

Kevin's face lit up. "You're Edna Madison's son?" He looked more like a love struck teenager than an efficient waiter.

Peg held back a giggle and winked at Max. "And *he* plays, too," she offered.

Kevin's eyes lit up. "Is that right? I wish you had told me earlier. I'm sure my boss would like to have heard you play. He came in just as your mom was leaving last night. Tell her hello from me."

"I will, but I'm sure she'll be back, and," he looked at Peg, "we will, too."

Peg's heart skipped a beat as she cautiously nodded. "The pheasant was the best I've ever had."

"I'll pass that on to the chef. Will there be anything else?"

"Just bring the check, Kevin." He handed him the credit card.

They sat for another half hour and listened to the woman play show tunes and a little Mozart. She asked if they had a request.

"One song for the road," said Max. "How about *All The Things You Are*?"

"An old one, but a good one." She nodded, turned a few pages and started to play.

Peg's heart skipped a beat as she remembered sitting in the student cafeteria listening to the song. Max had watched her from across the dining hall during the entire song. She could feel her face turning pink. "She's very good, isn't she?" said Peg, trying to keep her attention on the soloist.

It wasn't until he saw Peg's face blush that he wondered if she remembered hearing this song in the cafeteria at college when he was so totally smitten with her. If she did remember, it seemed to embarrass her. Best not to mention it. He gave the pianist a nod of approval when she finished the piece and put a five dollar bill in the large glass bowl on the piano. Kevin brought the check and Max signed the credit card slip.

When Kevin saw the gratuity, his eyes opened wide. "Thank you, sir."

He leaned closer to Kevin. "The name is Max. Drop the *sir*, please."

"Yes, sir." When he realized what he'd said, he quickly corrected it. "Yes, Max."

Peggy excused herself to go to the restroom and Max walked up to the front for their coats. He hadn't been standing there two minutes when he heard a gushy voice behind him, a voice he didn't want to hear. His whole body stiffened. What a way to end a perfect evening!

"We meet again, Maxwell." Veronica Tillman, dressed to the hilt, put her hand on his arm. "I didn't know you came to places like this. Won't you join us at our table?" She pointed to the rear of the room.

Max shook his head. He couldn't believe this. First at the store, then at the hospital, and now here. "Oh, Mrs. Tillman. I didn't see you. Have you been here long?"

"No. We just came in ten minutes ago. Won't you join us?"

He made it a point to look around, hoping to see Peg coming back from the restroom. "Isn't your husband with you?"

She waved her ringless hand in front of her face. "I'm divorced, Maxwell. Didn't you know that?"

"Uh, no, I didn't." Of course, he knew. How could he not know the way she kept flinging herself at him?

"So," she moved closer to him and hung on his arm. "So you thought I was married. No wonder you wouldn't give me the time of day. You see there is no reason we shouldn't see each other socially. Please join my best friend and me at our table."

"Thank you, but I'm waiting for someone." He couldn't help the way his words came out abrupt and bit cutting.

"Bring him along," she said, not about to give up. "My friend isn't attached either, if you catch my drift." She batted her eyelashes at him.

Max finally caught a glimpse of Peg behind Veronica. She couldn't stop grinning. She wiped the smile off her face and stepped forward, claiming his other arm. "I'm sorry to have been so long, darling." She was gushing as well as, if not better than Veronica did. "Will you forgive me?" She had just the right adoring look in her eyes.

Who'd have known Peg had that hidden talent? "Of course." He pulled out of Veronica's grasp put his arm at Peg's back. "Peg, this is Veronica Tillman, a customer at my store." He nodded towards Peg. "Margaret Swenson." He added, "Enjoy your dinner, Mrs. Tillman." They left Veronica standing with her mouth hanging open. He helped Peg into her coat and guided her out the door before he let out a sigh of relief. "I don't know what I would have done if you hadn't come along. How did you know I was in trouble?"

Peg laughed, but her eyes showed sympathy. "The look on your face was priceless. You looked like a caged animal. I hope I didn't misread you." She looked into his eyes, genuinely concerned.

He grimaced. "Not at all." He told her about meeting her at the hospital last night, and about her advances at the store.

"Well, maybe she'll think we're an item and quit bothering you."

"That would be great, but that woman is very aggressive."

"Why don't you simply tell her that you're not interested?"

"I've tried, but she's a customer, and I don't think she hears what she doesn't want to hear. Haven't you heard *the customer is always right*?"

"I see your point. If you just lost *her* business, you'd probably survive, but one person, especially a woman like that can cause a lot of trouble for you."

"It wasn't as if I didn't let her know that I'm not interested in a relationship. I don't think she likes to admit defeat."

"Well, just look what a prize she's working for." Peg batted her eyelashes like Veronica had done earlier.

Max laughed, a little embarrassed. They talked about college days, little things they remembered about each other and funny things that happened in some of their classes. They recalled the college band tour when half the band almost ruined a hotel room. It seemed the boys had started an innocent pillow fight and the activity snowballed into a full fledged brawl.

Max was pensive when they were close to her apartment. He'd had such a delightful evening with Peg. He couldn't understand how Peg's husband could cheat on her and leave her. "You must have been devastated when Dennis left you. How did you get through the hurt and betrayal?"

Peg turned to him. "I knew God was with me. My faith got me through it."

"Hmmm." He berated himself for asking. Max didn't want to tell her about the loss of his faith. She wouldn't understand. He remembered how she threw herself into the Bible class. Come to think of it, he was that way once. That was a long time ago.

"You don't look very convinced."

He turned his head back to watch the road. "Oh, I have no doubt that your religion helped you, Peg."

She could tell how uneasy he was. He didn't want to talk about this, but she couldn't just drop it. "How about you? Didn't God help you through your tragedy?"

Talk about stupid! He mentally hit his head with the heel of his hand. He didn't know how to answer. He didn't want to mislead her and he couldn't lie to her, so he felt he had to tell her the truth. If only he hadn't invited this question. "God didn't help me, Peg." He wasn't able to keep the anger out of his voice. "God let a beautiful woman in the prime of life get shot to death. How could He help me?"

It was Peg's turn to remain silent. She couldn't explain it, but she couldn't drop it. "So you believe God *planned* your wife's death?"

He felt the anger he'd felt three years ago. His lips clamped tightly together. "He let it happen," he ground out between his teeth.

Peg looked down at the floor of the car. "So some young man needed money and tried to get it the only way he knew how. That certainly didn't make it right, but suppose the boy was mentally ill or on drugs. Do you really think God would plan a thing like that? That doesn't even mean you can assume He *allowed* it to happen. I understand it's very hard to accept, but God gave us brains, Max, and--"

"Don't bother trying to explain it, Peg" His words came out more harshly than he'd intended, but every time he talked about God, it seemed he couldn't help himself.

"Have you seen the boy who did this? Have you talked to him?"

Max shook his head. "I couldn't even go to the trial because Sam was sick and I couldn't leave her." He shook his head. "She needed me, Peg. She couldn't stop crying. I couldn't help her, but I had to be there for her. It was only when I held her in my arms that she calmed down." He sighed deeply. "My wife was killed, leaving me with a daughter to raise by myself. That's just the way it was." He pulled up in front of Peg's two-family house. "Let's not talk about that." He pointed out the window to her two-story stucco duplex. "We're home."

She wanted to know how he felt about the boy. Naturally, it was a horrible thing to do, but was he able to forgive him? She doubted it. What could she say? Although she could think of a few bible verses, she knew quoting scripture would certainly send him running. She sighed. "Yes, we're home."

Relieved that he could change the subject, he studied her home. "Nice house. Have you lived here long?"

She shook her head. "I just rented this place a year ago. I got tired of apartment living. I wanted my own place, but I can't afford it on my salary. Renting isn't so bad." She picked up her purse, ready to get out of the car. "Want to come in for coffee?"

"I'd better not tonight." He opened his car door. Without thinking, he said, "I'll take a rain check if it's okay with you." If he didn't want any more talk about God, why did he bother asking for the rain check? He'd bet anything the subject would come up again if they kept seeing each other.

"Sure thing." She waited for him to come around to her side of the car. It felt so strange to have a man open her car door for her. She was perfectly capable of getting out by herself, but she was sure she'd hurt his feelings by doing so. His hand was warm on her back. What a glorious feeling it was.

When they were at her door, he kissed her on the cheek. "Thanks for going out with me, Peg. I can't remember when I felt so relaxed." *Except now.* "I really enjoyed the evening. Can we do it again?" *Only without the religious talk.*

"I'd like that. I had a wonderful time, too." *I hope you mean what you're saying.*

"How about tomorrow? We could go to an early brunch, say at eleven."

She looked hopeful. "Tomorrow is Sunday, Max. Church is at ten-thirty." Her words sounded as if she expected him to know that. "I sing in the choir," she explained softly.

Now what? He should have known. "Ah," he uttered. Best forget that idea.

"But you could come to church with me and we could leave from there."

She might as well have kicked him in the stomach. Everyone knew that Max Madison didn't go to church. Hadn't he just told her about his lack of faith? "No." He didn't want to be alone tomorrow but he wouldn't give in and go to church, not even for Peg. "Maybe I could pick you up here at noon." He watched her expression. She was, no doubt, disappointed, but there was no point in skirting the issue. He wouldn't give in to her suggestion, but he wanted to see Peg again.

She hesitated before answering. "I suppose that would work."

He found he couldn't ignore her disappointment. "Is my lack of faith going to keep you from seeing me?"

Her expression softened. "Of course not. You're just misguided. Somebody didn't do a very good job of explaining God's part in a tragedy like yours. How can I hold that against you?" A simple *Do unto others...* allowed her to agree to see him again. She couldn't help wondering *if* he could change, but she couldn't help *hoping* that he could.

He was relieved, yet a little concerned that Peg might try to convert him to her way of thinking. "Noon?" At least she hadn't quoted scripture to him. He'd balk at that.

She smiled. "Noon it is."

He kissed her cheek again. "Goodnight, Peg."

"Goodnight, Max. Thank you again." He left her standing just inside her doorway. She had thought he might kiss her on the lips. She really wanted him to, but he probably wouldn't on their first date. Still, it wasn't as if they hadn't known each other before.

Actually, she had to admit that they probably didn't know each other after so many years apart. She had changed and she was sure he had, too. She went inside and closed the door. Maxwell Madison was in her life again, but she was going to be very careful not to get carried away this time. When he hadn't asked her out again, she left college hurting like she never thought she could. She later chalked it up to nothing more than a teenage crush, but when she saw him again at the hospital, she realized it wasn't just a crush. She had always wanted to be part of his life. It just hadn't happened. Did they stand a chance after all these years? She hoped so.

Max had kissed her on the cheek, turned on his heel and abruptly walked away from her. "Idiot," he said to himself. What made him ask her to brunch right after she told him about her faith in God? Did he want another do-gooder in his life? Hadn't he had his fill after Bernice was killed? Hadn't the minister come to talk to him, almost begging him to come back to church? Even his friends from church and his neighbors meant well, but nobody understood. Nobody *could* understand who hadn't suffered the same kind of loss. Sure, people died every day, but how many of them were gunned down in cold blood so senselessly by a good-for-nothing hoodlum? What if the kid had been desperate for money? That didn't and never could change what he did.

After a great deal of soul searching, Max decided that once he'd seen Peggy at the hospital, he didn't want to walk away from her, even if they couldn't agree on the matter of religion. He only hoped that he wasn't letting himself in for another broken heart, and he certainly didn't want to mislead Peg. She as much as admitted that she was seriously interested in him in college. He had definitely been attracted to her and wanted her even now as more than a friend.

He thought about their college days. He had really thought he loved her then. Silly as it seemed, he didn't have to have a bunch of dates to know she was the girl for him. They'd been together in classes and at functions where the band played and, of course, at Bible Study. They seemed to hit it off right from the start. What if she hadn't gotten the flu that night? Might he have been married to her by now? If so, that would have saved *her* a lot of agony. On the other hand, he would not have married Bernice, nor would they have had a daughter. Oh, Peg might have had his child, but it wouldn't have been Samantha. He couldn't imagine life without his beautiful little girl who was growing into a beautiful woman. Even though he realized she'd grown up, it was still hard for him to accept. She would *always* be his little girl.

He reached his house, wondering how he got there. He hadn't even been conscious of driving the distance from Peg's house. Driving while so involved in your private thoughts could be dangerous. It was a good thing his instincts worked for him, and it was probably pure luck that there wasn't much traffic on the road. Next time, he'd be more careful.

Next time? Suddenly, it occurred to him that Bernice, on the day she went to the store, might have thought about a *next time*. But she would never have a *next* time. How did any of us know if there would be a next time? He shook off the thought and went into the house feeling none too happy about his thoughts. Was God behind them? Was his dream connected to these thoughts? Was it his dad's voice that he heard in the dream?

CHAPTER EIGHT

▼

Michael accepted Edna's invitation to attend church with her. She had wanted to make lunch for him, but he convinced her to accept his invitation to Sunday Brunch at a restaurant near the hospital. That way, they could visit Samantha shortly after she would have had her lunch.

Michael found the service inspiring. The pastor's message made him feel almost guilty for not attending church on a regular basis. In fact, since Carol died, he just drifted away from the things that meant so much to them. His most vivid memories of church were of Carol's funeral. It was such a sad day that he didn't want to deliberately recreate his devastation. Perhaps he'd been wrong. The minister pointed out the importance of the parishioners supporting each other and he had to admit that he missed that. In no way did he blame God for Carol's death. He accepted that there was a time to live and a time to die. Whether it was predetermined or not, he didn't know. It didn't matter to him.

The ladies at the church had served coffee and some sweets after the service to allow the members the fellowship the minister believed so important; but all he wanted to do was go home to be by himself. He knew he wouldn't be alone, though, because the boys were there, and as devastated as they were about losing their mother, they were worried about him. Somehow, he couldn't hide his grief from them, but grieving was a natural thing. The emptiness that followed might not have been, but he was doing something about that now. It felt good. Did he have it in his power to do something about it all along?

His thoughts came back to the present when Edna introduced him to several friends. He noticed Judd and Mary up front speaking with the organist. One thing about Judd, he thought, was that when he was involved in something, he was right up there ready to serve wherever and whenever he was needed. He admired that.

"Would you mind if we went into the Fellowship room?" asked Edna. "If you have coffee, I can speak to Miriam Collins about next month's Salad Supper. I'll just be a minute."

"No problem." Before he had taken his first sip of coffee, two people had introduced themselves. After that, Judd and Mary spotted him and came right over.

"Well," said Judd, "I see Edna managed to drag you back to your beliefs."

Mary, who looked more beautiful than ever with her short brown hair and skin that never seemed to age, scolded Judd for his insensitive remark. "We're happy to see you here, Michael." She hugged him and kissed his cheek lightly.

"You get more beautiful every time I see you."

"You say that every time you see me, Michael." She gave his arm a little punch. "I expected to see you earlier this morning. Didn't you sleep well?"

"I slept great." *That is, the few hours that were left of the night, but I wouldn't have changed a thing.* "You were gone by the time I came downstairs."

She nodded. "We had a meeting before church. Will you join us for lunch?"

"Thanks, but Edna and I have plans." Before Mary could include Edna in the invitation, he clarified their plans. "We're going to the hospital to see Samantha and work in a brunch someplace."

"I was just telling Judd that I hope I get to see you sometime," Mary teased.

He looked at her out of the corner of his eye. She couldn't have forgotten, or did Judd forget to tell her? "Judd told you that I'll be moving here, didn't he??"

She nodded. "Yes. I hope you haven't changed your mind. We don't see you nearly often enough."

Michael smiled sheepishly. He hadn't been in town long enough to run over and see her, not after he'd met Edna.

"If things keep going the way they are," Mary teased, "you'll probably be so occupied that we still won't see much of you."

Judd tweaked his wife's nose. "Quit fishing, Mary."

Mary blushed and batted Judd's hand away. "I just want to say that Edna is one of the loveliest ladies I know."

Michael smiled. "I agree."

"You agree about what?" asked Edna, who had approached from behind, unnoticed.

It would never do to let her know they were talking about her. Just as he thought of a comment, Pastor Paulson introduced himself.

"Great sermon," said Michael as he shook the minister's hand.

"Thank you. Are you visiting our fine city?"

"I hope to do more than visit. I'm considering moving closer to Judd and Mary."

The pastor nodded. "And to our lovely Edna, I see."

Michael felt his face get warm. Was he so obvious? He tried to sound innocent. "I don't know what makes you say that."

"Oh, Michael," Mary's words came out with a little laugh, "you are so diaphanous."

Diaphanous? Was that a word he had heard before?

He must have looked puzzled because she leaned closer to him. "Transparent," she whispered.

Judd tried to keep the smirk off his face. "She's adding a new word to her vocabulary every week. Last week she was talking about graminivorous cows." He waited for Michael to comment, but Michael just shrugged with a questioning expression. "Animals that feed on grass are graminivorous."

"Ah." What more could Michael say? He moved his gaze to Edna. "I think we should be going."

"Yes, we probably should." She hugged Mary. "It was nice seeing you, Mary. We haven't talked in ages." She turned to Pastor Paulson.

"I'll call you about the details of the Salad Supper." He nodded and turned toward another couple.

Mary took Edna's hand. "We'll have to get together sometime, maybe for lunch on one of the days you work."

Her lips pulled together as she shook her head. "I don't leave the office at noon."

"I know, dear," Mary patted her hand, "but nothing prevents me from bringing lunch in, does it?"

"And you know," added Judd, "how she loves to fuss in the kitchen inventing new dishes." He eyed his wife as he directed his words to Edna. "Of course, you take your chances."

Mary's fist connected with his arm in a good natured punch. She smiled at her husband sweetly, and then turned to Edna. "Tell Sam I hope she feels better soon."

"I will." She turned to leave.

Michael took Edna's arm as they left. "See you later," he said.

"I should hope so, unless you intend to come in late and leave early every night you're here," teased Mary.

Michael laughed as they went out the door.

Edna waved to Sheila who was standing outside with a man Edna hadn't seen before. It hadn't been that long since the church supper, and Sheila hadn't mentioned a man in her life. Was this something new? Perhaps he was a relative.

"I'd like you to meet Jacob Tyler," said Sheila to Edna. *Should I know the man with Edna?* "Jacob, this is my employer's mother, Edna Madison."

Jacob shook Edna's hand as she introduced Michael to both of them.

"Are you from out of town?" Edna asked Jacob.

"No, but I've just returned after being out of town for a few months."

"And Michael, is it?" asked Sheila. "Are you from around here?"

"At present," said Michael, "I'm in the process of relocating. Edna's employer is my brother-in-law."

"Oh," said Sheila in an enlightened tone. She turned to Edna. "So you've known him a while."

Sheila had to ask, but why should she feel awkward about it? Michael is a new friend I met. That's all there is to it. Edna shook her head. "We just met recently."

Sheila asked about Sam, and Edna told her about their experience last night. She asked Edna to convey her sympathy before they said their goodbyes and went to their respective cars.

Samantha pushed her tray away. She had almost cleaned her plate, not that there was very much on it to begin with. She usually had a small appetite unless she didn't know what to do with herself, like when she was on vacation last winter and a snowstorm kept her trapped at home alone for three days. Her dad had gone to St. Cloud for the day, but he hadn't made it back to Minneapolis before the storm hit. She was bored. By the second day of the storm, the phones didn't work, but unlike many homes in neighboring areas, she was thankful to have electricity. She'd heard on the radio that several suburbs were without power, but she was able to cook and bake all three days, and ate most of her creations.

Sam had turned backwards trying to find the waste basket to get rid of her napkin when she heard someone enter the room. She assumed they were bringing Katie back from x-ray.

"How are you, Sam?"

She looked up to see Doug Daily, the handsome intern. "Hi." She wasn't sure she wanted him to call her *Sam*, but she sort of liked the way it sounded when he said it.

He grinned. "I see you didn't object to my shortening your name."

She shrugged. "My friends dubbed me Sam when I was young."

"I forgot," he said with tongue in cheek. "You're *much* older now."

Was he teasing her or flirting with her? She couldn't quite tell, but she sort of wished it were the latter. "You can't have that many years on me." She looked at him as if sizing him up. "You're what . . . forty-six?"

He laughed heartily, licked his index finger and scored her point in mid air. "Good one." He sighed. "I'm twenty-eight."

"Hmmm. I would have sworn you were older. You seem far too wise to be so young."

"I suppose I have to give you that point, too," he conceded.

Her chin raised partly in stubbornness, partly in defiance. "I happen to be twenty-two, so you don't have *that* many years on me."

"I'm just teasing, Sam. You didn't tell me if you mind that I call you Sam."

"As long as you don't call me Sammy, I guess it's okay." She added softly,

"Thanks for asking."

He grinned. "You're welcome."

"What brings you in here? You're not assigned to the surgery floor, are you?"

He smiled. "I told you I was going to come and see my friends. Where's Katie?"

"They came for her as soon as she finished eating. I think they took her to x-ray." Her expression was grim. "Anything new on her folks?"

"Possibly. It's too early to tell, but it looks like her dad might be snapping out of it. When he's conscious, they'll be able to determine if there was brain damage."

"Oh, I didn't even think of that. I was just concerned if he'd live or die."

"I know. Katie's been a brave kid, but she'll need a lot more courage. They may have to put her in a foster home until her parents are dismissed from the hospital. That could be weeks or months."

"That would be awful. Can't you do something?"

"Me? I'm just a lowly intern."

"You're a resident physician, now."

He nodded sheepishly. "Yeah, I guess you're right, but what can I do?"

"Keep her here."

"You must know that a hospital can't afford to keep patients longer than necessary. Already, they're keeping her here for some mysterious ailment that may or may not actually exist." He hoped he could trust Sam not to say anything to anyone about this. "They moved her out of Pediatrics when they felt she was well enough to be discharged. Some doctors and nurses seem to be doing a little cat and mouse thing with her. Or so I suspect."

Sam's lips formed a wide grin as she nodded her head. "They're human."

"But don't get your hopes up, Sam. It's only a matter of time before they'll have no choice but to cut her loose."

"Is somebody going home?" asked Edna as she and Michael entered the room.

Doug and Sam both shifted their attention to the older couple. "Hi."

Doug picked up Sam's chart and checked the data. "It's possible. Her temp seems to be back to normal. If it stays that way, they'll probably let her go sometime tomorrow or the next day."

Sam's face was grim. "We were talking about Katie. Do you know she'll have to go to a foster home until her folks recover enough to take care of her?"

"Oh dear," uttered Edna. "Well, foster homes aren't always as bad as the ones that are in news reports."

A little uncomfortable, Sam shifted in bed. "I know, but she's so worried about her parents and then to have to go to strangers? It isn't fair."

Edna sighed and patted Sam's hand. "Life isn't always fair, you know."

A flicker of sadness replaced the outrage in Sam's eyes. She looked at Doug. "Isn't there anything we can do?"

Michael stepped forward. "Couldn't she stay with people she knows?"

Doug had overstepped his position by confiding in Sam. Now the information had gone farther. Doug exhaled a breath he didn't even realize he had held. He was sure he had many lessons to learn before he would become the confident doctor he hoped to be one day. "If one of her parents regains consciousness enough to give permission, then it would be a matter of finding someone willing to take her in. That's her only hope."

"But she has no relatives and when I asked her why her friends didn't come to visit her, she said they had just moved from Ohio, and she didn't know anyone yet. I'm sure there are no friends who would be willing to take on the responsibility."

Edna spoke up. "Well I certainly would be willing. She's such a sweet little thing."

Michael squeezed her shoulder. "I'd be willing to help while you're working."

"First things first," said Doug. "Let's pray that her folks will be able to give the permission she needs."

Edna shook her head sadly. "They will, no doubt, be skeptical about letting her go with people our age."

Sam had a determined pout on her lips. "I'm sure Dad wouldn't mind if she stayed with us."

Doug squeezed Sam's hand. "Let's give it some time. I'll let you know as soon as there's any chance something like this would work." He waved his hand as he left the room. "See you later."

"Well, well, well," teased Edna. "It looks like the young doctor is interested in more than your medical condition." She winked at Sam.

Sam blushed. She had secretly developed a crush on him, but she'd never admit it. She was beyond the age of crushes and should know better than to get involved with a man so quickly. "I doubt it. He probably came looking for Katie."

Edna winked at Michael with a glint in her eye. "Uh-huh."

"Gram," Sam changed the subject, "can I ask you a personal question?"

Michael loosened his tie uncomfortably. "I'll go down to the gift shop."

"No, don't leave. Really, I just need to talk to someone."

"And you can't talk to your father?" asked Edna.

Sam looked horrified. "He's the last one I can talk to."

Edna showed deep concern as she moved closer to Sam. "What is it, child?"

"You know how Dad feels about God since Mom was killed." Her eyes were sad. "He doesn't go to church. He won't talk to a minister. He wants nothing to do with God. He says God is responsible for Mom's death."

Edna nodded sadly. "I know."

"You didn't lose your faith when Grandpa or Mom died, Gram. Why not?"

Edna wanted to be careful the way she explained. "Grandpa had a bad heart, but concerning your mother, I don't believe that God *allowed* that young boy to shoot your mother. I think that He has to let people live their lives. We're not puppets on strings that God controls. He doesn't decide our fate. He gave us brains, and He allows us to use them. Sometimes it's right, sometimes it's wrong." She sighed. "It's such a difficult subject, honey."

"I think your grandmother's right," Michael interjected. "If God gave us brains, but didn't let us use them, why bother to give them to us in the first place?"

Sam was silent for a moment. "It's so hard to decide. Sometimes, I almost believe Dad is justified in feeling the way he does. It's hard to see him so bitter; on the other hand, what you're saying makes sense."

Edna pushed a strand of Sam's hair off her forehead tenderly. "It really does. At least, to me it does."

"I wish Dad could see it that way." Sam felt so helpless. She knew she couldn't help him, especially since she wasn't sure just what she believed.

Michael knew what Max was feeling, but to him, it seemed like Max should have been able to see things more clearly by now. "Maybe someday he will."

Sam looked at the couple with admiration. "You two are so wise."

"Hmmm," uttered Michael. "People always say *Wisdom comes with age.* I think that the reference to age involves many decades of listening and learning. If we listen, and weigh the concepts, we might be lucky enough to see actual results. It is through that process that we gain wisdom." He winkled at her. "It takes a little more than age."

"So you're saying that *that* process allows us to form our own opinions?"

"Exactly. When you've lived as long as your grandmother and I have, you have many opportunities to see if your opinions were right or wrong; or sometimes, you learn that *conflicting* opinions each worked for different people."

Sam scratched behind her ear in confusion. "Thanks a lot. You make it sound like there is no right or wrong."

Michael shook his head. "I didn't say that exactly, Samantha. I said *sometimes* there's no one answer. And it's true. Sometimes there is no right or wrong. We are all entitled to our own opinions. Who's to say which one is valid? That's what makes life so interesting. We're individuals. We form some of our opinions at a very early age, and some in our adolescence. Believe it or not, your grandmother and I are still forming them at our age. We never cease to learn unless our minds are no longer able to function." He glanced at Edna. "Sadly, that can happen any time."

"Wow. That's a lot to think about. Thank you."

A nurse wheeled Katie to her bed and helped her into it. "Hi."

"Hi, Katie." Edna waited until Katie was in bed and then she picked up the sack she had put down on Katie's table. "This is for you, young lady."

Katie's eyes opened wide. "For me?" She looked at them all.

"Open it," prodded Edna.

When she looked inside the sack, her eyes lit up. She pulled out a portable CD player with earphones. "I always wanted one of these." Her eyes were bright with delight.

"We didn't know what you like to listen to, so we brought you a contemporary CD and a classical one. We can add to your collection as soon as we know your tastes."

Katie was so excited about the gift that her hands trembled and Michael had to help her open the package and put the earphones on her. She put in a CD and the widest smile formed on her lips. "Thank you." She looked up at Michael and then to the others. "Thank you so much."

"You're welcome," they said in unison.

They talked for another few minutes before Edna said they had to leave. She kissed Samantha's cheek. "I love you, dear. I'm so glad everything turned out so well. Just think what could have happened if Michael hadn't convinced me to call 911."

"I suppose. I really didn't want you to, you know."

"I know. You were frightened."

Sam bit her lower lip as she nodded.

Michael squeezed her hand. "Did I hear that young doctor call you Sam? May I call you that, too?"

"Except for family, I haven't been called that since I was in high school."

"Do you dislike it?"

She shook her head and then shrugged. "It depends who calls me that. I'd like very much for you to use that name, Mr. Richards,"

"I will if you will call me Michael."

She smiled. "Thank you, Michael."

"We must run. You let me know what I can do to help," Edna said as she surreptitiously glanced toward Katie. "Your dad will have to open the store in the morning, but if he's tied up when you come home, I'll be happy to pick you up and stay with you until your father gets home."

"I won't be bedridden. They've been having me walk around already."

"We'll wait and see. Enjoy the service here, dear. Tomorrow, you may be on your own." They said goodbye and left.

Reluctantly, Doug walked into ICU. No matter how hard he tried to ignore the obstruction in his chest, he couldn't forget how his grandfather had died. The Intensive Care Unit was wonderful in attempting to save the life of the man who was so very special to him, but it hadn't worked. Doug was young when the accident had happened, but he would never forget the loss he suffered when he was told they couldn't save the man he loved so dearly. Would he ever forget the feeling? He sighed. No, he could never forget that. That's why he became a doctor. It was a tribute to his beloved grandfather.

He shook off the powerful emotion and talked to the nurse attending Katie's mother. There was just enough change in her condition to give them hope that she would regain consciousness in time. He then checked on Katie's father, who surprisingly had also shown signs of improvement, although it was doubtful how long it would take for him to speak.

"Give it time," said the attending nurse. He'd used those exact words when he said them to Katie earlier.

Katie, however, may not have time. In a way, it was too bad she wasn't actually running the mysterious fever, which Doug doubted was genuine, but he wasn't about to say anything. Doctors took an oath to heal their patients, and sometimes, the healing process involved more than physical care. Katie needed to be with people she knew, and right now, the hospital staff was all she knew.

If one of Katie's parents had the ability to give permission, even if it was done verbally with witnesses, the nice older couple or Sam and her dad would take her in and care for her. It was too bad that they couldn't just send Katie home with Sam. She'd be great with her, but Sam had a life of her own.

It wouldn't be long before she'd leave to finish her clinicals. He smiled when he thought of Sam. She was different, cute, special. He'd never asked her where she was taking her training, but he assumed it was in Minneapolis. He wasn't pleased with the thought that if she were out of town, he wouldn't be able to ask her out, and he fully intended to ask her to dinner very soon. *Don't borrow trouble. If she came back to live with her father, she wouldn't be going out of town.* He sighed with relief. Even if they both would be busy, he had a feeling that she would make time for him. He hoped it wasn't just wishful thinking.

Max and Peg had had a wonderful Sunday Brunch. They talked about college days and what had happened in their lives through the years. Life, they decided, was filled with unexpected turns, both pleasant and unpleasant, some devastating. Even so, life went on. Often, depression got the best of each of them, but they managed to pull themselves out of it, Peg with her faith, and Max by sheer determination. Never had Max come quite so far out of his dark moods as he had since he found Peg again.

"My parents," said Peg, "are divorced and I seldom see them. Mother blames me for Dennis leaving me for another woman." She had told her that she could have held him, had she wanted to. From that moment on, she realized that her mother wasn't interested in her happiness. "She wanted her own level of comfort, no matter what it cost me." She hung her head. Peg would never understand why anyone would want a man who cheated on her? How could her mother even suggest it? Her dad was just resigned to the fact that his daughter was no better at marriage than her mother was; therefore, he also held her responsible for the breakup.

Max couldn't understand that. "What do you talk about when you're together with your parents?"

"We're never together anymore. Mom is remarried and Dad is shacking up with women half his age." She closed her eyes and bit her lower lip. "I no longer have a family. I'm better off without them."

Max frowned and shook his head sadly. "I've been fortunate. Dad was faithful to Mom until the day he died, and she," he smiled affectionately, "is the most gentle soul I've ever known." He looked at the scraps of food left on her plate and grinned. "Have you had enough?"

She laughed. "I got carried away. I've had way too much and it won't look so good on my hips."

"Hmmm. I was thinking just the opposite. You aren't a pound heavier than you were in college. In fact, I think you lost weight. Was that Dennis's doing?"

"Are you asking if I ate my heart out after the divorce?" He nodded. "No, I ate, but maybe out of stubbornness. In a way, I refused to give in to my anger and bitterness." Before he could speak, she went on. "I was hurt, Max, but I found it easier to deal with the whole thing with anger and judgment."

"Judgment?"

Her eyes narrowed with a sly, almost facetious look. "Well, of course. I knew Dennis was going to hell."

He laughed. "Remind me never to cross you."

She laughed, too. "I promise I won't wish that on you. You'd have to do something pretty low down and dirty to affect me that much, and," she added as her eyes met his, "I don't think you have it in you."

He raised his eyebrows with a hint of humor. "You don't think so, huh?"

Her voice was soft, but had a tone of determination. "I *know* you don't."

Max checked his watch several times. He was nervous and his voice was unsteady when he spoke. "How would you like to spend part of the day visiting your place of employment?"

The warmth in her smile put him completely at ease. "You want to take me to visit your daughter."

He nodded. "Good guess. You don't *have* to go along, but I'd like you to meet Samantha. Besides, she wants to meet you."

"Oh?" Her eyes opened with surprise. "You've told her about me?"

He didn't say a word, he just grinned as a faint pink showed on his face.

"Won't she resent me? I mean, if she misses her mother, she won't want to know that I'm dating her dad."

"Samantha has begged me to . . . how did she put it? Oh yes, to *embrace life* again. She moved back from Duluth after-- after it happened. She refused to leave me alone. I felt guilty, of course, but I couldn't make myself refuse her. Maybe I wanted to believe that she needed me as much as I needed her at that time." He looked down at his empty plate before he looked up and his eyes met hers. "She's one special girl, Peg."

Peg smiled. "I'm sure she is. I'd love to meet her."

A short time later, they were at Sam's door. Both girls had their eyes closed. Katie had her earphones on, her head resting against her pillow.

Max took Peg's arm. "Maybe we should come back later," he whispered to Peg.

She shook her head. "They're not sleeping," she said softly as she took his hand and pulled him into the room.

Max frowned. "How do you know?" he whispered.

She pointed to Katie. "That is not an expression of someone who is sleeping. Look at her. She's enjoying what she's hearing." She pointed to the earphones. She turned toward Sam. "And *her* respiration is not that of a sleeping patient."

"You can tell that just by looking at her?" he asked no longer whispering.

When she heard his voice, Sam's eyes flew open and her face brightened. "Dad. How long have you been here?"

"Not long. You must have been miles away, honey. Where'd you go?"

She shrugged. "Just thinking about what will happen in the near future." Her head tipped toward the other bed, letting them know she was referring to Katie.

"Peg," he said as he took her hand and pulled her close to Samantha's bed, "I'd like you to meet my daughter, Samantha. Sam, this is Margaret Swenson. We call her Peggy or Peg."

Sam reached her hand out to Peg, who shook it warmly. "It's nice meeting you. Dad says you're a nurse."

She nodded. "I'm in Pediatrics right now. He tells me that it won't be long before you get your degree."

"May tenth. I'm so excited." Her face turned serious. "That is, if they let me finish after missing so much."

"I'm pretty sure you can make it up. Have you found a job yet?"

Sam was surprised with the question. "So soon?"

"It wouldn't hurt."

"I want to work in the ER." The words that once were filled with determination, sounded not quite as confident as they had earlier.

"Really? I wouldn't have thought-- " She stopped herself suddenly so as not to discourage Sam. "Well, you can't try to find a job too soon, but I think you'll need some extra training for the ER."

She sighed. "I know, and I'm not sure I want to spend that extra time doing it right away. Maybe I'll have to let it go for a while. My main concern is to get my degree. Do you have any idea how long I'll have to stay home to recuperate?"

"I'm sorry. I don't know what your doctor will say. From what your dad told me, they got you into surgery just in time."

"Yes. So you're saying that my recuperation time is going to be a little longer than routine appendectomy."

Peg shrugged. "I'd assume so. The best thing to do is to ask your doctor next time he comes in." She saw the disappointment in Sam's eyes. "You'll learn very quickly that as a nurse, you won't try to out-guess the attending physician."

"Well, anyway, Doug thinks my doctor will let me go home soon."

The lines on Peg's forehead deepened as she tried to remember someone with that name. "Doug?"

"Dr. Daily," she said trying to hide her obvious fondness. "He was with the ambulance and the paramedics."

Peg nodded. "Young, tall, dark hair, handsome as all get out?"

Sam smiled and her face turned a tell-tale red. "That's him."

Peg repressed the grin that wanted so much to form on her lips. "He's nice."

She tried to sound barely interested. "Do you know him?"

"I've worked with him." She winked. "I understand he's available, too."

"Oh? I didn't know." Sam tried to look like she didn't care, but Max and Peg knew better.

"Oh," squealed Katie. "I didn't hear anyone come in."

Peg looked over at her, surprised to see the girl who had been in Pediatrics a few days ago. She went over to her bedside. "Katie Jordan? I didn't recognize you with those earphones on your head. How are you doing?"

Katie held her arms out for a hug. "I missed you. They wouldn't let me come and see you."

"Well, they should have told me where to find you. I thought you'd been discharged. How long have you been on fifth floor?"

"They brought me up a few days ago. I lose track of time."

Peg brushed Katie's hair behind her ear. "That's nothing unusual when you're in the hospital."

Her eyes opened in an innocent appeal. "Have you heard how my folks are?"

"Sorry, honey, but I've been working nights. Haven't they told you anything?"

Katie bit down on her lower lip. "Dr. Daily said there's hope. Do you think he's just saying that?"

She shook her head emphatically. "No. You can believe him." She was still puzzled as to why Katie was still in the hospital, and on fifth floor at that. They should have kept her on the pediatric floor where she belonged. The last she saw of Katie, she had only the broken arm to contend with, unless she was running a fever or there was a complication from the surgery. Everyone was pretty closed-mouthed about it or Peg would have heard she was still here. Poor Katie. She was so very vulnerable. She had no one but her parents.

Max took in the whole conversation. "So you two are already acquainted?"

Katie's eyes lit up. "She's my favorite nurse. She took care of me the night of the accident. I couldn't remember what happened, but Peggy helped me to remember. She'd tell me what was happening with Mom and Dad." Her lower lip quivered. "I wish they'd get better, Peggy."

Peg folded her arms around her. "Keep praying, honey."

Max stiffened. He looked at Peg and scowled. How did she dare tell the child to pray to a God who let his wife be killed? He turned to Samantha and made an effort to speak with her. "How are you feeling, honey?"

She giggled. "You always ask me that."

He shrugged. "So, answer it."

"I'm fine, Dad. I'm ready to come home."

Katie's expression turned solemn. "You're going home?"

"Maybe." Sam had to soften the blow. "They haven't said for sure."

"Then where will I be?" She was close to tears.

Peg ran her hand down Katie's silky hair. "Probably right here. You'll get another roommate." Peg put her finger under Katie's chin and raised her head to eye level. "I'll even come in and see you now that I know you're still here."

Katie's mouth formed a perfect pout. "I'll miss Sam."

"I'm sure you will." Peg stroked Katie's cheek.

Max moved over to Katie's bedside. "How about if *I* come to see you as soon as Samantha is able to take care of herself?" He reached in his pocket and took out a small box. "Which reminds me, Peg and I stopped at the gift shop. They didn't have any game boys or anything that would work for you, so we got you this." He handed the dark blue ring box to her.

Katie's left arm was in a cast, but she could use her fingers to hold the box while the other hand raised the cover. She took the ring out. "It's beautiful," she squealed.

"It's supposed to change its color with your moods. There's a little slip of paper in the bottom of the box explaining which color means what."

"Thank you." Katie was genuinely happy and put the ring on her finger. The stone gradually started to change to a shade of green.

"There," Peg pointed to the ring, "it's already showing that you're in a good mood." She blinked her eyes to hold back tears. She always got emotional where Katie was concerned.

Katie grinned, but kept her eyes glued to the stone.

Max kissed his daughter on the cheek. "I think it's time for us to leave, honey."

Sam nodded. "I'm getting sleepy anyway."

Max nodded knowingly. "It must be the company."

"Oh Dad, you know better than that."

Peg hugged Katie before moving over to Sam's bed. She took her hand. "We both know it's the after affects of the surgery."

Sam nodded. "I'm sorry. Maybe we can visit longer some other time."

"Don't be sorry. We have things to do now, but I'll see you again, I'm sure."

They said goodbye to the girls and left.

When they were in the car, Peg grabbed a tissue and dabbed at the moisture in her eyes. "Poor Katie. They'll have to send her to a foster home until her parents either snap out of it or the unthinkable happens."

"That's tough all right."

"Yes, it is. I wish I could do something, but unless one of her parents regains consciousness, Social Services will place her in a foster home. God forbid if neither one makes it."

Max just nodded. What could he say? He was well aware that it was still a possibility that if nothing else, complications could cause their deaths. It still irritated him that Peg had been so sincere about asking Katie to keep praying. Didn't she realize how cruel it was to give the child hope that could be shattered at any minute?

He wanted to bring it up and tell her how he felt, but he didn't want to spoil their time together. It troubled him to think that they were so far apart in their thinking. Still, he wasn't willing to give her up now that he'd found her again. He had a feeling of doom in spite of the joy he experienced when he was with Peg. What would happen was anyone's guess.

CHAPTER NINE

▼

As expected, Dr. Coleman discharged Sam on Tuesday on the condition that she would call him immediately should she start running a fever again. She was to take it easy for six weeks.

"*Six weeks?*" she almost shouted. "I can't miss training for that long."

"You won't have to miss your training for that period of time, but you will have to refrain from lifting for a while. I'll write an explanation to your instructors," the doctor assured her. "As rigid as the rules might be, don't forget that these are medical people who know the consequences of going back to your duties too soon."

She didn't have to stay in bed, but not being able to lift meant she couldn't take care of the patients assigned to her. She wouldn't be able to sneak back to her clinicals early. Most of the time, working with patients involved lifting, and she didn't think there was any way she could be excused from doing it.

She was worried that she wouldn't graduate after all, but she wasn't going to think about that right now. She'd be glad to get home.

When the doctor left, Doug dropped by her room. When he found her smiling, he grinned. "I take it Dr, Coleman cut you loose."

"He sure did, but he said I can't go back to my clinicals for a while. If I could sit at a desk and study, he would have let me go back early."

He nodded. "What did you expect?"

She shrugged. "I guess I figured..." She laughed as she let her words trail off. "I thought that I was an exceptionally fast healer."

He chuckled. "One good thing about this happening is that you have first-hand experience as a patient. Do you think that will help you when you take care of your future patients?"

"I don't think that applies to me. I want to work in the ER."

He stared at her in disbelief. "You're joking, right?"

"No," she snapped. "I'm not. I want the urgency and excitement of the ER."

He nodded, wondering why anyone would want a steady diet of that kind of stress. She was, however, entitled to her own opinion. If everyone wanted the same job, there'd be many jobs that would never be filled. He shrugged. "You're entitled to your own opinion."

"Yes, I am." Her words were short and almost belligerent.

He wasn't doing it consciously, but he realized that he'd criticized her. Should he politely back out of the room? Not yet. He went over to Katie. "Hi there, little angel. How are you doing today?" He picked up her chart and noticed the consistent 99.7 to 99.9 temperature record. He'd dearly love to take her temp himself, but if he found the chart to be inaccurate, he'd have to report it. After all, the nurses could be trusted, couldn't they? At least Katie was among friends, and right now, that was important.

"Sam's going home." She said glumly.

"I know," he moved closer to her, "but *I'll* still be here."

"You're not my roommate." Her lower lip stuck out in a pathetic pout.

"No, but I'll come to see you everyday."

Katie tried to smile as she moved her head slightly in a nod. "I love Sam."

Sam looked over at her, her heart almost breaking. "Katie, I'm going to come and see you, too."

Her mood brightened a little. "Will you really?"

"As soon as I can walk the distance from the entrance, I'll have Dad bring me."

Doug chimed in. "I'll even wheel her in a wheelchair if necessary."

Katie's expression mellowed a little before she asked the usual questions. "How are Mom and Dad? When can I go to see them? You could take *me* in a wheelchair."

"I know how you must feel, honey, but we can't have you going into ICU with your fever, even if it is low-grade." At least the false reports served a purpose. This wouldn't be a good time to see her parents.

"I'd be okay."

"It's not for your sake, Katie. The patients in ICU can't be exposed to any infection or anything like that. It could cause them a big set-back or worse." That much was true and he hoped Katie would accept it.

She hung her head as tears ran down her cheeks. "Okay."

Sam got out of her bed and went over to Katie. She sat on her bed and wrapped her in her arms, stroking her hair. "It's okay, Katie. I promise, I'll come to see you, and Dad said he'd come. And Peggy will come in everyday that she's working, I'll bet you have lots of friends here."

Katie was still sobbing. "I know, but I miss my mom and dad."

Sam held Katie close, her head tucked under Sam's chin. There was nothing she could say that would make Katie feel better. Why did she want to even try? Katie missed her folks and that wouldn't go away. She was glad that Katie couldn't see the tears in her eyes. "I know you do. Just be patient, Katie. Just be patient."

She shook her head. "I don't think God hears me. I pray so hard every night."

Oh dear. What could she say when she wasn't firm in her own beliefs? At times, she wondered if her dad was right. "I know you do."

Sam was thankful when Doug spoke. "And He does hear you. Just remember that He has his own way of doing things. He acts in His own time."

Katie sniffed. "Whatever that means."

The expression in Sam's eyes told Doug that she was at a loss. Why would that be? He knew her grandmother went to church, but maybe Sam didn't. He'd have to ask about it later, certainly not now. "I have to leave you two girls. I'm at the hospital to *work* today. I'm scheduled to see a crabby old man about sticking to his diet. He likes cake and candy and all sorts of sweets."

Katie's sobs stopped. "Can't he have them?"

Doug shook his head. "He has diabetes so he shouldn't have sugar. Some of us know what's good for us, but we *like* the things that aren't good for us."

"Like Black Cherry Chocolate ice cream." Her tongue swept between her lips.

Doug laughed. "Exactly." He waved as he left the room. "See you two later."

"But--" He was gone before Sam could tell him she wouldn't be there. Funny, but now *she* felt like crying, too. That was silly. She had gone all these years without a man in her life. She had decided that she didn't want a relationship like her parents had, the kind of relationship that caused so much pain when something happened to the other person. It practically destroyed her dad when her mother was killed. She sighed. Maybe it was just as well, but she would miss seeing Doug. She got sort of attached to him during her stay at the hospital. How could that happen in three short days?

Sam was still holding Katie when she realized Katie wasn't sobbing anymore. She released her and handed her a tissue. "All better?"

Katie dabbed her eyes. "I guess so, but I *will* miss you."

"And I'll miss you, too. We'll just have to call each other on the phone until I can come and visit you." Now, she had to change the subject and get the spotlight off Katie's problems. "Tell me about Peggy. She seems to be very nice."

Katie's eyes lit up. "She's super. Your dad likes her."

Sam had been hoping that Peggy would be a good influence on her dad. "Yes, I think he does," she said thoughtfully.

Katie frowned. Sam didn't sound that interested. "Don't you like her?"

"Of course I do, but I just met her."

"But you look like you don't really like it that your dad likes her."

Sam scowled. "Why would I look like that?"

Katie shrugged. "I don't know. Don't you want your dad to like her?"

"I've been hoping for a long time that he'd get interested in a woman." She sighed. "He's been so out of it since my mom died."

"That must be hard. I hope *my* mom doesn't die." Suddenly panic struck her.

"You think she'll be okay, don't you?"

"Oh, Katie, I'm not the one to ask. I'd like to think that both of your parents will be okay, but I don't know any more than you do. Just don't borrow trouble. Don't go through life worrying about hundreds of things that may never happen. When they don't, you wonder why you spent so much time worrying. Deal with the disasters of life if and when they happen. Do you understand what I'm saying?"

Katie nodded. "Just act like nothing happened."

"No, not exactly. Just don't sweat the stuff that hasn't happened yet."

"*Your* mom wasn't killed in a car accident," she argued.

Sam wasn't sure just exactly what Katie meant by that. She really didn't want to go into the explanation all over again. Maybe Katie forgot what she had told her before. Maybe she couldn't handle the horror of it, but she had to repeat it or it could undermine the advice she'd just given her. "No, Mom was shot by a kid who robbed a convenience store. I didn't have a chance to worry, Katie. My dad came home and had to tell me she was dead, that I'd never see her again. She was always there when I left for school, but suddenly, I didn't have a mother anymore." She hoped she didn't goof up.

Her eyes were wide with concern. "I'm sorry, Sam."

Sam took a deep breath. "It's okay. It's been a while since I told anyone about it."

Katie tried to smile. "I shouldn't have asked."

"I'm glad I told you because I found out that it doesn't hurt as much as it used to." She nodded, proud of herself. "I'm really glad I told you." *I think I learned something about myself. No wonder I'm not an optimist. I'm afraid to hope for the best because bad things just happen and you're stuck with them. You have to deal with whatever it is.* She wondered if she would ever feel comfortable hoping for the good things in life to happen. If she did, would she be struck down with tragedy as she had been when her mom died? She sighed. That would be too hard to deal with. She thought back to her teens, to a time before her mom was killed. How did she react to life back then? Was she afraid to hope? Hope—faith. They were such heavy words to her.

Katie put her arms around Sam because she looked so sad. "I'm glad you feel better talking to me." But she didn't believe it. This time it was Katie's turn to change the subject no matter how curious she was.

Max was at the store when Sam called and informed him that she would be free to leave the hospital sometime after lunch.

"I have to wait until Sheila shows up, honey. She has an appointment with the doctor. I can't ask her to postpone it because it took them three months to work her in. Dermatologists are few and far between in this city. Are you sure you don't want to go on to medical school to be an MD?"

"Dad." Sam laughed. "Can you really imagine me examining skin conditions?"

He laughed. "No, I can't. What do we do about getting you home? Sheila's appointment is at two. She should probably be back by three, maybe a little later."

"Oh, I can wait." But she really wanted to go home.

"Maybe your grandmother can pick you up. She's not working today."

"That's an idea, but really, Dad, I can wait for you."

"Call her. If she can't, -- hang on, honey." She could hear him telling a customer he'd be right with him. "Call me back if she can't pick you up, okay?"

"Okay, Dad. Thanks." She hung up.

Sam couldn't reach her grandmother and she was about to call Max again when Peggy stopped in to see Katie.

"And how are you girls this morning?" she asked cheerfully.

Besides Sam's "Fine," she heard Katie's less than enthusiastic, "Okay, I guess."

Peggy gave Katie all her attention. "That doesn't sound too encouraging. Is something wrong?"

"Sam's going home today." She was sulking.

Peggy nodded her sympathy. "And you'd rather that she stay in the hospital, get her temperature taken, eat hospital food, be subjected to umpteen million tests and get shots." She nodded her head as if she understood fully that Sam should choose staying in the hospital over going home. "I can see why she'd rather stay here."

Katie hung her head. "I know. I'm being selfish, but I love Sam."

"And I love you, honey," Sam replied. "I feel bad that I'm going home but--"

Katie shook her head. "Don't feel bad. I'm old enough to know better. I'm sorry, Sam." She raised her head courageously. "I'll be okay."

"I can't go home until Dad gets here." She looked at Peg. "The woman who works for Dad won't get to the store until after three. She has a Dermatologist's appointment at two."

"Trust me, Sam, if she has a two o'clock appointment, she may not be at the store by three, unless it's just down the block."

"No. I think her clinic is downtown." She began to understand what Peg was saying. Not only would the appointment take time, but the travel and parking added to it.

"Listen," said Peg, "I get off at three. Why don't I take you home?"

"Oh, don't be silly. I can wait for Dad. You'll want to get home and--"

"No, Sam. I would love to see where you live, and you could probably do with a nurse around for a little while before your dad comes home. Right?"

She hardly thought she needed a nurse. After all, she was a nurse herself, but she had to admit that it would be nice to get to know Peg a little better without her dad being around. "Are you sure?"

"I'm positive." She looked at her watch. "I have to get back to my floor. I'll pick you up as soon as I get off." She turned to Katie.

"And I'll stop in to see you tomorrow. Is there anything I can bring for you?"

Katie shook her head and watched Peg leave the room. She was going to quit being such a selfish kid. She should be happy for Sam, and she was. Besides, Sam said she'd come to see her. She was going to act more grown up so Sam would like her, sort of like a girl friend instead of like a little kid. She sure wished someone would come in and give her some good news about her folks.

Peg pulled up in the driveway of the pale green split level house. "What a lovely home you have." She commented.

"Dad designed it. His best friend was an architect, so he sat down with him and told him exactly the way he wanted it. At least, that's what I was told when I was little. I called him Uncle Ben even if he wasn't related to us. He said Dad was so good, he should have been an architect."

"But he's such a wonderful musician. It would have been a crime had he gone into anything except music."

"That's what Gram said; still, we all know he's good at a lot of things."

"Really?" *Like what*? she wondered.

Sam was tickled that Peg was interested in her dad. "He made a lot of things in the house. You'll see wooden bowls and lamps and serving trays made out of cedar. He even made the nicest shadow box. It's so intricate. I don't know how he did it."

In spite of Sam's arguing, Peg wouldn't let her carry her overnight case as they went into the house. Sam unlocked the door and invited Peg inside.

The living room was huge with a high ceiling decorated and supported with walnut colored rafters. "Impressive," she said. The fireplace seemed to be the focal point of the room. At least, that's where Peg's eyes went immediately. The furniture was tastefully done in neutral colors, shades of ivory, tan and brown to complement the taupe carpet. There were accessories in gold and an occasional splash of red. Four steps led up to the dining room and Peg imagined the kitchen must be somewhere close to the dining room. Sam explained that the bedrooms were also on that level off to the side of the house over the garage. Below the dining room area there was a family room half a level below the garage.

Peg pointed to the living room. "I suggest that you sit down for a little while and let me get you some coffee, tea or a soft drink."

"You don't have to wait on me, Peg."

"Nonsense. I do this all day, as you will--" She stopped speaking suddenly. "I forgot. You want to be in the ER. You won't have the chance to wait on anyone. Well, that can wait until you get married."

Sam shook her head. "I don't think so."

Peg had a smirk on her face. "You're not going to wait on your husband?" Peg was surprised, but then, she had heard many younger girls talk about how they were going to train their men to do all the things that Peg always thought came naturally to women. Maybe times have changed.

"I'm not going to have a husband to wait on." Sam's face seemed emotionless, but Peg caught just a hint of something in her eyes, sadness or perhaps a hint of pain, but enough to prompt her to ask questions.

"No husband? Isn't it too soon for such a decision? You're what? Twenty- one?"

"I'm twenty-two, but no." She took a ragged breath. "I just don't want to go through what Dad did when Mom died. It nearly killed him."

Peg could understand how it would cause a youngster such an emotional upset to have something so violent happen to her mother. If only Sam had been able to overcome the grief and the nightmares over something so horrible. She wouldn't stand a chance if her *father* couldn't get over the tragedy. Somehow, she thought Max had come a long way, but his reaction must have influenced Sam. If something didn't change her opinion soon, she might never change her mind. She frowned. Hadn't she gotten the impression that Doug was interested in her, and as more than just a patient? "I'd reserve judgment for a while, Sam. I don't mean to tell you how you should think, but your dad might snap out of it, and you might welcome the thought of a husband and children."

*I'm a fine one to talk when I won't ever marry again. Maybe Sam's
pretty smart after all.*

Sam was deep in thought. Yes, she really wanted children, but
her family would hardly hold still for having a single mother in
their midst. And she had no desire to go into a marriage without
love. Besides, how would she explain that to the groom? *Yes, I'll
marry you, and I want children, but don't ask me to love you,* or
maybe, *Get me pregnant and you can go your own way,* or, *Let's
just live separate lives.* Well, none of the above. She had no logical
answer. Her plan would stand as it was. No husband, no children,
period. She would have to go through life with friends. Suddenly
she longed for a close friend in whom she could confide. She had
no one to talk to, not on *this* subject. Maybe if she knew Peg better
. . . Still, would she be able to tell Peg what was in her heart?

Max knew he was running late. If Veronica Tillman hadn't
stopped in, he would have been home by four; but he could see
from the look in her eyes that Veronica was out for blood. She came
into the store, looked around, evidently didn't see the woman he'd
been with the other day, and pounced on him without warning.
He remained calm, at least on the outside. He interrupted her and
told her that Sam was discharged from the hospital today. Just as
Sheila returned, he said he'd have to leave but that his assistant
would be happy to help her. He rushed out the door before she
could object.

He felt pretty proud of himself. His strategy was to keep talking
so she couldn't get a word in edgewise. Having left before she could
say anything, she couldn't claim that he mistreated her or hurt her
feelings. He'd been polite but rushed.

He saw Peg's car in the driveway. She'd left room so he could
drive into the double garage. He smiled. Why did that make him
feel good? He felt like he'd felt back in college *before* he'd asked her
to the party. He sighed. That was water under the bridge. This was
today, and he was happy. He couldn't remember the last time he felt
so excited about seeing anyone. He rushed into the house before
Peg had a chance to leave.

"Hi. Anyone home?" He *knew* they were.

"We're in here, Dad."

He joined them in the living room. "How are you feeling, Sam?" He waited until Sam answered that she was fine and then turned to Peg. "Thank you for bringing her home. I owe you."

She nodded, but with a glint in her eye. "Don't worry. I intend to collect for it."

He should have winced at the thought; instead, he grinned.

Sam looked from Peg to her dad and back again and started to get up. "I'm a little tired. Maybe I should go lie down."

Peg threw her a stern look and stood up. "Not before you eat. I didn't go to all the trouble to cook you a meal just to have you duck out on me."

She really was hungry, but she had wanted to leave them alone. "If you insist."

Peg glanced at Max. "Would you like to wash up before we eat? I've got things pretty well ready."

"Sure. I'll only be a minute." He went up the stairs to the bathroom while Peg and Sam followed him as far as the dining room on their way to the kitchen.

"Sit down, Sam. What would you like to drink?"

She sat down, itching to set the table, but she knew Peg wouldn't let her. "I think I'd like a glass of iced tea."

Peg put some water on the stove and started to look in the cabinets for the tea.

"The right door over the stove." Sam figured she wasn't good for much, but she could at least give Peg directions where to find things.

"Thanks." Peg took the tea bags out. "One iced tea coming up."

"Better make that two. That's what Dad usually drinks."

"Make that three. I'm rather fond of it myself."

"You're fond of what?" said Max coming into the room. He looked at the partially set table and went to the cabinet to get plates and silver. "Something smells really good."

Peg shrugged. "It's just a casserole." She bowed her head, praying silently.

Sam hadn't noticed. "Just a casserole? We don't have enough of those to suit me. Suddenly I'm starving."

"Hmmm." Hadn't Max just heard her say she wanted to lie down? Strange, but after having had surgery, he guessed she was allowed to change her mind, so he didn't comment.

Sam ate a hearty meal, fully enjoying Peg's cooking. Peg had warned her that her stomach might not react normally, but she had no problem with it.

Max had told Peg a few humorous anecdotes about Sam's childhood, so the mood was light throughout the meal. When they had finished the meal, Max took the plates and put them into the sink. When Sam offered to help clear the table, she was told in no uncertain terms to rest. When she decided to go to her bedroom, Max escorted her to see if there was anything he could do to help. By the time he returned to the kitchen, the table had been cleared and Peg was just finishing the dishes.

"You're an efficient woman, Peg," he commented.

She shrugged with a smile. "I generally get the job done right away," she said.

"Come into the family room and talk to me . . . if you have the time."

She nodded. "I like your house, Max. It's homey." She looked around the room
that was directly below the dining room. "I can see your influence here."

"Why," he teased, "because there's a hint of music in every corner?"

She had noticed the piano in one corner, an organ opposite it and pictures and figurines of instruments scattered around with a bust of Chopin on the mantle over the fireplace. "Two fireplaces? That's pretty special."

"Pretty necessary when the power goes off in below zero weather."

She shrugged. "I just use the gas stove."

"I can see you on a bear rug in front of the stove." He chuckled. "No offense, but that's why I put in both fireplaces. They came in handy a few times."

They sat down in the two chairs in front of the fireplace. Peg was determined to bring up the subject that had bothered her for some time now. "You said you don't go to church, Max."

His whole body stiffened. "That's right. I have no time for a God that didn't give a second thought to taking a life so ruthlessly."

Peg could understand how he'd feel that way. She had certainly seen enough of the impact that tragedy had on the lives of the survivors. How could she explain it away? "Do you really think God wanted that to happen?"

"Maybe not, but why did He *allow* it to happen? Why did He let her go into the store right then? Why did He allow that kid to have a gun? I've asked hundreds of questions since that awful day, but I have no answers." His eyes challenged her.

She was quiet for a moment. "I've seen tragedy replaced by wonderful things. Had it not been for the tragedies, those wonderful things would never have happened." She took a deep breath. "I once saw a woman being brought into the ER from a serious car accident. She never regained consciousness, and when she took her last breath, her husband was angry, like you. They did an autopsy because the other driver had been at fault, and it had to be proven that the accident was indeed responsible for her death. During the autopsy, however, they found that the woman had an inoperable brain tumor and she would have suffered a slow agonizing death had she lived. In a way, the husband felt it was merciful of God to allow her to avoid all the pain and suffering."

Max was quiet. Finally he sighed. "Well, nothing like that happened here."

"You can't know that. You don't know what was in store for her. None of us knows what's ahead for us or for our loved ones. We have to trust Him, Max. You may never know why it happened, but it did, and God didn't cause it. It's too bad you can't take comfort from Him."

Max stood up and walked to the fireplace. "It sounds good, Peg." His comment was cynical. "I wish I could believe it." He sighed deeply. "I was taught all about God, but I can't believe what I was taught. Not any more." *Don't talk about it anymore. Don't spoil what we have together.*

She could feel his hostility. Discouraged, she got up to leave. "I'd better get home. I have some things to wash out yet tonight." *Or tomorrow night or the next night. Best I leave now before I say something to make him back off forever.* That thought didn't appeal to her at all. She wanted desperately to say something that would bring him back to God.

He stood up when she did. "Peg, I can't thank you enough for coming to our rescue today and for cooking a great meal for us. We really enjoyed it, but then, you could tell that by how much we ate."

"I don't often cook something like that for myself. It was fun."

"Really? Then we'll have to do it more often. What else can you make?" His lips couldn't keep from grinning briefly until he remembered the rift that would always be between them. Religion was important to Peg. He could see that. He shouldn't encourage more contact with her, but it was difficult not to. He liked her a lot, perhaps too much.

She was encouraged that he might want to see her again in spite of his wanting to avoid the subject of religion. "I know you're teasing me, but I would love to, Max. Just let me know when." She had a sinking feeling inside, a feeling that warned that she should not get involved any more than she already was, but she couldn't help herself..

Max took her coat out of the front closet. He held it for her and as he wrapped it around her, he turned her to face him. "Thanks again." He lowered his head to kiss her lightly on the cheek. Once there, he couldn't resist and placed the kiss on her lips. "Hmmm." He had an indescribable feeling, but he knew better than to linger. If he'd deepened the kiss, he would have wanted more. Now wasn't the time to pursue anything like that. Maybe there'd never be a time considering the difference in their religious beliefs. He laughed to himself. Very simply, she had them. He didn't.

"Goodnight," she whispered as she backed away from him and turned to open the door. "Tell Sam to call me if she needs anything."

"I will." Their eyes met. For the briefest of moments, he wanted to pull her back inside, but he didn't. He wanted to tell her that their differences could be overcome, that they could live with them, but he didn't know if that was possible. Better let her go. "Good night, Peg."

She drove off with overwhelming disappointment. She could sense when Max stiffened and the mood between them had changed. What was she to do? She couldn't renounce her beliefs because the man she loved-- she stopped in mid-thought. She *did* love him. She realized that she had never lost her feelings for him. All those years away from him, finishing her education at a different college, working, even marrying a different man, Max was always in the back of her mind. That might even be why she hadn't been able to keep Dennis from falling for another woman. Had she not tried hard enough? Had it been more her fault than his? No. If she were being honest with herself, Dennis *always* looked at other women. She thought it was harmless at the time. She started the engine and drove off. *Please, Dear Lord, let Max know Your Goodness and Grace again.* She knew he'd been strong in his beliefs in college because they both belonged to the Bible study group. But now? She stood by her door and wept bitterly.

By the time she was able to see enough to unlock her door, her thoughts went back to Dennis and she realized that he had always enjoyed the attention of other women, even before they were engaged. She thought it strange that she hadn't felt any jealousy. Shouldn't she have been jealous of his ogling and flirting with pretty women? She frowned. There was only one explanation. She hadn't loved him the way she thought. That was probably why she was able to channel her emotions into anger rather than hurt, not to say that it didn't hurt her ego when he left. Wouldn't anyone hurt when a relationship was severed, even if they were no more than friends?

That was beside the point, she thought as she hung up her coat and walked into the kitchen. What had she wanted in the kitchen? She sighed and sank into a chair by the table. What was she going to do about Max? She had been so hopeful when they found each other again. He was even more handsome than he was when he was younger. He'd been sweet and attentive, but what now?

If she were going to fantasize, she could see herself living with a man who no longer believed in God. She could devote the rest of her life to changing his mind, but she knew that wasn't realistic. It would be Max who would feel the strain of not believing as she did. She would be a constant reminder of his tragedy, of his feeling of betrayal. That would eventually drive him away from her, and she didn't think she could take that again. She remembered how it had hurt when Dennis left. It was inevitable that Max would tire of her preaching and leave. What if she tried to change his mind and he decided that they should go their own way? What would it do to her when again, Max was no longer in her life? She didn't want to feel that pain again. Even if she was young then, her pain was very real.

She remembered when she was in college. Karen, her best friend was dating a man who didn't believe in God. Whether he was an atheist or an agnostic, it didn't matter. Everyone in their Bible study told her to get out of the relationship. She insisted that she could make him believe in God. They said the odds were against that. Most marriages that weren't based on a common religious belief ended up in divorce. Karen hadn't listened and she married him the following summer. What ever happened in her marriage?

Her thoughts flew to the memory of her parents arguing. She could still feel the helplessness and hopelessness that a child felt in that situation. She shivered as she remembered going into her closet and covering her ears to avoid the loud arguments.

Although she was pulled in two different directions, Peg knew what she had to do for his sake as well as her own. She couldn't be that involved with Max. It would be certain heartbreak, not only for her, but for him, too. Could she remain just a friend, knowing how she felt about him? Could she walk away and never see him again? She could still feel his lips on hers, no matter how quickly the kiss was over. She wanted so much to keep his lips on hers longer, to feel that special closeness that she'd always dreamed about. Had she gotten herself involved again, not knowing what a gigantic problem she was facing? There was no one to ask, no one to guide her . . . except God. She prayed with her whole heart, knowing that God would answer through His Wisdom. He'd answer her prayers the way He thought best for her. She had never doubted her faith before, but now she wondered if she could put her whole life into God's hands. She needed her faith to stay as strong as it had always been. She put her head down and cried, for she was sure that she'd lost her last chance at happiness.

CHAPTER TEN

▼

Peg almost cried as she walked into Katie's room. She looked so small and vulnerable in the hospital bed. Her eyes were red and there were patches of moisture on her cheeks where tears hadn't quite dried. She stared out the window at nothing. Poor thing. She must be so frightened and alone.

Peg made an effort to put on a cheerful smile. She really had to work on it during the week that had passed since she'd made dinner for Sam and Max. He hadn't called her since that night. She really didn't expect that he would even if she had fully intended to be only friends with him. That didn't mean she accepted it graciously. She'd fought with herself, telling herself that many couples had different opinions. Just because it was religion, did that mean the rift between them was too great? Some of her married friends even went to different churches. Their marriages didn't seem to suffer from it, at least, not that she knew about, but others seldom see the whole picture, those problems they keep from family and friends.

No amount of rationalization would fix this problem. She knew why she had made her decision. She tried to tell herself that it was for both their sakes, but in all honesty, it was for his sake, not hers. She'd been the one to decide against seeing him again. She'd left the back door open so they could be friends. She'd loved him for a long time, a love that she now knew could never be; yet when Max came back into her life, she had hoped for– well, for something that wouldn't happen after all. She felt so let-down that she wanted to join Katie and cry with her.

She tried to put on a big smile. "Hi, Katie. How are you today?"

Katie's eyes brightened just a little. "Okay, I guess."

Peg sat on the edge of the bed, something she couldn't do if she had been on duty. "You don't sound like it."

Katie shrugged her shoulders. She didn't want to talk because she knew she'd start crying, and she didn't want to cry again.

"Nothing new with your parents?"

She shook her head. "Can't you find out anything for me, Peggy? Nobody tells me anything." Her lips quivered. "Dr. Daily says they're as good as can be expected."

Peg nodded at the standard answer that was used extensively around a hospital. "That isn't all bad news, you know." Peg happened to know that at this very minute, a Neurologist was examining Katie's dad to see if the signs they had seen earlier today were significant. Her mother seemed to be on the brink of regaining consciousness, but nobody wanted to get Katie's hopes up just to have them crushed if the news wasn't favorable. She'd been a brave little girl since the accident.

The hospital was now insisting that they discharge Katie to Social Services. Everyone tried to stall. Peg was almost certain that some of the doctors actually contemplated manufacturing evidence that she had some unexplained ailment that would allow her to stay. Needless to say, they had already been doing that. It wasn't exactly wrong, the way they thought about it, because the welfare of a young patient was at stake. Now, however, the hospital was tired of waiting and felt she no longer needed to be in the hospital. Even when they were told the circumstances, it seemed they didn't have a heart, and that was sad.

"Did you go to the ICU to see them?" she asked eagerly.

"Not today, honey." She put her hand on Katie's shoulder and squeezed lightly. "They're pretty strict about letting people in there." She hoped Katie accepted the fib.

"But you're a nurse," she argued, lower lip protruding.

"True, but my job is on another floor. They know I don't belong there." She had to change the subject. It wouldn't be good for Katie to think anyone could get her information anytime of the day or night. It was too risky should something suddenly happen to either parent. "Have you had any visitors today?"

She nodded as her mood perked up a little. "Doug came to see me and Sam is coming tonight."

"She is? That's great." Peg was pleased to hear that Sam was able to leave the house. "How is she?"

Katie's forehead crumpled with furrows of curiosity. "Haven't you seen her?"

Peg kept her voice steady and nonchalant. "Not for a week. Is she okay?"

"She doesn't like her crutches. They hurt her arms."

"A lot of patients complain about that. Maybe not men. They don't want to ruin their image by complaining that they can't handle something like that." She brushed a strand of hair behind Katie's ear. "You'll be happy to see Sam. Uh- does Max bring her?"

She nodded. "He brings me stuff like fruit rollups and sweets that are healthier than candy, but that's okay. I don't miss eating candy . . . much."

Peg chuckled. "That's thoughtful of him." Dare she ask? "How is he?"

Katie studied her. "Haven't you seen *him* either?"

Peg held tears back. She shook her head and pretended that her attention was on something on the end table.

"He looks tired, and not as happy as he was before. It must be hard for him to take care of Sam." She suddenly changed the subject. "I wish Mom or Dad could wake up so they can say they'll let me stay with Sam."

"I don't blame you for not wanting to stay in the hospital forever."

Katie shook her head as tears formed in her eyes. "They're going to send me to a strange place, to people I don't even know."

"Who said that?"

"A Social Worker was here this morning." Her lower lip started to quiver.

Peg rubbed circles on Katie's back. "Oh, honey, they're just trying to do what's best for you."

"I know." She started to sob, not being able to hold back her tears. "Why can't they trust Max and Sam? Sam's grandmother said she'd come over and stay with me, or that I could stay with her when Max is at work. Michael even said he'd help and Doug said he'd help them. And he's a *doctor*."

"You know that I would help, too, honey, but they have to wait for permission. There are rules and the hospital has to follow them."

She pouted. "They're stupid rules."

Peg chuckled softly. "I agree with you. Sometimes they don't seem like very good ones. Be patient, Katie."

Doug came into the room. "Well, look who's here. How are you Peg?"

Her voice was soft. "I'm fine."

"Ha!" He let out one quick sarcastic laugh. "You look like you haven't slept in days. Look at the circles under your eyes. Are they working you too hard?"

She hung her head briefly before she raised it and looked into his eyes. "It's not work related."

"I see. You have come down with a mysterious ailment the name of which escapes me at the moment."

"I doubt it."

He looked her squarely in the eye. "I'd say it has to do with a certain male."

She moved to the window and made herself busy straightening the blinds. She didn't want to tell him how much she missed Max. Even his gentle teasing hurt. That's what she deserved for fantasizing the past few days. "Have you seen Sam lately?"

"I spoke with her on the phone. She seems to be doing well. She even came to see Katie," he glanced at Katie.

"She's coming tonight, too." Katie had thought Peg would see Sam every day. She wasn't sure what this conversation was about, but something was different. She knew Peggy liked Max. Maybe she liked him too much. Katie was sure that Max liked Peggy, and liked her a *lot*. It was all so confusing. Well, what did she know?

She was just a kid and nobody told kids anything. If she couldn't figure it out herself, she'd never know a single thing.

"Anyway," he went on, "I think I'll surprise her one of these days and drive over to see her. She doesn't live far from here, does she?"

Peg laughed and narrowed her eyes at him slyly. "As if you haven't already gotten her address and driven by the place a few times."

"Who, me?" He was the picture of innocence. How did she know? Has she seen him driving by?

Peg faced him head on. "So you're not going to call her first?"

He held her gaze as long as he could, but finally moved his eyes toward Katie. "And spoil the surprise? No way."

Peg shrugged. "I have to get going." She took Katie's hand and gave it a squeeze. "Hang in there, honey."

Katie nodded.

"I'll walk you out." He ruffled Katie's hair. "I'll stop in to see you tomorrow."

"Yeah, if I'm even here," she said glumly.

"What does that mean?" he asked.

Katie motioned to Peg. "Ask her. I don't want to talk about it anymore." She turned toward the window.

"Okay, squirt. See you tomorrow."

As soon as they were in the hall, he asked about it and Peg explained about Social Services having talked to her.

"I was hoping it wouldn't come to that." He walked her to the entrance of the hospital. "I'm going to check out ICU. Catch you later."

A short time later, he went to talk to the nurse who was assigned to Albert and Laura Jordan. Their cubicles were side by side so they could leave the curtains open between the two units. The nurse had just finished marking Albert's chart. "Nothing has changed?" he asked.

The nurse raised her head to greet him. "On the contrary. Albert seems to be coming out of it, but he's not making sense. He mumbles, but nothing coherent."

"And what about her?" He tipped his head toward Laura.

"We think she'll be conscious anytime now. All her reflexes are responding and her EEG looks good."

Doug sighed with relief. "A little prayer might help. Their little girl is scheduled to go to Social Services tomorrow."

The nurse nodded. "In that case, a *lot* of prayer would be better."

"Thanks." He waved his hand and left.

Judd put the folders on top the file cabinet and went to the closet to get his coat. "Time to close up and go home, Edna. He watched her finish up a loss report on the computer to send in to the company.

"Big plans for the weekend?" he asked.

"Michael seems to have something planned." She shut down the computer.

He sat on the edge of her desk. "You and Michael have become a couple. I think that's nice. It's good for both of you."

She could feel her face turning pink. "We're just friends, Judd."

He looked at her out of the corner of his eye. "Could have fooled me."

She could feel her cheeks turning from pink to red. "Really, Judd, at our age, who thinks about romance?"

He raised his eyebrows. "Who said anything about romance?"

"I–I thought you implied--"

He laughed. "Michael is right. You really are cute when you blush." He took Edna's coat out of the closet and helped her into it. "Just teasing." But as she watched, the teasing light in his eyes turned dull and concern replaced the humor. "Is it just men who fall in love so quickly at our age?"

"What do you mean?"

"Michael is smitten with you."

She laughed nervously. "Smitten?" She hadn't heard that word for years.

He gave an affirmative nod. "Definitely smitten." He motioned her to sit down, which she did while he stood in front of her. "I talked to Michael when he first came to Minneapolis, the day he saw you at your desk." He held up his hands to ward off a comment from her. "I know. It's really none of my business, but I was concerned that he'd get you all excited and get your hopes up only to have them smashed. I asked him not to hurt you." His lips turned up ever so slightly. "I didn't realize that I'd have to ask the same of you."

She stiffened. "What exactly are you saying, Judd?"

"That I don't want him hurt any more than I want to see you hurt." He took a deep breath. "It may be hard for you to believe, but my brother-in-law has shown the first signs of being involved in life again. He's been barely existing since Carol died, going through the motions of eating, drinking, sleeping and just getting through each day. You should have seen him, lethargic, listless, much like you were when you first came to work here."

She nodded, understanding what he was saying. She had to admit that she knew that kind of *existence* all to well.

"He's fallen hard, Edna. If you don't return his feelings, I suggest you let him know before this goes any farther."

"But we're only friends," she insisted.

"Do you really believe that? Perhaps you had to know Michael before." He patted her shoulder. "I care a great deal about both of you. Nobody has more right to happiness than the two of you, and I happen to think you can have that happiness together. And I know that Michael thinks so, too."

Her head snapped up, her eyes challenging him. "How do you know that?"

"Because he still hasn't found an apartment. I think he's stalling until he sees how you feel about him."

Her forehead was furrowed with lines. "But he never even approached the subject of anything more than friendship. That is, not directly. I suppose he might have implied something like that, but it's been so long since I've been with a man . . ." she shrugged.

He pursed his lips. "Do you suppose he's scared?"

"How do you mean scared? Scared of what?"

"That you don't feel the same way."

Edna sat for a moment as if in a trance. Did she want Michael to be more than a friend? She had been flattered by his attention, and she enjoyed being with him, but the thought of anything physical made her weak. She could imagine herself running away from the relationship, but that vision disappeared instantly. Lost in thought, she remembered the times he had touched her hand or her back when they were walking. She *had* been excited. He had made her feel feminine and *special.* Even so, was Judd talking about marriage? Why on earth would anyone want to marry a woman who was turning seventy this year?

"Edna?" Judd had waited for a comment, but as he saw her staring into space, he knew that he'd started her thinking. He only hoped that the result was what he had hoped.

She shook her head to shake off her thoughts. "Uh, yes. I – don't know what to say, Judd."

"Perhaps you would be better off talking to Mary about this. If you don't want a man's opinion--"

"Oh, no," she interrupted quickly. "It isn't that. I just can't believe that any one would . . . are you talking about marriage or just a companionship type of relationship? There are many widows in our building who carry on a relationship with men who come and go steadily. They don't live together, but they're always with each other going to plays, movies or just out to dinner. You know what I mean?" She sighed with exasperation. "We've only known each other a short time, Judd. You can't honestly think--"

"I can, and I do. I know Michael. He needs you in his life. If you don't need him in yours, now is the time to let him know."

She nodded slowly, understanding what he was saying, but she couldn't quite believe that Michael was that involved with her. She didn't want to hurt him. In fact, when she thought about it, if he left Minneapolis today, she would miss him terribly. What was wrong with her? Had he somehow sneaked by her defenses and made her vulnerable? Had she gradually become part of this *couple* as Judd called them? Had she fallen into the same dependency on Michael as she had with Fred? When Fred died, she had no purpose. She swore she would never depend on any man's love that much again.

"Well, what do I know?" he said, concerned that he had said too much. "That's just my opinion." He took her purse off the desk and handed it to her. "Time to go home. I didn't mean to upset you, Edna. You know how much Mary and I value your friendship. You're not just an employee, you know."

"I appreciate that." She stood up. "Thank you for telling me, Judd."

"Do you mean that? You're not going to do something foolish, are you?'

Her eyes settled on his. "Like what?"

"Like breaking it off with Michael?"

She shook her head. "I don't think I could." There was a hint of humor in her eyes. "My boss wouldn't like it."

"Edna, I--"

She laughed half-heartedly. "I'm joking, Judd." She took a deep breath. "If I were to be totally honest, I guess I'd have to say that it would hurt me a great deal if Michael suddenly left town." *And I'm not sure I'm comfortable with that.*

Judd laughed with relief. "I don't think you have to worry about that." He looked directly into her eyes. "Do you think you could somehow let him know that you're not planning on telling him to, how do the kids say it, *buzz off?*"

She laughed. "I assure you that I won't tell him to *buzz off.*"

"Tell him that." He turned off the lights. "Let's call it a day." After locking up he walked her to her car. "It was a lucky day the day I hired you, Edna Madison."

She smiled warmly. "It certainly was for me." She slid in behind the wheel. "Goodnight, Judd, and thank you."

He nodded. "Goodnight." He closed her car door and went to his own car as she drove off.

A short time later, she pulled into her assigned parking space in the apartment lot. She had such a strange feeling. Did it have to do with Judd's talk about Michael? No, she knew that affected her, but that wasn't what bothered he right now. It was Katie. She didn't know why, but she had the definite feeling that Katie needed her. Call it woman's intuition or what have you, she had to see Katie tonight.

As much as Michael protested, she had invited him for a simple dinner. She had seen him at least three or four times a week since he came to town. She did wonder what his intentions were, but she wasn't going to waste any time thinking about it until she knew for certain. If she learned anything in her almost seventy years, she learned that worrying and speculating did very little good. She dealt with a problem when it became a problem, not before.

She sighed as she took the steaks out of the refrigerator. Is that how she looked at this friendship, this *relationship* with Michael? A problem? Was it really, or was she hiding behind that thought, afraid to hope that it would be more than a mere friendship? She laughed to herself. She was doing the exact thing that she thought she'd learned not to do. *Don't speculate*, she told herself.

She took the low fat cheese and potato casserole she'd made the day before out of the refrigerator and put it into the oven. What would happen if Michael really was thinking about marriage? Could she live with a man again? It seemed like she'd been totally independent for so very long. After Fred died, she had felt lost and so very alone. Nothing could penetrate the depression and loneliness, but now, she had become accustomed to being alone and found it difficult to think about sharing her space, so to speak, with someone else. Was that reality or just a reason not to hope for anything more?

Was she afraid to be disappointed or hurt if things didn't work out? Perhaps she should just stop thinking about it and let whatever will happen, happen.

How could she have come to this? She had always wanted someone to care for. No, she had always *needed* someone, somehow giving her the proof necessary to convince herself that she was put on this earth for a purpose, that she had worth and value to someone.

She frowned as she assembled the salad. Where had she gotten her poor self-esteem? Had her parents not told her what a special child she was? Well, perhaps not often enough or they weren't convincing enough. She had grown up with the notion that she had to prove herself worthy of their love and attention, often falling short when her parents were preoccupied with matters of finances and work.

Then there was her older sister who had been ill and so often needed the attention of her parents. They said Esther's lungs hadn't developed properly because she was born prematurely. As a result, much of the parental attention went to Esther. It wasn't that she was exactly jealous of it, but she often felt left out.

She had tried so hard to please them with her music, but they were too preoccupied with Esther's painting to pay much attention her. She wasn't good enough.

The ringing phone shook her into the present. Michael was downstairs waiting to be buzzed into the building, which she did. A short time later, she was opening the door to let him in.

Snowflakes on his jacket sparkled in the light. "Is it snowing?"

"It is, and it's getting cold." He shivered as if to prove it to her.

"Come in. Dinner's almost ready."

"It smells delicious, Edna." He took off his coat and hung it in the closet next to hers. "We could have gone out, you know."

She laughed. "I wanted to cook for you, but time was short because of work, so I decided on steaks."

He grinned and quickly made a sulking face. "What a hardship." He sighed dramatically. "I guess I'll just have to suffer." He laughed. "What can I do to help?"

"Open the sparkling grape juice?"

"Gladly." He looked at the table in the dining area. She had a floral centerpiece in the middle of the lace tablecloth and candles that weren't yet lit. You're going all out with this."

"I hardly do it anymore. It feels good. I love to cook."

"But when you worked all day, it doesn't seem fair to you."

"I made the casserole yesterday. I'm just heating it up."

He set the open bottle on the table. "Isn't there anything else I can do?"

"Thank you, Michael, but I really have everything ready. Let's sit down and start with our salads." Michael said the prayer before she put the salads on the table. "I hope you don't mind my jumping up to check on the steaks once in a while. I believe in eating steak when it's hot, so I refuse to make them and let them get cold until we're ready for them."

"I agree, but I could do the jumping up for you."

She looked down at her waistline. "I really think I need the exercise. My weight has been steadily climbing. It must be old age."

"It's more difficult to lose weight as we get older, isn't it? I can remember when I could eat a banana split after a large meal and not gain a pound. Now, I think twice about having a scoop of ice cream."

"You have nothing to worry about, Michael. I think you look wonderful." As soon as she'd spoken, she wondered if she was being forward? That wasn't at all like her.

"In that case, I'll eat to my heart's content."

When they had finished the steaks and casserole, Edna took the plates into the kitchen and replaced them with smaller plates.

Michael looked at them. "I don't think I could eat another bite right now."

She smiled. "I don't think I could either. Should we wait and have cake later?"

"That sounds wonderful."

She poured more coffee and suggested they take it into the living room.

He studied her for a moment. "Is something troubling you, Edna?"

She marveled at the fact that he was so insightful. "In a way. I have the definite feeling that I should go to the hospital to see Katie." She shook her head. "What's worse, I haven't the slightest idea why."

"Woman's intuition. I'll be glad to take you. In fact, I've been thinking that Katie needs all the friends she can get. Trust your intuition."

"It's more than that. I just can't explain it."

"Then don't. Should we go now and come back for cake?" That was sneaky, he knew, but the more time he could spend with Edna, the sooner he could convince her that they belonged together.

"Let's finish our coffee and I'll put the dishes in the dishwasher."

A few minutes later, they were on their way. Michael looked over at Edna. "Samantha seemed troubled about her father's religious beliefs." Michael didn't want to pry, but he was interested.

"Max should have come around by now, but he felt that God betrayed him. I'm not only worried about him, but I'm concerned that Samantha is questioning her faith because of her father's reaction. I don't know what to do to help except to pray about it. Somewhere inside, I know he hasn't strayed so far from God that he can renounce Him."

He nodded. "I somehow don't think that trying to *make* Max accept God is the answer. Acceptance has to be on his own time and he has to be ready. I'll pray about it, too. Right now, it's Samantha who needs reassurance."

He turned into the parking lot and parked. "Sometimes these things are best left up to God, but it doesn't hurt to show a good example."

She nodded as they walked into the hospital. "You're right. That's about all we can do. Youngsters don't take kindly to preaching from their elders."

"How well I know."

They were just outside Katie's room when Lorna motioned them away from the door, out of earshot. "Katie has to leave the hospital. The Social Worker is picking her up in the morning."

"Oh, no." Edna closed her eyes and shook head. "Isn't there anything we can do?"

Lorna's smile was sad. "Outside of kidnapping her tonight, I don't know what."

"The poor little thing." Edna put her hand on the nurse's shoulder. "It isn't fair when there are so many of us who are willing to keep her until her parents are better."

"Perhaps if we spoke with the Social Worker."

Lorna shook her head. "We've already tried that."

"Suppose," said Michael as an idea unraveled, "that I was a distant relative, perhaps her grandfather's brother, her great uncle, I believe."

Edna studied him. "You'd do that? But how could you prove it?"

"They would have to take my word for it. I will have come in from out of town."

"Michael, you don't even live here."

"All the better. I will be--" he looked at Edna cautiously, "staying with you since Katie's parents are in the hospital and that way, I can keep her in the city to be close to her parents."

Edna thought about it. Could it possibly work? "But surely they'll ask for proof."

"Hopefully, by the time they learn the truth, her parents will be able to communicate with the authorities."

Edna inhaled deeply. "I don't know. Isn't that a criminal offense?"

Michael shrugged. He looked at Lorna.

"Don't get me involved. If you're related to the girl, you're entitled to care for her. Who am I to say what you should do?" She walked away from them as a doctor entered Katie's room.

Michael put his hand on Edna's arm. "We'd better wait out here."

She nodded. A short time later, Lorna entered the room saying, "You called for me, doctor?" She closed the door behind her.

Edna frowned. "I wonder what's going on. I hope there aren't any complications."

"I think Lorna would have told us." He threw up his hands and spoke accusingly. "Look at us. We've learned from experience that worrying does no good. What are we doing?"

"I know what you're saying, but I can't help it."

Michael put his arm around her shoulders and pulled her close to him.

It wasn't long before the doctor left the room and Lorna stuck her head out the door. "Come in. Katie has something to tell you."

The second they were in the room, Katie blurted out her happy news. "My Mom is awake and she can talk." She was so excited that her little body was actually shaking.

Edna, noticing the tears running down Katie's cheeks, rushed over to her and held her in her arms. "That's wonderful news, Katie. I'm so happy for you."

"Thank God," said Michael in no more than a whisper. A moment later, when he'd had the time to think over what he had offered, he realized how foolish his plan really was and he knew that he could have been in serious trouble. Now, all it took was to convince Katie's mother that there were people who would care for her daughter.

Edna looked from Michael to Lorna. "Would this be a good time to call Max?"

Michael was thoughtful. Just because the woman had regained consciousness, was no reason to think that her thought process would be adequate enough to make a decision as to Katie's welfare. "You mean to speak with Katie's mother?"

She nodded. "If Social Services will be here in the morning, I think it's crucial."

Lorna agreed. "That's true, but I doubt that they'll let anyone into ICU to speak with her."

Katie had been so happy, but the adults in the room didn't seem to share that happiness. They acted as if she wasn't even there. "What are you talking about? Aren't you happy for my mom?"

Edna put her arm around Katie's shoulders and hugged the little girl. "Of course we are, honey, but unless you want to go with the Social Worker, we're going to have to do something soon."

Katie sat up straight and nodded. "I almost forgot about that."

"We'll do everything we can."

Michael ruffled her hair. "You know that we'll do our best, don't you?"

She nodded and her lower lip trembled. Before she could say anything, a nurse wheeled a patient into the room. It was a woman with white hair. Katie's heart sank. She thought she'd get a roommate, maybe someone Sam's age. Oh well, she had more important things to think of now.

"We have to leave, honey, but we'll be back in the morning. When you're lying here, just remember that we'll be busy trying to get things settled so you can stay with Sam for a while." She kissed her cheek. "Get some rest."

Michael kissed her cheek as well. "We'll do our best, Scout's honor."

"Were you a Boy Scout?"

Michael turned back momentarily. "I was a talent scout. Does that count?"

Katie giggled as the adults left the room.

"She'll be okay," said Lorna as they walked down the hall. "You know, getting in to see Mrs. Jordan isn't going to be easy. I don't know what to suggest."

Edna squeezed Lorna's arm. "I have an idea." She smiled kindly. "Thank you for all your help and concern."

"I wouldn't be a nurse if I didn't care."

"I know." They left Lorna at the nurse's station and went to the nearest waiting area to use the phone.

Edna dialed and anxiously waited.

There was finally an answer. "Hello."

"Samantha, it's Grandma. Is your father home?"

Sam's voice was filled with concern. "What's the matter, Gram? Are you sick? Did something happen?"

"No, no, dear. It's Katie. The Social worker is coming to take her to a foster home in the morning."

"Oh, no. They can't do that."

"They can, but there's been a development that could save her. Katie's mother regained consciousness."

"I know," answered Sam, "but they said she didn't make sense."

"That has apparently changed. Someone has to get in to see Mrs. Jordan and convince her that Katie would be better off with you. That's why I need to talk to your father. Isn't he there?"

"He's here, and so is Peggy." Her voice changed to a whisper. "I think Peggy came when she thought Dad wouldn't be here. They act so . . . cold. Not even like friends."

"Oh, dear, I was hoping everything would work out with them. Well, I need to talk to him or her."

"Maybe they'll have an idea how to get Dad in there. Wait just a minute."

Edna heard Sam calling her father in spite of her hand covering the receiver.

"Hello, Mom. Is something wrong?"

"Max, dear. I think you should go to the hospital to see if you can talk to Katie's mother. She regained consciousness and somebody needs to convince her that Katie should not have to go to a foster home of Social Service's choosing."

"I agree, but ICU isn't a place for non relatives."

"I know, but can't Peggy help?"

He was silent for a moment. Peg had come to see Sam, and she had hardly said a word to him since he returned home. Her eyes looked like she hadn't slept any more than he had the past few days. But now wasn't the time to think of their problem. "Yes, I think she can. Peggy," he called. "Listen, Mom, I'll talk to Peg and call you back and let you know what she thinks."

"I'm not at home, Max. Michael and I are at the hospital. We're leaving shortly."

"All right. Leave it to us, Mom. I'll call you at home if I have anything to report."

"Please," she begged, "no matter what happens, call me, son."

"I will. Now go home and relax. You're too old to keep pace like you were still a youngster. You've had a full day."

At first, Edna was insulted, but she knew Max was right. She couldn't do all the things she'd done when she was younger, and she definitely felt better if she limited her outside activities. Still, Katie's welfare was at stake. "Please, call me. I'll worry until I hear something from you."

"Come on, Mom. What did you always tell me? Don't worry. Wait until something actually happens."

"I know, dear. It's just that it is *definitely* time to worry when a Social Worker is breathing down Katie's neck."

"Trust me, Mom. I'll do my best to take care of it."

"Thank you, Max." She hung up and turned back to Michael. "He and Peggy will figure something out . . . I hope."

He hugged her to him and spoke softly into her ear. "You know, you might put a little faith in God. He's been known to work wonders."

"You're right, of course. Let's go home and pray, Michael. And then we'll have some cake."

"I like the way you think."

CHAPTER ELEVEN

▼

Peg didn't ponder the wisdom of being with Max. She'd come over to see Sam, certain that Max wasn't home, but he had been. She couldn't waste her time thinking about that. Right now, Katie needed her, and that was more important than her problem. She and Max headed for the hospital as soon as he'd hung up the phone. Peg wasn't happy that she had ended up with Max again when she'd resolved not to see him anymore. All she wanted to do was visit Sam. Her intention was to keep her company at a time that she didn't have to see Max. Was that fate? She hardly thought it was God's plan for her.

Max's frown hadn't left his face since he'd hung up the phone. "I don't see what there is that we can do if I can't get in to see Mrs. Jordan. She's not about to give permission for her daughter to stay with people she doesn't even know. Besides, is her brain functioning enough to make a valid decision? "

"We can only hope so. I'm sure the nurses on this shift will let me talk to her. I've kept checking on the Jordans in ICU since I had Katie on the Pediatrics floor."

"What good will it do for you to see her?" Max knew he was impatient.

Peg shrugged. "Let's wait and see. A little pray—er--" She stopped speaking abruptly, remembering Max's lack of faith. "Let's wait and see. Okay?"

Max wasn't going to worry about Peg's opinion of him. He didn't want to open up that can of worms. She was a wonderful, caring woman, but she put too much stock in a God who could betray you in the blink of an eye. He sighed. "Whatever you say," he replied dryly and shifted his attention from her to the road..

They practically ran into the hospital. Max followed her down the hall to the ICU. It seemed so sterile, he thought, immediately feeling stupid because naturally everything in a hospital *would* be.

"Wait here," she said as she walked through the double doors.

He paced the floor by the entrance for what seemed like hours, although it was probably no more than five minutes. What was taking her so long? What if Mrs. Jordan slipped into a coma or worse yet, died? He didn't want to think about it, but he had to face reality. It was possible. Things like this happened everyday. People died everyday. People got shot everyday... God let them--

"Max." Peg stood at the doorway. "Come here. You can't go in to see her, but I want you to stand by the window to her unit so she can see you. It might help." She took his hand and immediately felt the warmth and strength that she longed for. Ignoring her emotions, she led him down a narrow hallway, stopping by a window that enabled the woman to see him.

"What good will that do? You can't tell anything from the way a person looks."

"Trust me, Max." She squeezed his hand before she let it go and went back into ICU to the woman's bedside.

He didn't like what he saw when he looked at Katie's mother. Her face was marred with cuts and large bruises, and her arm was in a cast. She was hooked up to medical equipment with all sorts of wires and tubes. He shivered at the thought. It was a pretty gruesome picture, but the woman looked at him and seemed to try to smile as he watched Peg talking to her. Before long, two other nurses went to her bedside. Peg was talking to them. They smiled and nodded and left the unit. A minute later, Doug came in. After greeting Mrs. Jordan, he and Peg were talking. He wished that he could read lips. Doug nodded and smiled as he patted the woman's hand and spoke with her. It was hard to tell anything from the woman's face, probably because the bruises must hurt if she smiled or even moved her mouth to talk.

Doug left and another doctor came in. As Max watched the conversation, he was tense. If only he could hear what was being said.

"Relax, Mr. Madison." It was Doug who had come to talk to him.

"Dr. Daily," he said as he shook his hand. "What's going on in there?"

"I believe that Peg is getting permission for Katie to go home with you. I hope that's why you're here."

"Yes." He sighed with relief. "That's great, but how is she doing it? Is Peg--"

"She's talking to Mrs. Jordan and telling her about you and Sam. If that doesn't work, we'll try to get special permission to put you in a gown and mask and get you in to see her, but it looks like she won't have to do that." He pointed to the others in the room. "Getting permission is the first thing. Having witnesses to Laura's consent is necessary because she's unable to write. The doctor attending her also has a tape recorder going so they'll have proof of her consent for Social Services." His head gestured toward the doctor examining Laura's eyes as he spoke to her. "The doctor has to give his opinion that she is mentally able to understand and act intelligently."

"I wouldn't have believed it. It looks like they covered all the bases."

Doug laughed. "I'm sure they did. Tell me, how is Sam?"

Max patted Doug's shoulder. "She's doing just fine."

"Do you think she'd mind if I dropped over to see her?"

Max smiled. "I think she'd like that."

Doug couldn't help grinning but he was a little skeptical. "Really?"

Max had frown lines on his forehead. "Why would you think she wouldn't?"

Doug grimaced. "You weren't there the night we took her to the hospital."

Max chuckled. "No, but I heard about it."

Doug's mouth stretched over to one side. "From your mother?"

He shook his head. "No, from Sam. She's really embarrassed."

"Oh," he said softly, but repeated louder as if more enlightened, "Oh. What would you think about tomorrow night? I could check on her as well as Katie, that is, if she's going to be there by then."

"Sounds good." Their eyes followed a smiling Peg walking toward them.

"It's all settled. Laura was doubtful at first, but I told her how upset Katie was about going to a foster home. She said, 'Foster home? No. Don't let them do that.' When she saw you and I told her about you and about Sam being her roommate, she was grateful and happily gave her permission."

"Can the Social Worker object?"

"Hardly. Katie's mother has stated her wishes. There's no way they can object. She gave her permission, witnessed by nurses and a doctor. They're out of it now."

Max took Peg's hand and led her away. "Let's go tell Katie." He turned to Doug. "We'll see you tomorrow night. Oh," he added, "come for dinner. I'm cooking, so it'll be simple," he looked at Peg, "unless Peg takes pity on us."

Peg was silent for a moment. All her resolve left her when she thought about the happy occasion with Katie and Sam. She didn't want to miss it, no matter what. "You twisted my arm. I'm working, though, so it *will* be something simple." She'd just have to deal with her feelings for Max. She could do it . . . couldn't she?

"I'm sure Mom will contribute. She doesn't work tomorrow."

"I see," said Peg, pretending to be insulted. "You just invite women who can cook for you."

He laughed. "Works for me."

She laughed. "Me too."

"Since it's a joint effort, can I bring something?" asked Doug.

Peg studied him. "Can you cook?"

He looked insulted. "Can I cook? You're asking me if I can *cook*?" His chin went high in the air. "I'll have you know that I . . ." his shoulders slumped, "can't even boil water."

They all laughed.

Doug left them as they entered the elevator. "You'd better tell Katie the good news before visiting hours are over."

Peg looked at her watch. "You're right. Thanks, Doug."

"See you tomorrow."

They were quiet when they entered Katie's room. Her roommate was sleeping and they didn't want to wake her. Katie had her earphones on and didn't see them come in.

Peg walked up to her and put her hand on Katie's good arm. "Hi," she whispered.

Katie took her earphones off and started talking excitedly, but quieted down when Peg put her finger up to her lips and motioned to her sleeping roommate.

"Did you hear? God answered my prayers. Mom can talk. They said she's going to be all right unless she gets compi --- compli-ca-tions."

They nodded. Max wasn't going to inflict his opinion on her. He was certain that God didn't have anything to do with saving her mother, but he wasn't about to burst her bubble. She was happy. He stepped forward. "Would you like to come and stay with Sam and me until your mom is better?"

Her face lit up. "Does that mean I don't have to go with the Social Worker?"

"That's right, honey." Peg was almost as elated as Katie. "I got your mother to give Max permission to take you home."

Katie beamed from ear to ear. It suddenly faded. She looked at Peg with begging eyes. "Can't I see my mom?"

"Not yet, honey. I'll let you know as soon as it's possible. Just remember that there are reasons. We don't want to do anything that will set her recovery back." She was almost sure that they would allow her to look through the window the way Max had, but a picture like that would probably stay with Katie for the rest of her life. More than that, Katie was still looking rough. Her mother might get too emotional about seeing her. Her doctor would tell them when the time was right. With such serious injuries, everything had to be considered.

Katie looked at Peg. "Is my dad any better?"

"Actually, he is a little better, honey. They think he'll snap out of it pretty soon. The swelling has gone down, and that's a good sign. He's improving. They're watching him carefully and they haven't had to do surgery to relieve the pressure." She smiled. "They're taking very good care of him."

Katie wasn't too sure that she believed Peg, but what could she do? She was just a kid, and they didn't tell kids anything. Well, at least not everything. *When I grow up,* she thought, *I'm going to tell my kids the truth, no matter what.*

The intercom announced that visiting hours were over. Peg and Max hugged Katie, and Max promised to come and pick her up the next day.

"Why can't I go with you now?"

"The doctor will have to discharge you from the hospital. Everything goes according to rules. We talked about that. Remember?"

Katie nodded. "In the morning then?" she asked excitedly.

"I don't know, honey. I hope so. I'll come as soon as the doctors say I can spring you from this joint." Max sounded like a gangster and watched as Katie giggled. That was better. "We want to do everything according to the rules."

She wasn't sure she could wait, but she nodded and waved the fingers on her good hand. She wished they would let her talk to her mom before she left, but she wouldn't want to cause her to get worse. Maybe she didn't want to see her the way she was right now. She got used to seeing herself with the bruises, but she wouldn't want to see her mom that way. Maybe her mom would feel bad if she saw her daughter with bruises and a cast. She'd wait. She was just glad that her mom was going be all right. "Thank you, God," she whispered.

On the way home, Max was trying desperately to think of something to say. Peg had said she didn't want to see him again, but something always threw them together. Why was that? It may be uncomfortable, but he wasn't going to deprive Sam and Katie of the friendship of a wonderful woman. And she *was* wonderful in every way except one. He took a deep breath and glanced at her. He wanted to be with her, but their conversations always led to God. Couldn't she leave Him out of it?

Peg sat quietly wondering if she could go on running into Max every little while. What did she have to do? Get a job at a different hospital? No! She would not be stupid and run away like she had when she was in college. Maybe God was trying to tell her that if she hadn't run away to another college, they might have had a future together. Had she taken full control of her life instead of looking to God for guidance? Had she ever prayed about it? No, she didn't think she did. She took her life into her own hands and made a big mess of it. What was she going to do? Maybe she'd learned a lesson. She bowed her head and silently prayed, putting her life into God's hands.

Michael and Edna sat at the table, each with a piece of cake in front of them. Both of them only picked at the cake. It wasn't that Michael wasn't eager to eat it, but Edna's concern for Katie kept him from enjoying it. They had sat at the table in silence for almost half an hour. He was about to speak when the phone rang.

Edna jumped and answered it. "Hello?" she asked it as a question, hoping it would be Max.

"This is Peggy."

"Do you have news for us?" Edna asked breathlessly.

Michael was concerned that this was upsetting Edna too much for her age. Who was he to talk? He was older than Edna. He watched her expression carefully, concluding that she was hearing good news.

She hung up the phone and turned to him with a smile on her lips. "Max will bring Katie home tomorrow. We're all invited for dinner." Her face became serious. "Michael, perhaps you shouldn't be involved. You have been so concerned and even now, you look so worried. I don't think this stress is good for you."

Michael laughed heartily. "I was thinking the same thing about you, but it sounds like the stress is over."

She smiled. "I think you're right."

"As for dinner, I'd love it." He took her hands in his. "I have to ask you something, Edna."

She looked up at him curiously. "Is it something serious?"

"Yes." He led her to a chair and let her sit down, still not letting go of her hands. "You know that I'm planning on moving to Minneapolis. I'm not sure how you feel about it, but Edna, I want to get to know you better. I'd like to be more than a friend. If you're against it, I want you to be honest and tell me."

Edna was quiet for a moment, a moment too long for Michael to wait for an answer. He let go of her hands and stood back. His expression was part hurt, part regret. "I'm so sorry, Edna. I shouldn't have backed you into a corner like that. You may not want a relationship with me or any man for that matter." He turned away.

She shook her head and reached for his arm. "It's true that I have learned to live alone, and I wouldn't have considered more than friendship. I enjoy being with you, but I don't know if--" She stopped to rephrase the thought. "Michael, I think you're a wonderful man, and it would hurt me if you were to walk out of my life."

He sighed. "That's at least something."

"Can you be honest with me? What did you have in mind?"

He looked at her and started to laugh. "I didn't think of an illicit affair, if that's what you're worried about."

She laughed as heat crept up her face. "I should hope not."

"You are such a beautiful lady, Edna. I wouldn't insult you that way. No, I want us to get to know each other and if we both agree, I had thoughts of our spending the rest of our lives together."

"The rest of our lives," she said thoughtfully. "Somehow, that doesn't have the same meaning as it might have had fifty years ago. That's sad."

"I don't think it's sad. I think it's wonderful. We're older and wiser now. What we do with our lives can mean so much more than it did back then."

"Well, we are older. but--."

He shook his head. "You know what they say. You're not getting older, you're getting better."

"Then why is it that I feel like I'm not getting better, I'm just getting *older*?"

"Because, dear lady, you don't see you with my eyes." He bent down and kissed her cheek, looked into her eyes and kissed her lips. "Mmmm. I may be old, but I can still enjoy a kiss."

Oh, my. What a wonderful feeling, but she wouldn't tell him.

He must have known what she was thinking. "And you did, too, Edna Madison. You kissed me back."

Her lips twitched, trying not to smile. "I did, didn't I?"

"Now that you didn't send me packing, I'll have to find a place to live. Would you mind if I moved into this building, that is, if there's a vacant apartment?"

"Why should I mind? I'd like that."

"And you'll be retiring soon and have a lot of free time. I'd like nothing better than to spend that spare time with you."

She had a glint in her eyes. "We'll see," she teased. Was she being foolish? He hadn't mentioned marriage. That was a good thing, because if he had, she might have rejected the whole idea. After all, they had just met. The thought of spending time with Michael was nice. He was a good man, an excellent companion, and she enjoyed being with him. For now, she wouldn't think any farther than that. Still, should she tell him her concerns about actually sharing her life and her home with a man? Not now. She didn't think she could manage that kind of an arrangement, but she didn't want to mention it. Michael wanted companionship, no more. And they were compatible. She'd leave well enough alone. Besides, she needed to pay some attention to Max. She had hoped things were working out with Peg, but it certainly hadn't look like it this past week.

It had taken three hours to finally get Katie discharged from the hospital. It was not the usual red tape that prevented it from going smoothly, but the many employees who knew of Katie's situation came to wish her well. Although they all wished her well, some brought gifts and gave her their phone numbers in case she ever needed anything. Others spoke with Max so they could make sure he was going to treat her right.

Dr. Emily Carter, Katie's doctor came to get her in a wheelchair. She said she couldn't take her into the ICU cubicles, but she was going to let Katie look through the window at her mother. The nurses had been careful to situate her mother in a way that Katie wasn't able to see the worst of her mother's bruises.

Katie, of course, wasn't satisfied, but was grateful that the doctor had let her see for herself that her mother was there and was able to see her. She was even able to lift her hand and wave to her daughter. Katie tried to hold back the tears so her mother wouldn't be upset. If she saw Katie crying, she'd feel bad that she couldn't hold her and comfort her the way she always did. She'd missed her mother so very much, and she had tried to stay brave. After all, she told herself, her parents were in the same hospital as she was. Just because she couldn't be with them didn't mean that she would never see them again, even if she had felt like that sometimes.

"Don't let me regret this," said the doctor noticing that the tears were going to flow anytime. "I thought it would be good for both of you to see each other, even if you can't be close to her."

Katie nodded as she wiped a stray tear with the tissue the doctor had handed her.

The doctor smiled down at her gently. "Wave to your mom and I'll take you back to your room. Try to smile, Katie. That will be the best medicine for her."

Katie did smile as she waved. The minute Katie was out of the ICU area, the tears started. "I'm glad I got to see her," she sobbed. "I wish I could see Daddy, but at least Mom waved to me. She was hurt really bad, wasn't she?"

"Yes, she was, but she's getting better every day. It won't be long and she'll be in a room, and then you can visit with her every day." She wheeled Katie back to the nurse's station. "You can look forward to that day, Katie, but you have to be patient, even if it's hard." The doctor saw Max waiting for them. "She's all yours, Mr. Madison. I'll expect her in the clinic in about ten days. Call and make an appointment."

"I'll do that, and thank you, doctor."

She bowed her head slightly, acknowledging his thank you. "Be good, Katie."

"I will. Thank you for letting me see my mom." Drying her tears, she turned to Max, her eyes hopeful and excited, yet sad. She felt guilty for leaving her parents in the hospital; but going with Max would be so much better than having to go with the Social Worker and live in a house with strangers. She would be able to see Sam every day, and she liked that idea. "Are we going home now?"

"We certainly are. Are you ready?"

"Yes, please."

They took the elevator down to the main floor and Max left Katie with the nurse while he went to get the car. When he pulled up in front of the building, they were already outside waiting.

The nurse helped Katie into the car while Max put her things into the back. There was something missing, he thought. Katie didn't have a *suitcase* or anything except the gifts she had received. He'd have to take Peg and shop for things that Katie would need like clothes. All she had was the clothes that some of the ladies from the Auxiliary had collected. The clothes that she'd had on at the time of the accident had been ruined. If Sam could go shopping, she'd know what to get, but Peg would know, too. Besides, it would give him another excuse to see Peg. It was strange since he had decided not to see her any more; still, he looked forward to seeing her and being with her again. He missed holding her and kissing her. Why couldn't he stop thinking about her? He knew well enough that he didn't like talking about God, but the desire to see Peg again seemed to be stronger, nullifying his decision. What was he going to do?

"Here we are," he announced as he drove into the driveway.

Katie's eyes opened wide in wonder. "*This* is where you live?"

"This is home. Wait here." He got out and walked to the other side of the car and opened the door with a flourish. He bowed and held out his hand to her. He felt like a Queen's aide helping his mistress out of the car. "This way, young lady."

Katie giggled. He carried her things in one hand and held onto her good arm with the other, letting go only to open the door.

"Welcome home," said Sam who had been waiting for hours.

Katie rushed right over to her for a hug.

"How do you feel, honey?"

Katie shrugged. "I feel okay, I just..." her lower lip trembled. "I just hated to leave Mom and Dad there."

Sam looked at her tenderly. "But you knew you had to." She gave her good arm a little squeeze. "Just think ahead to when *they* can leave the hospital, too. Meanwhile, don't let it spoil your recuperation."

"Okay," she said softly.

"Come on." Sam took her hand. "I'll show you to your room." Sam climbed the steps slowly to avoid the pain in her side. The incision still bothered her when she made fast moves or stretched a little too far, but it seemed that when she was rushed, she did just that. She knew it wouldn't last, but she'd be careful for a while.

They reached the first doorway on the left. "This is it. I hope you like it."

Katie walked inside and looked at the frilly white curtains that let the sunshine spill across the dusty rose bedspread on the full-sized bed. "Wow!"

"I figured I'd use the bedspread that looks like Black Cherry ice cream."

Katie giggled. "It really does look like it." She looked around at the pale rose walls and the burgundy chair by the window. There was a dresser, a chest of drawers and a desk not far from the chair. "Is this your room?"

"No. Mine is across the hall." She pointed out the doorway.

"It's beautiful. Are you sure I can stay here?"

Sam frowned. "Why on earth not?"

Katie shrugged.

"Is everything okay?" asked Max as he brought Katie's things in.

Sam had a glint in her eyes. "Katie isn't sure we want her to stay in this room."

"Really?" He bent down slightly so he could catch her attention and look into her eyes. "Why not?"

"It's so nice."

"Good. You deserve *nice*." He turned to Sam. "I'm meeting Peg at three so we can go shopping. Is there anything you want me to pick up for you?"

"Black Cherry Chocolate ice cream," they said at the same time and laughed.

"I guess I can mange that. I was thinking more of shampoo or toothpaste," he looked at Katie. "Do you have special brands that you like?"

"I've got the stuff from the hospital. That's okay for me."

"I can get whichever brand you usually use, Katie."

She hung her head. "I don't want you to spend money on me."

"Hey," he said softly, "I *want* to get you what you'd like, but you have to tell me the brands. I don't do very well guessing about things girls like."

"We always get whatever's on sale. Honest. The stuff from the hospital is good enough."

He studied her for a minute, shot a look at Sam and winked at her. "Well, we'll fly blind then. See you later." He left the room.

"What does *fly blind* mean?"

Sam smiled. "You've never heard that expression? In this case it means going shopping and not knowing what to get, more like guessing."

Katie's eyes started to tear.

"What's the matter, Katie?" She put her arm around the girl's bony shoulders.

"Everyone's been so nice" She wiped her hands over her cheeks. "I hope they'll be that nice to Mom and Dad."

Sam smiled. "You can count on it. Now, Miss Jordan, would you like to rest until dinner time?"

"Can I call it supper? We always call it supper. Dinner sounds like we're really rich and spoiled."

Sam laughed. "Supper it is. How about resting?"

Katie shrugged. "Can't I just watch TV while you rest? I had to rest so much in the hospital. That's all I did."

"I'm with you, Katie. I hadn't planned on resting, either. Should we go down and see what's in the fridge? Did they feed you lunch?"

"Sort of," she answered shyly. "I was too excited to eat."

"Then let's go see what we have and take it into the family room to watch TV or play a game or something before I put a casserole into the oven. You can help me with that. Together, we'll do what neither one of us can do alone. We don't want to eat too much now, though, because everyone is coming for din-- supper." She took Katie's hand and led her down the stairs.

"When I grow up," said Sam inching down the stairs, "I'm going to go down these steps like a human being instead of like a snail." It was good to hear Katie giggle. She was glad her dad brought her home.

Peg was surprised when Max had called about going shopping. Since she'd told him she wasn't going to see him anymore, her first thought was to ask if he didn't understand English, but that was too much like a snotty kid's remark. When she thought about it, she realized he really did need help with shopping for Katie. How could she refuse? After all, it was really Katie who needed her. She avoided thinking about how much she'd missed him and how excited she was to be with him again. Couldn't she ever stick with her decisions? Was it possible that God had a hand in their lives? Was it His plan to throw them together so often? She chose not to keep that thought and end up disappointed. Best to just go with Max willingly.

Peg chose some contemporary clothes for Katie, some jeans, slacks, a shirt and sweater and a pretty purple dress (Katie's favorite color). She picked up panties and anklets, but she couldn't buy shoes. She should have asked Max to find out what size, but shoes were so iffy. She could always do that later. Maybe, if she waited a few days, she could take Katie with her.

Max waited patiently, marveling at the ease with which Peg chose items, not hovering over any one item for more than a minute. She was efficient and seemed to have fun shopping for Katie. He enjoyed watching her. Peg was a very special woman, a very special woman he wanted in his life; but he didn't know how to accomplish that. She was perfect in every way except one. How could he put up with her constant prodding to get him to turn back to God?

He needed to get his mind back on shopping. He spotted a purple knitted scarf, mittens and cap set, picked it up and took it over to Peg. "It still gets cold. Do you think she'd like this?"

Peg almost squealed. "She'd love it. Oh, Max. She's going to be so surprised. I can't wait to get home."

He smiled at her enthusiasm as well as her use of the word *home*. He knew that she meant *his* home, but it sounded nice. "Do we have everything she needs?"

"For now. I can always pick up some things later." She was thoughtful. "If they live in Forest Lake, it's too bad we can't get the key and get some of her things from their house. Maybe I'll talk to her. Forest Lake isn't that far."

"For all we know, the key to the house could have been lost at the time of the accident. Still, there must be some way to get into their house. It would really be good for Katie to have her schoolwork. She's bound to get behind. I don't think she'd enjoy spending another year in her grade."

"I'm sure she wouldn't. Let's try to find out. Not tonight, but soon."

He agreed. Half an hour later, they carried packages into the house. Max detected the aroma of food coming from the kitchen. "Sam must have started our dinner," he commented. "Can she do that?"

Peg laughed. "As long as it doesn't tire her too much and remembers not to lift anything heavy, she'll be perfectly fine."

He narrowed his eyes and frowned. "Like in lifting a pan?"

She looked very serious. "Only if it's filled with lead; otherwise, a pound or two won't hurt her. If it hurts, trust me, she'll stop in short order."

They found the girls in the kitchen, Sam cutting vegetables for a salad and Katie stirring something on the stove.

"Hi, you two busy beavers."

They both turned toward Max and Peg. "Hi. What are all those packages?"

Peg stepped forward and handed Katie one of them. "They're things for Katie to wear so she doesn't have to live in what she's wearing."

Sam smiled. "That was thoughtful. Nothing I have would have fit her. I wondered if I'd have to take out the sewing machine and make over some of my clothes."

"No need. They watched as Katie opened the first sack and held up the dress.

"Ohhhhhh. My favorite color." She looked at the purple garment and held it to her chest. "It's beautiful." Her cheeks were moist with tears. "You didn't have to buy me anything."

"That's not all." Max handed her another sack. They all watched her excitement as she opened each and every one. "They're all so pretty. I don't know what to say." She wiped her tears.

Sam smiled and hugged her. "Just say thank you and let's get this meal ready."

Katie hugged Max and Peg. "Thank you so much."

"After we're done eating," Sam told her, "we'll take them upstairs and I'll help you try them on."

By six o'clock, Edna and Michael arrived with food ready for the table. By six-thirty, they were all seated, all except Doug who had called saying he'd be delayed a while, not sure that he would be able to get there at all. Max was going to start eating, but Edna touched his hand as she asked Michael to offer the blessing.

"Gladly." He bowed his head. Knowing that Max no longer believed in God, he silently prayed that he would say a blessing that would be meaningful to Max. "Lord, we thank you for taking care of the two girls at our table tonight, that they will be healed under your care. We ask that you keep watch over Katie's parents and heal them. We thank you for the many blessings in our lives, and with Your help, we can overcome the tragedies we've experienced. Bless the food that has been placed at this table. In the name of Jesus. Amen."

Edna watched Max out of the corner of her eye during the prayer. She noticed his jaw tighten when Michael had mentioned tragedies, but she saw no further reaction.

Peg served Katie before she passed the food around the table.

Max kept the conversation light, teasing Katie once in a while when he saw her staring off into space. She must have thought about the many times she sat at a table with her parents. At least he was able to snap her out of it for a while. She'd be all right as long as she knew her parents were no longer in danger. He hoped that there wouldn't be any complications that would keep them from improving.

Peg, Edna and Michael started the dishes while Max finished clearing the table.

Sam took Katie upstairs to model her new clothes. For each outfit she tried on, she came downstairs to show them, hugging each of them excitedly every time.

Edna and Michael left, promising to come over on Thursday to visit. Sam and Katie went upstairs to get ready for bed while Peg and Max went into the family room.

"It's too bad Doug couldn't make it. I think he's interested in Sam."

Max didn't react to that statement one way or the other. He hadn't really given a thought to Sam leaving home one day, but he had to accept that it *would* happen. Why did he have this sick, empty feeling in his chest? "Did something come up at the hospital?"

"They needed a doctor to go with the helicopter. There was a bad accident, and Doug was the only one available right then." She looked at the pictures on the wall of musical instruments, some of which she had never seen before. "That was a nice dinner," said Peg as they sat on the sofa.

"It was," Max said, "but leave it up to Mom to make sure we had a prayer."

She watched him carefully before responding. "Max," she started softly and sympathetically, "you can't expect others to forsake their beliefs because *you* believe differently."

He sighed. "I know. It's just so--"

"Max," she interrupted, "tell me something. Haven't you found any good things in life since you lost your wife?"

His eyes stabbed hers, as if to challenge her. "Like what?"

She shrugged. "Like your mother learning to manage her life after depending on your dad so heavily."

He shrugged. "She learned in order to survive."

"Oh, I don't know. She could have asked you to take care of everything. Instead, she learned, and she has a job. Most women her age are enjoying retirement." She couldn't stop now. "What about your beautiful daughter? Don't you consider her--"

"You know how much I love her," he snapped. "What's your point?"

She was silent for a moment. She'd better not stay here. She didn't want another argument, but she couldn't help offering that last comment. Why had she never learned to keep her mouth shut? "Well, you're going to have to find the good things yourself. Once you discover them, they'll make sense." She got up to leave.

Max wasn't sure if he was relieved, angry or what. "You're leaving?"

"I work in the morning," she said in a cool manner. "And so do you, but I have to be there by six-thirty."

He nodded and followed her to the foyer, retrieving her coat from the closet.

"Thanks for coming," he said none too gently as he held her coat for her. "Thanks for shopping, cooking, cleaning, and . . . preaching." He watched her out of the corner of his eye. *What's the matter with me? Why did I have to say that? I don't enjoy feeling like the bad guy all the time. Can't anyone understand?*

"I guess I deserved that." Her voice was soft, but she turned her head so he couldn't read her expression. "Goodbye, Max."

Goodbye? That sounds so final. He took her arm to pull her back to him and turned her so she faced him. "I appreciate your concern, but I can't suddenly change my way of thinking."

"Max, have you been to church at all since that awful day?"

He shook his head. "No!" The word was emphatic.

"What does your reaction do to Sam's faith?" *I had to open my big mouth again. Why don't I learn?*

He looked past her, but he wasn't seeing anything. "I never thought about it. It's her decision what she believes. I think Mom influences her a lot."

I sure hope so. She said nothing except, "Goodnight," and walked out the door.

Max had intended to kiss her goodnight, but her attitude tonight was so different. Besides, that *goodbye kept playing over in his mind.* He was confused. She'd been so caring, and understanding. What happened to change her so suddenly? He knew the answer to that. It was Sam. Did he really influence what Sam believed? Did he even know what she believed? Was Peg really blaming him for Sam's religious beliefs, or lack of them? He was able to squelch the feeling of guilt that tried to surface. In its place, he could feel anger rising in him. So be it. "Goodbye, Peg," he said to himself with a certain finality, wanting to slam the door behind him; instead, he stood stiffly in the doorway and watched until her car was out of sight.

Frowning, he walked back into the house and upstairs to his bedroom. His temper made him strip off his clothes more roughly than he'd intended. His clothes off, except for his boxers, he sank onto the bed and put his head in his hands. What was the matter with people? Why did everyone have so much faith in the God who had proven to be unreliable? Why couldn't they see how many people died needlessly? Why did babies die in their cribs without even being allowed to live long enough to utter a word? Why did God allow those parents to suffer such a devastating loss? Why did God let good people die and bad people live?

He laughed to himself. In his psychology classes in college he remembered learning that mentally ill people thought everyone else was wrong, but they themselves were right. Even if ninety-nine people thought differently than one mentally ill person, it meant only that ninety-nine people shared the wrong opinion. Ninety-nine against one just made the ninety-nine more stupid and the one more intelligent. He frowned. Could it be that *he* was wrong? If so, God had better do something, and soon, if he hoped to salvage his relationship with Peg. That thought stopped him cold. A few minutes ago, he had said goodbye with the intention of not seeing her again, and now he's thinking of saving the relationship?

Faith was a belief in something you couldn't see or hear; but he *needed* something tangible. God had to know that Max had to be *shown*. He couldn't just take the word of others after what he'd been through. What was he thinking? That God had goofed? Hardly, yet down deep, was he hoping that that had been the case so he could freely pursue Peg? What was happening to him? Was he softening after all these years?

He lowered his head to the pillow. Peg's question gnawed at his conscience. He was angry, but he had to think about Sam. *What does your reaction do to Sam's faith*? Just because he doesn't pray, does that mean Sam doesn't pray? He told Peg that his mom influenced Sam. What a defensive remark to make. *Did* his mother influence Sam? He hoped so. He closed his eyes and tried to relax. He suddenly sat up with one thought coming to the surface. Why did it concern him that Sam might accept *his* doubts? He frowned and slid back down on the pillow. If he truly didn't believe in God, why should he care? Did he ever deny the existence of God? No. He realized that he didn't. He just didn't *trust* Him anymore. He hadn't prayed since Bernice's death, but he knew God was there . . . for someone, just not for him.

After tossing and turning and seeing Peg's image for what seemed like hours, he finally fell asleep in the wee hours of the morning.

CHAPTER TWELVE

▼

Doug had missed the dinner at Sam's house and had been busy every night since. He finally had a Friday night to himself. Did he dare show up at the Madison house without calling first? No. They might not be there. Both Sam and Katie would be able to leave the house now. He picked up the phone and dialed. His heart sank when the phone rang five times. He was about to hang up when someone answered.

"Madison residence," said the little voice trying to sound grown up.

"Katie? It's Doug-- uh, Dr. Daily."

"Hi."

"How are you feeling?"

"Fine. Did you see my mother?"

"I did. And I saw your dad, too. They are both improving. I'll talk to their doctor and see if we can take you to the window again sometime soon."

"When are you going to ask?" She was excited.

He laughed. "I'll have to wait for a day or two. There's a little problem that's going to keep your mom in ICU for a while longer, but I'll keep you posted, okay?"

"What kind of problem?" Her voice was trembling.

"Nothing you'd understand, honey. Just give it time."

"But it's been so long." She whined, sounding close to tears.

"Trust the doctors, Katie. They're taking very good care of her."

"But things can happen, can't they? Bad things."

"That's true, but they don't foresee anything like that now."

Adults didn't tell kids everything. Maybe things were worse than he was telling her. "Is my mom talking better now?"

"She is, and she asked about you today."

That seemed to get her attention. "What did you say?"

"I told her that you're with people you really like."

"Did you tell her that Grandma Madison comes to stay with me, too?"

He laughed. "I told her everything I know. She's concerned about your schoolwork. I told her that I might stop at your school on my way up north next week. Do you think your teacher would give me your books and assignments?"

"I think so." Katie was pleased. It would be fun to do her studies again. She'd missed something and she wasn't sure what it was. She loved school and really enjoyed learning. "What about my dad?"

Doug hesitated for a moment. "He's conscious, but you know that."

"Can he talk now?"

"Well, he tries, but his throat is pretty raw from the tubes--." She didn't have to know that the sounds that came out of his mouth didn't sound at all like words. He didn't want Katie to know all the gruesome details. It was common procedure in the hospital, but it could intimidate the toughest of people, and probably scare a youngster to death. "It will take time, honey."

"Okay. Goodbye."

"Wait, Katie," he yelled. "Don't hang up."

"What?"

"Is Sam there with you?"

"Uh-huh."

"Well," he waited, but she didn't say anything. "Can I talk to her?"

"Okay. Just a minute."

Doug could hear Katie's footsteps. She's a cute kid, he thought.

"This is Samantha."

He laughed. Didn't Katie tell her who was calling? "Sam, it's me, Doug."

"Doug." She sounded pleasantly surprised "How are you?"

"That's *my* line."

She chuckled. "Okay. *You* ask."

He laughed. "How are you, Sam?"

"I'm fine. I think I have permission to go back to training in a week if I'm careful. I can at least observe so I don't lose so much ground."

"That's pretty unusual."

"It is, but when you have an influential doctor making a request like that, I guess they listen."

"Hmmm. That's great– isn't it?"

"Yes. I need to get back."

"Still counting on the ER?"

"Well, maybe not right away. I'd need special training, but I guess you'd know that. How is the residency going?"

"Actually, pretty well. It's the evenings that kill me."

"Do you have night duty?'

"Sometimes, but there are always meetings I need to attend. I think it's my mentor's idea to keep me out of trouble."

She laughed. "I suppose you know all about Katie's parents."

"I just told Katie the latest."

She laughed. "Unless something happened recently, she knew the latest this afternoon."

"The little stinker didn't let on that she knew."

Sam was thoughtful. "I think she was testing her information," she whispered. "I'm not sure she always believes the reports."

"I suppose that's understandable. Nobody told her anything concrete for quite a while. Listen, I was wondering if I could come over and visit for a little while. If you're busy, just say so."

"We're not busy. Gram and Michael are coming over later to play Monopoly with Katie."

"Fun," he said dryly.

She laughed. "I know. No, I'd be very happy to have a visitor."

"Am I supposed to feel flattered that the only reason you want me there is to get you out of playing that boring game?"

"If you think that, I'll have to think up a way to change your mind."

"Hmmm. That sounds interesting. What did you have in mind?"

"Oh," she thought for a while, "maybe I'll give you a piece of chocolate cake with ice cream."

"It's a deal, as long as it's Black Cherry Chocolate ice cream."

She laughed. "You heard about that, huh?"

"I did. Uh -- Sam, your dad won't mind if I come over, will he?'

"Why should he? Besides, he's taking Peggy to Adam's Haven tonight. That's the restaurant that Gram and Michael found so enjoyable."

"Hmmm. An *enjoyable* restaurant? I think in terms of food. Well, never mind. I thought they weren't seeing each other anymore."

"I know. Something came up and I guess they want to talk about the problem."

She heard his page over the intercom in the background. "I have to run, but is seven o'clock okay?"

"It's fine. I'll see you then."

"Okay. Goodbye." He hung up, pleased with himself.

Peg was nervous. She really didn't think Max would call after the way she spoke to him. How could she be so brutally honest? She *had* to be. She'd thought it over and decided that she had to do something that would shock Max back to the person he was all those years ago. She shook her head because she knew very well that that wasn't possible. They were not the same people they were in college. They had both changed, had both gotten older and more mature, she hoped. Tragedy had struck both of them, but they managed to go on with life.

What was Max thinking and feeling? How should she act? She sighed with disgust. *Act?* Was she thinking about presenting an image that wasn't her? No. She had to be true to herself. If he didn't like her for who she was, it would be his tough luck. She wasn't about to try to be the woman he wanted her to be. If she had learned anything in life, it was that she had to be herself, no matter what. *Lord, please help me to be the kind of woman Max will listen to. Please let him open his heart to You.*

The doorbell rang and she took one last look at her emerald green pant suit. It was not too dressy, but dressy enough if Max was taking her someplace special. She took a deep, calming breath as she opened the door.

He smiled and nodded when he saw her, his eyes sweeping over her from head to toe. "You're beautiful."

"You say that every time you pick me up." She smiled. "Come in."

"Am I early?" he asked.

"No. You're right on time. I take it my pant suit is acceptable?"

"It's great. We're going to Adam's Haven."

"I like that place. I just wish your mother were there to play for us."

"We'll ask Mom and Michael to come with us sometime when things settle down at the house."

Peg sighed with relief. At least he didn't intend to stop seeing her, but was that a good thing? What had happened to *her* decision not to see Max anymore? Hadn't she thought it was best to break up with him? God knew she didn't want to; but she worried about how their differences would affect their relationship. Was she betraying God? No. God would never think she was betraying Him by asking for His help for Max. God knew what was in her heart, but would He think she was wrong? Was Max a lost cause?

He helped her on with her coat and they left.

He didn't know what to say. Peg seemed to be enjoying the scenery as they drove, or maybe it was her way of keeping occupied so she didn't have to talk.

The silence got to him. "I've missed you, Peg." *That was a stupid thing to say.*

"I've missed you, too." She sighed.

"I know we have this difference of opinion between us, but I want you to know that I do believe there is a God." He shook his head. "I just don't think God wants to hear me. If He won't give me the time of day, why should I--" He stopped abruptly, hitting the steering wheel with his hand. "That's stupid. He betrayed me. Pure and simple." He shrugged. "Maybe we shouldn't talk about this right now. Let's table it and enjoy the evening."

"Someday, Max, something will happen and you'll know that God really is on your side. He just has a bigger picture in mind. We can't all have what we want, and God isn't responsible for some of our stupid mistakes. He gave us brains. He expects us to use them and He *lets* us use them. He doesn't control our thinking."

Max took a deep breath. That was a lot to absorb and he wondered if he could, but he didn't want to think about it right now. Maybe having this talk wasn't a good thing. He was with Peg and he wanted to enjoy her company, not her preaching.

Before they knew it, they were parked at the restaurant.

She looked at the beautiful structure. "I still don't know why I didn't know this was *here*."

"Don't feel bad. I didn't either until Mom told me about it. You don't mind coming here again, do you?"

She shook her head. "Not at all. I love this place. It's beautiful and the food is wonderful."

He got out of the car and went around to her side to help her out. They were soon seated at a table near the piano.

Kevin approached them. "It's nice to see you again."

They smiled and accepted the menus he handed them.

Kevin looked at Max. "Would you like something from the bar?"

Max looked at Peg. "Just some green tea, please," she said.

Max ordered coffee for himself and looked at the menu.

Peg closed her menu. "I already know what I want."

Max looked up with raised eyebrows.

"The poached salmon," she said.

He nodded. If he wanted to eat a healthy meal, he should probably have the same thing, but he had his eye on something else. "I'm thinking about the Beef Wellington."

"Oh, Max, you would have to mention that. I'm really trying to eat healthy."

He knew that he should, too. "Let's split our meals half and half. That way, we can indulge and still eat healthy. It's a compromise."

Her eyes sparkled. "I like compromise."

As before, they enjoyed the meal and kept the conversation light. Max knew that they thoroughly enjoyed being with each other. The circumstances didn't matter. Their difference of opinion didn't even seem to matter most of the time. So what was he going to do about it? It was too soon to declare himself, but it wasn't as if they hadn't known each other for many years. Well, technically, they hadn't been in touch, and granted, people change, but not that much. A leopard doesn't change its spots. Peg was a wonderful girl in college and she was a wonderful woman now. Maybe that's what scared him. *Maybe she doesn't find me so wonderful anymore. Maybe she doesn't want to be with anyone who doesn't believe in God, whose faith isn't as strong as hers.* He looked over to find her watching him.

"Is something wrong?"

He shook his head and became conscious of having drifted off in thought.

"Nothing. Everything is great." He looked at the piano when Kevin returned with the check. "No music tonight?"

"The woman has been ill. We almost thought of calling your mother last night to see if she'd like to help us out."

"She'd like that, Kevin." He took out his card and wrote her phone number on the back. "I won't say she'll do it, but it doesn't hurt to ask."

Kevin smiled from ear to ear when he walked away with Edna's phone number.

Peg studied him. "Are you sure you should have done that?"

He laughed. "No, but at least she'll feel flattered to be wanted. Mother has been feeling her age lately. Her boss is retiring and she's so sure she won't be hired anywhere else that she won't even try."

"Then maybe you did her a favor. It sounds like they need someone here. *You* could have played."

"We'll leave that to Mom." He stood up. "Ready to go?" He pulled her chair out for her. They said goodnight to Kevin, promising to come back again and they left.

When they were on their way home, it bothered Peg that Max looked so serious. She'd been kidding herself all along. She thought she could just be friends with Max, but that was impossible. She wanted him to hold her and kiss her. She wanted to be with him in the morning when she woke up and at night when she went to sleep. Obviously, he didn't feel the same way. He had been too quiet, too thoughtful. She wanted him in her life, but she knew she couldn't have him. A thousand conflicting emotions rippled through her like a mallet sweeping across the bars of a xylophone. Better to end it now before she got even more involved.

"I think we should stop seeing each other, Max. It just isn't working, is it." It wasn't a question.

Max stiffened and frowned. He'd thought Peg was having a good time. She enjoyed the dinner and the conversation, although a little slow at times, seemed to flow smoothly. She probably decided that their differences were too great to overlook. As much as he hated to admit it, she was probably right. He wouldn't argue. He nodded. "Don't forget that you left a cake pan at my house."

Devastated because she hoped that Max would at least try to persuade her not to end the relationship, she turned her head toward the window so he couldn't see her tears. She should have known better. Good things didn't happen to her. She had flashbacks of the many disappointments she'd had during her lifetime, starting with her sister's illness, her parents divorce and her own failed marriage. What could she expect? Neither of them spoke. The silence was as potent as a funeral dirge.

The evening seemed long. Doug had called that he had to work for another two hours or so because of a last minute emergency. He asked if a little after nine would be too late to come, but he couldn't do more than estimate the amount of time he would be tied up. Although she was disappointed, she said it would be fine. She ended up playing Monopoly after all, but it wasn't so bad when she was able to keep her mind on the game. Michael and Edna made the game almost fun. Of course, not as much fun as she would have had if Doug had shown up, but she would have to wait. Katie was having a good time, and that was important.

Sam followed Michael and Edna out the back door where Michael had parked the car. He and Edna commented that it was almost nine and time for old people to leave. Katie was in the family room sitting in the big chair directly in front of the TV when the local news came on. She leafed through a book and was only half listening when she heard something that made her take notice. They had said something about an accident that had happened sometime ago. "The victim died very suddenly tonight," said the newscaster, "leaving his wife who was still in ICU in a state of shock. The attending physician will give a statement as soon as he's available."

Katie sat motionless for a moment, thinking over what she had heard. *Husband died---accident sometime ago--- wife in ICU in shock.* Katie's hand flew up to her mouth and she cried out, "Daddy." She jumped up, faced one direction, then the other and ran to the door, then back to the room. Nobody was in the living room or in the kitchen. She had to do something, go someplace. "Daddy," she cried, ran out the door and out onto the street. Tears blinded her and she couldn't think straight. She didn't know how, but she had to get to the hospital.

Sam had come back into the house after saying goodnight to Edna and Michael. She had gone to the kitchen to get a soda for Katie when she heard her yelling. She ran toward the family room just in time to see Katie running out the front door to the street. "Katie?" she called after her. "Katie, stop!"

Max and Peg were just driving up when they saw Katie running out into the street. They looked at each other. Then Peg's hand flew to her mouth as she realized that Katie didn't see or hear the truck that was backing up. It looked like it was heading right for her. Max slammed on the brakes, but before the car had even stopped, Peg jumped out and ran toward Katie who seemed to be looking straight ahead of her. Fear ran through her as she saw Katie running right into the path of the truck

Peg felt like she was running in slow motion. This couldn't be happening. She screamed and threw herself at Katie to knock her out of the way of the truck. She felt Katie move but Peg tripped and felt herself falling. She felt pain as her head struck something hard before everything went black.

Max froze. Katie, although dazed, was safely on the other side of the road, but Peg was lying on the street. The truck driver was standing over her.

"Oh, my God. Oh, my God." He kept repeating it over and over.

Max ran to her and bent down beside her. "Call 911," he yelled to the stunned truck driver. Max glanced at him and repeated the order louder. Finally the driver pulled out a cell phone.

By that time, Sam had reached him. "Is she okay, Dad? Is she?"

Max shook his head. "I don't know." There was blood on the side of her head. He was relieved when he felt her pulse and could see that she was breathing. He took out his handkerchief, glad that it was clean and unused and put pressure on the wound. He glanced up at Sam. "Take care of Katie."

"But--" Sam wanted to check Peg, but reluctantly left Peg's side, knowing that Katie needed attention, too. Katie was sitting on the curbing, dazed. She was shaking and crying uncontrollably. Sam reached out to her. "What happened, Katie?"

Katie couldn't stop crying. Sam wrapped her arms around the little girl. She seemed to be in shock. What on earth happened to cause this? She was just out of the room for a short time. "Katie, tell me what happened."

Katie, still shaking and sobbing, stared straight ahead without speaking.

She tipped the little girl's face up to look into her eyes. "Katie," she said firmly, "you have to talk to me. Tell me what happened."

Katie put her head on Sam's shoulder. "Daddy," she said. "They said Daddy died." She couldn't stop crying.

Sam couldn't believe it. "Who said that?"

"The news," she sobbed. She put her arm around Sam and held on to her.

Sam couldn't believe it. "The news said your dad died?"

"They said that there was-- an accident sometime ago." She sobbed some more. "They said -- the husband died-- and his wife--

was in ICU-- and she was in shock." Her voice became frantic. "I have to see my mom." She started to get up.

"Stay with me, Katie. You're shaking. We'll find out about it in a minute."

Katie looked around, coming out of her daze. When she saw Peggy on the street, she screamed her name and tried to get up. Sam held Katie's little body to her own. She didn't want her to see the blood on Peg's face. This was no time to be subjected to more tragedy. She'd had enough of that.

Just then they heard the sirens and the ambulance drove up. Two paramedics went right to Peg and asked Max to stand aside. They took her vitals and examined her.

Max paced behind the ambulance. He felt helpless. He hadn't known what to do to help Peg and now, they didn't even let him near her.

"What happened?" asked one of the paramedics.

"She was trying to get a little girl out of the way," Max explained. "The girl didn't see the truck backing up."

The truck driver was shaking his head. "I didn't see her. Honest, I didn't even know she was there until I heard a scream. I slammed on the brakes." He ran his hand through his hair. "She's going to be all right, isn't she?"

They didn't answer him. "Let's get her to the hospital." They put a collar on her neck and carefully transferred her to the gurney.

"May I go along?" asked Max, sick with worry.

"Are you a relative?"

"No."

"I'm sorry, sir. Maybe you'd like to follow us to the hospital."

He nodded and watched them as they raised the gurney, rolled it to the ambulance and folded up its legs before sliding it into the ambulance.

"Take her to Center City Hospital."

They started to object. "But--"

Max interrupted. "She works at that hospital. Take her there." His tone left no room for an argument.

They nodded as they closed the doors.

"I'll be right behind you."

"We're going along, Dad." Sam had her arm around Katie.

He shook his head. "I don't think that's a good idea. "

"I do," she said firmly. "Katie thinks her dad died."

"What?" What next? "How? Did someone call?"

Sam held up her hand as if to top his many questions. "She heard something on the news. Dad, I think she's in shock. Look at her eyes." Katies eyes were staring straight ahead but not seeing anything. "They can examine her there. If the report is true, she's going to be heartbroken. Give me a minute to get our coats. We need to keep her warm."

Max took off his coat and wrapped it around Katie while Sam ran into the house. "Come on, honey, let's get you into the car. It's warmer in there." He guided a hesitant Katie to the car and had opened the door when Sam returned with their coats. Here," she said handing Katie's coat to her dad.

On the way to the hospital, Max tried to question Katie about the news report. By that time she was sobbing only intermittently and was able to tell him what she had heard. "That doesn't mean it was your dad, honey." He parked the car in the lot closest to the ER and they rushed into the building.

"But they said there was an accident sometime ago. They--"

"There are so many accidents every day and so many hospitals in the city. Let's not borrow trouble. As soon as we get upstairs, Sam will take you to the nurse's station at the front of the building and ask them to check with ICU. I'll be in the ER waiting for news about what's happening with Peg."

Sam was concerned as she noticed Max's drawn face, white with fear. "Will you be all right, Dad?"

He nodded. "Go," he said gently and shooed them toward the nurse's station.

Katie's feet wouldn't move. She looked up at him. "I want to wait with you," she said, grabbing his hand.

What brought that on? He reached over and squeezed her shoulder.

Her eyes begged him to let her stay. She had to find out about her dad, but she knew Peggy was hurt bad. "I have to know how Peggy is. It's my fault that she got hurt."

He put his arms around her. "It wasn't your fault, Katie. You love your parents and you were reacting to the news you thought you heard."

"I didn't *think* I heard it. I *did* hear it," she insisted. "I didn't want to hear it, but I told you what they said."

"Okay, calm down." He plunked her down in a chair in the waiting room.

"What are you going to do?" whispered Sam.

"I'll find out once and for all. She needs to know." He left them and headed around the corner.

"May I help you?" asked the nurse behind the desk.

"I hope so. I have a little girl in the waiting room who is sure she heard a news report that her father died. They were in an accident a while back, and her parents were both still in ICU when I took her home with me. Is there any way to find out for me? Their name is Jordan."

The nurse looked up at him. "You say they are in Intensive Care?"

"Yes." He again explained what Katie had heard.

She punched in three numbers and waited. "This is Carla in admitting. Do you have two patients by the name of Jordan in ICU? Husband and wife." she added. She waited. "Their condition? ---- Their daughter is down here. --- I see. --- No, she heard a news report about a husband dying, leaving his wife in shock." She smiled and looked up at Max. "Thanks, Jenny." She hung up the phone. "Mr. and Mrs. Jordan are, if you'll excuse the expression, alive and kicking."

"Thank you. I'll tell Katie right away. I don't suppose there's any way of letting her see for herself."

She took a deep breath. "I'll see what I can do. Her name is Katie Jordan?"

"Yes. She's in the ER waiting room. Right now, I have to get back there. There's a special-- well, it's a long story. Thank you again." He left and returned to the waiting room where Katie and Sam sat.

"Your folks are fine, Katie. It was somebody else."

She closed her eyes.. "Are you sure?" *Thank you, God.*

"I'm sure. Why don't you just sit here and wait. I have to find the information desk." He left them to find out Peg's condition. This was so frustrating. He should be able to be with her, wait with her.

"She won't die, will she?" Katie asked Sam.

What should she say? She could tell it was serious, but the thought of promising a little girl something for which she had no control? She couldn't do it. It wouldn't be fair. "I hope not, Katie. She was breathing and she had a pulse. Those are good signs."

Katie hung her head and tears started to slide down her cheek. "You're a nurse. You should have taken care of her instead of me."

Sam shook her head. "Dad told me to take care of you. Besides, I don't think I could have knelt down with this incision." She didn't want Katie to feel guilty.

Max returned and fell into a chair. "They won't let me see her."

"I know, Dad." Her words were sympathetic.

"They won't even tell me anything about her."

"It's too soon for them to know anything. Besides, you're not related."

"I should have lied," he said defiantly.

Katie looked up at him. "You could tell them you're married."

Max frowned and looked. "Where did you come up with an idea like that?"

"Peggy said she had a crush on you lots and lots of years ago. She said she would have married you if you'd asked her." She covered her mouth. "Maybe that was a secret." She looked at Sam. "Will she be mad at me for telling?"

After watching her dad's grumpy expression, she shook her head. "I'm sure she won't be mad, Katie."

She sighed. "What's taking so long?"

The nurse who called herself Carla came into the area. "I take it the little bird sitting in the corner is Katie Jordan," she said. She walked right over to Katie. "I see you have a broken wing."

Katie giggled bashfully.

"Would you like to come with me to see your mother? Of course, you can't go in, but you can see her through the window."

She jumped up and stood right in front of Carla. "Can we, really? I did that before I was discharged from the hospital."

"Well, these people probably want to wait down here to find out about their friend, but I'm on my break and I'd be glad to take you up."

Katie looked to Max and Sam for approval. They both nodded.

Before they knew it, she was at the elevator waiting for Carla.

Sam's eyes opened wide. "Oh, my gosh," Sam blurted out. "I forgot all about Doug coming over."

"What about him, honey? Wasn't he there?"

"He said he was still tied up, but he thought he could make it by about nine." She looked at her watch and it was already nine-forty-five.

Just then, Doug rushed into the waiting room. "What happened? I got to your house to see you, but you weren't there. Your neighbor said an ambulance took someone away. Is Katie hurt?"

He sat down beside her while Sam and Max explained.

"Katie's okay, you said?"

Sam looked him in the eye, hoping he would suggest examining Katie when she returned. "She was in shock for a little while, but I think she snapped out of it. We kept her warm." She didn't want her dad to be worried about Peg and add more concern for Katie. She hoped that Doug had gotten her message.

Apparently he did. He nodded. "I'll check her over when she gets back."

Max was pacing the floor. "A nurse took her up to see her mom." He became agitated as his eyes met Doug's. "Can't you find out anything about Peg?" Max begged.

Doug was already at the door. "I intend to." He left them and after showing his ID badge to the security guard, he went though the double doors to the ER.

Max couldn't think straight. The tension was giving him a headache and he felt like he was crawling out of his skin. What if Peg didn't snap out of it? It looked like she had hit her head on the curbing when she fell. The whole thing happened so fast, he didn't know if he could relate it accurately. He didn't actually see what happened, but he could guess.

Doug came back frowning. "It's a waiting game, Mr. Madison."

"Call me Max, please. I take it she's still unconscious."

He nodded. "Sometimes it takes a long time to--"

"Don't sugar-coat it," he snapped. "Is she going to make it?"

Doug inhaled deeply. He sympathized with Max, the worry so obvious in his crazed eyes, but he had to be honest. "I don't know at this point. We have to wait."

Max got up and walked to the window. He turned back to Doug. "What is it that we're waiting for?"

"For some response or for her to regain consciousness. Head injuries are tricky. No doctor will give you a prognosis until all the facts are in. They're running some tests now." He motioned Max to sit down and sat down beside him. "Do you want me to wait out here with you?"

He closed his eyes and shook his head. "No, go back to Peg. Just come back and keep us informed, will you?"

Doug squeezed Max's shoulder as he looked at Sam. She nodded her head, her eyes pleading as if he were able to control what was happening in the ER.

Max and Sam waited in silence for what seemed like hours, but it was probably no more than twenty minutes. Sam had tried to talk to him, but words didn't come.

"There's a chapel down the hall," Sam finally said softly.

"I don't need a chapel," he snapped.

Sam nodded, but remained silent. She was helpless. He was hurting, probably like he hurt when her mother was killed. If only he could ask God to help; but what if God didn't listen. Her dad had said He didn't hear him before? She stood up and walked down the hall and back. Her side was a little sore, but it was nothing compared to what Peg would be feeling. She stopped at the chapel door and went in. In spite of what happened to her mother, Sam had no trouble praying. The only problem she had was not knowing for sure that God heard her prayers. Her dad could be right, that

God hadn't listened three years ago. Maybe He wouldn't listen now.

Doug had come in just to check on them and left again twice, but there had been nothing new. He thought Max would feel better even if there was nothing to report. They always say *no news is good news*, but in a case like this, people tend to borrow trouble when minutes stretch into hours.

Max paced the floor until his legs ached. He stood at the window and watched the traffic drive by. He saw two ambulances, a police car, a medi-van and two private cars, followed by... What was the matter with him? It was like counting sheep. He was avoiding the one thing he'd been taught to do in any situation like this. *When all else fails,* his dad always told him, *pray, Son.* He could still hear his dad's loving voice. *God will help you.* In his dream, was his dad trying to tell him to forgive God? To forgive the boy who shot him? Or forgive himself for not being there?

It seemed like hours that he stood there. He knew Sam came back, and he heard the nurse bring Katie back, but he couldn't think. He should go to her, but he couldn't right now. Sam would have to take care of her. The more time that passed, the more he feared that Peg wouldn't make it. It had been different with Bernice. She was already gone when the police called him. It was strange, he thought, but when all was said and done, he never got a chance to ask God to spare Bernice's life. He frowned as if that one thought had a special meaning for him. Could it?

What was taking Doug so long? Why didn't he come back? He'd been gone a long time this time. Maybe things weren't going so well in there. He wasn't even going to think about that now. She'd be all right, wouldn't she? He shook his head. Where was Doug? Even when he'd had nothing to report, he'd come and talked to assure them. Why wasn't he here now?

CHAPTER THIRTEEN

▼

The minutes dragged, seeming like hours. Wearily he sat down, shoulders slumped, his body surrendering to the moment as he bent his head and covered his face with his hands. "Please, God, don't let her die. Don't let another woman I love die."

Katie was at his side, holding his hand. "I prayed for my mom and dad and they got better. I prayed for Peggy, too. Did you?"

He raised his eyes to look at her, but stared straight ahead as if looking through her. Her words sank in. More than that, the words he had just whispered sank in. "Yes," he muttered somewhat disbelieving. "I prayed."

Sam, although smiling, swiped at the tears she couldn't hold back. Her dad *prayed*. After all these years, he *prayed*. *Thank you, God. Thank you.*

The three of them sat huddled together, holding hands, each one saying a silent prayer for Peg's life.

Max opened his eyes and raised his head. A feeling of calmness had come over him, a peace that he hadn't known for many years. Suddenly, he knew that Peg was going to be all right. He was exhausted, but he sighed with a feeling of well-being.

The doctor came into the waiting area with Doug. "I'm Dr. Jamison," he said. "Doug tells me that you're Peggy's fiancé."

Max coughed as his eyes shot to Doug. Doug's eyes begged Max not to contradict him. He nodded as if asking Max to go along with it.

His face was white with fear and worry. He didn't know why Doug had said they were engaged, but he needed to find out how Peg was, so he bent his head in an *almost* nod. He avoided lying by not answering the doctor's question, but by asking his own most urgent question. "How is she, doctor?"

"She regained consciousness. A concussion isn't unusual in a case like hers. I'll want to keep her here for a two or three days. That was quite a bump on her head."

Max nodded. "She must have hit the curbing."

Dr. Jamison winced. "She couldn't have chosen anything harder. She's a little confused, but that should gradually improve. The laceration isn't as serious as it looked. Head wounds can bleed profusely. It's understandable that you'd be concerned about it. All in all, it's better if we keep an eye on her for a few days."

Max nodded. "May I see her?"

"Doug says she has no family here. I suppose you should relieve her anxiety." He smiled. "She mumbled your name a few times when she was regaining consciousness." He smiled. "You'd better go in."

Max reached for his hand and shook it. "Thank you, doctor."

Dr. Jamison nodded. "She's a good nurse." His eyes met Max's squarely on, but there was a hint of humor in them. "Funny she never mentioned being engaged."

Max looked a little sheepish and shrugged. "She didn't know," he mumbled. Nor did he, he thought.

"You'd better remind her," he winked, "or ask her, whichever the case may be." Grinning, he nodded as a final gesture before turning and walking down the hall.

Max looked at Doug and laughed. "Why did you tell them we were engaged?"

"You wanted to get in to see her, didn't you?"

Max nodded. "Where is she?"

He motioned toward the double door to the ER. "Come on. I'll show you."

Doug led him to Peg's bed, left him there and went back to examine Katie.

Peg's eyes were open, but she looked so small and pale lying there. She was hooked up to so much equipment that the tubes and wires almost looked like they were part of her body. It scared Max to think that her injury was so serious that constant monitoring was necessary. At the same time, he knew that she was being well cared for. "Hi," he said softly, covering her hand with his.

She smiled ever so slightly. "What happened?" Her voice was almost a whisper.

Max smiled down at her. "You saved Katie's life. Do you remember any of it?"

Her eyes searched his as if his held the answers to her questions. Then, it all seemed to make sense. "The truck," she said on a sigh. She suddenly realized the gravity of it and fear struck. "Katie! Where is she?"

Max gently touched her shoulder to calm her. "She's fine, honey."

She was silent for a moment. Did Max call her *honey*? She must have misunderstood. "Where is she?"

"Out in the waiting room. By the way, Doug told the doctor that I'm your fiancé so I could come in to see you. Apparently, only relatives are allowed in here."

She must have missed the fiancé part. "I don't have any relatives who'd care."

He had hoped she'd react to *fiancé*. "That's what Doug said."

A nurse approached them. "We're trying to get you a room, hon." She looked at Max. "You can wait with her for a little while if you want."

Peg didn't look pleased. "I have to stay?"

"'Fraid so," answered the nurse. "You'll like it here. We take good care of our patients."

"I know," said Peg dryly.

Max winked at the nurse. "She works here."

The nurse was surprised. "You do? Where?"

"Pediatrics."

"RN?" she asked.

"Yes."

"Well, we'll just take extra good care of you. Okay?" With a quick wave of her hand she left Peg's bedside. She whispered to Max. "Don't stay too long. She'll be tired."

Peg chuckled about the care the nurse had promised, but pain grabbed at her head.

Max was concerned. "Should I call the doctor?"

"No. The pain gets worse when I laugh, that's all." Her fingers carefully felt the area around the bump, not quite wanting to touch it directly. "That's why I have to stay?"

Max nodded. "That and a concussion."

"Oh." Her eyes were sad.

"It's for the best, Peg."

He sat with her quietly, and when her eyes drifted shut, he whispered, "I'll be back to see you after I take the girls home."

"Okay," she said on a breath.

Max could see that Peg was having trouble keeping here eyes open. He bent down and kissed her cheek. "I'll see you in a little while."

She blinked her eyes and closed them as he left the cubicle.

He heard Katie and Doug talking as he approached the waiting area.

"Don't worry, sweetie," Doug told Katie. "She'll be all right."

Katie grabbed Doug's hand to get his attention. "Why couldn't *you* be her doctor? She'd like that."

"Peggy needs a specialist." Doug answered.

"Like my mom and dad?"

His smile was warm. "Exactly."

Max sat down beside them. "They're taking her to a room."

Doug stood. "They'll want to watch her for a few days."

Max stood up and turned to the girls. "Let's go home. I want to come back and visit in a while."

"I should hope so. A fiancé would even bring her something special," he teased, "– like a ring."

Sam grinned when she saw the expression on her dad's face. It was one she hadn't seen for many years, if ever. Was he thoughtful? Embarrassed? If she didn't know better, she'd say he almost looked enlightened.

Doug put his hand on Max's shoulder. "Why don't you take Katie? I'll take Sam with me if you don't mind, unless you want me to take them both so you can stay."

"I need to stop at home, and I don't mind if you take Sam as long as you bring her right home. I don't want to leave Katie alone when I come back to the hospital."

"Of course you don't," he replied. "I just want to talk to Sam for a while. I'll even stay with the girls if you don't object. That way, you can visit to your heart's content."

Max glanced at Sam who didn't seem to object to Doug's suggestion. He held his hand out for Katie to take it. "Come on Katie. Let's go home and leave these two alone."

They were in the car when Max forced his mind away from Peg to glance at Katie. She looked skeptical. "What's the matter, honey?"

She shrugged. "Are you sure Peggy's going to be okay?"

"I saw her myself. The doctor told me he wants to keep her here for observation. That means they want to watch her and make sure she does what she's supposed to do. They won't want her to sleep for long periods of time."

"She could come home with us and she could sleep in my room. I'd make sure she didn't sleep too long."

He chuckled. "Bring her home, huh? Now there's a thought. Maybe we'll consider that when they discharge her." He smiled and patted Katie's hand. "The more I think about it, the more I think that is an excellent suggestion."

Katie grinned. "Do you like her again?"

"What do you mean? I *always* liked her." Too much, he added to himself. "What made you think I didn't?"

"You didn't look happy and you looked sort of like you were mad."

"I did?" He was surprised that Katie could read his moods. He hadn't been that bad, had he? Granted, he hadn't been in a good mood, but he never stopped loving Peg. Had he even stopped loving her all these years? Surely he loved Bernice, but . . . .

Life was so complicated sometimes. Was it possible that God thought they belonged together all along? God wouldn't plan something like a death to facilitate an end result. He'd have to think about that, but not now. It was too broad a concept to contemplate tonight, and right now, the possibilities seemed endless.

"Peggy wasn't happy, either. She said it was because she was working too hard, but I knew that wasn't the reason. I'm glad you like each other again."

He put his arm round her shoulders and hugged her. "So am I, Katie. So am I."

Edna tried to call Max for the last half hour. "Where could they be?"

Michael tried to keep from grinning. "Perhaps they had someplace to go. Do they always check in with you when they leave the house?"

"Of course not." She sounded outraged, but she had to admit that Michael made sense. "It's just that Sam was home when we left. I wasn't aware they were going anyplace. Someone would have told me."

"Really?" he teased..

Her chin went up defiantly. "Yes, really!"

He chuckled. "Don't get upset. I guess I'm not used to the lives of families being so intertwined."

Her expression softened. "I guess many families aren't so considerate. It's just since Fred died and since my health problems started, Max and Samantha let me know when they'll be gone. Their reasoning is that if I need someone, I call them, but if I know they aren't home, I won't waste time trying to call them and call 911 right away."

Michael's expression turned serious as he laced his fingers through hers. "That makes perfect sense, Edna. I'm sorry I teased you. I've pretty well fended for myself lately. Perhaps that's why I decided to move here."

She put her other hand on his arm. "I'm glad you did."

Michael had been thinking. Was this a good time to bring up their relationship? Was it too soon for Edna? Some people weren't able to decide something like that after such a short period of time, but he had known from the first time he saw Edna that he wanted her to be part of his life. He hadn't even considered to what extent. He just knew. "Edna," he took her hand, "do you think that you and I could--"

The ringing phone interrupted him. She excused herself, got up and went into the kitchen, leaving a frustrated Michael sitting alone.

He sat there, vacillating. Was it coincidence that the phone rang just then, or was this God's way of telling him it was indeed too soon? How was a man to know? He envied people who recognized God's work and accepted it without a doubt. He always questioned it. Why was that? Did he not have faith? He'd always thought of himself as a man with a firm belief in God, but lately, he wondered if coincidence didn't play an important role in his life. No, his faith was unused for a while, but still intact.

Edna returned with a serious look on her face and sat down beside Michael.

Michael took her hand in his. "What is it?"

"It's Peggy. She got hurt. It seems she fell when she saved Katie from being hit by a truck."

"What?" This was hard to believe. "Where are they? How are they? You said Peggy is hurt. What about Katie?"

"Katie wasn't hurt." Edna explained about their being at the hospital all this time. "Max said that Peggy has a concussion and a nasty lump on her head, but she's going to be all right."

"That's a relief," he said with a sigh. "How did it happen? You said it was a *truck*?"

"Katie heard a news report on TV and she thought her father was the man they were talking about. They reported his death and Katie was so shaken, she ran out into the street and didn't see a truck backing up."

"Why did she run outside?"

"I wondered the same thing, but she's young and acted out of fear. I suppose the poor girl was beside herself."

"I hope she learned that is wasn't her father."

Edna smiled. "A nurse took her to see her mother and let her peek in at her father. They both seem to be coming out of it. Their condition is no longer critical."

"That's good to hear. Katie is such a sweet little thing."

Edna nodded. "She's been such a frightened little girl. I'm glad things are looking up for her." She sighed. "You had started saying something to me when the phone rang."

"It can wait." He still hadn't decided if the phone call had been a sign from God or merely dumb luck. He'd have to ponder that. "I think it's time I went back to Judd's." He stood up to leave. "It's about time I find an apartment of my own, don't you think?"

"Is it uncomfortable staying with them?"

"Not at all, but I don't want to wear out my welcome. You know how it is when you have an extra person in the house."

"Yes," she said thoughtfully. A fleeting thought again crossed her mind as she wondered how she would feel sharing her place with someone after being alone for so long; but then, he wasn't talking about her. This was about Judd and Mary. "You're thinking that two is a couple, three is a crowd."

He chuckled. "I haven't heard that expression since Carol died, but I guess that about says it. They're not newlyweds, but they need their space."

Edna had a soft smile on her lips. "They still seem to be very much in love."

Michael nodded. "They've had their share of bad times, but their faith has seen them through their troubles. Somehow, I think the adversity, once resolved has made their marriage more solid. Their devotion to God and to each other is a joy to witness."

Edna sighed. "You and I missed that part of our marriages by losing our spouses, didn't we?"

He looked down at his shoes, contemplating the thought of saying more to her right now. "With our spouses, yes, but that doesn't mean that we can't experience that devotion with..." His words trailed off as he paused because he had wanted to say *each other*. He didn't know if he should. Instead he said, "Someone else."

Edna frowned slightly, not sure what his meaning was.

He kissed her on the cheek, but he wanted more than that. He moved his hand to the back of her head to pull her closer and covered her mouth with his. After a very long minute, he broke the connection and stared into her dazed eyes. "Goodnight, Edna," he whispered. "I'll call you." With that, he left.

Edna stood motionless, stunned by his kiss and shocked that she had enjoyed it so very much. She hadn't thought she would ever kiss a man again, except for the courteous peck on the cheek that was the custom with close friends and family. She began to realize that she was becoming accustomed to having Michael around and she enjoyed it. The thought of *sharing* her apartment with him might be a different story; besides, how foolish she was to think in those terms. Just because he kissed her, no matter how enjoyable that kiss was, didn't suggest any kind of commitment. She was really being ridiculous. She sighed, locked the door and went into the kitchen. Why was it that she could still feel his kiss on her lips? That was silly. She wasn't a teenager. Life wasn't like that anymore. She was almost seventy, for heavens sake. "Get real," she said aloud, but oh, it felt so good to be held in his arms.

Doug stopped the car in the driveway, leaving room for Max to drive out when he left for the hospital.

Sam looked at Doug. "You've been very quiet. Is there something wrong?"

"No. I have some things to say to you, but I don't know if it's too soon, or if I even have the right to say them."

Sam watched his expression. She didn't see fear or confusion. It was more like awkward indecision. She sighed. "Isn't it just best to say what's on your mind? I'm a good listener."

He laughed. "You weren't listening the first time we met."

She blushed. "I thought you forgave me for that."

"I did. It's just that this is sort of hard for me. I don't usually talk about feelings, but what I have to say directly involves them."

She waited patiently. Why did men have such a hard time with feelings? She noticed with her dad that he would be very quiet or sometimes grumpy, but seldom told her what was wrong. "I'm listening."

He took a deep breath and looked into her eyes, hoping to see what she was feeling before she told him to take a hike. "I really like you, Sam. I want to get to know you better. I want to know what your favorite color is, what you like to eat, what scares you, what makes you happy. I want to know what you have planned for your future. Where do you want to live? Do you ever plan on getting married? How do you feel about kids? Do you--"

"Whoa!" She couldn't handle all the questions and the implication at the same time. She was quiet for a moment. "I'd like to get to know you, too, Doug. I enjoy being with you when you're not diagnosing me and shipping me off to the hospital."

He grinned. "And doing it all wrong on top of it."

She blushed again. "Could we just forget about that first night?" she begged.

He shook his head. "Oh, no. I'll *never* forget that first night. You were so cute."

"Cute? That's what you call cute? How would you have thought of me if I'd been sweet and cooperative?"

"Hmmmm. We can leave cooperative for a later time."

"So what exactly are you trying to say?" She really wanted to know.

"Are you interested in pursuing a relationship?"

She was quiet, giving herself time to consider the extent of his meaning. "That," she started slowly, "depends on what you're contemplating. Just what does this relationship involve?"

He was confused. "What does any relationship involve?"

"What if your idea of a relationship involves a lot more than I'm willing to give?" What if he wasn't thinking about intimacy? That was stupid. He was a doctor. What doctor wouldn't think about the body? If he was thinking about hers, that simply wasn't going to happen. She reserved that part of a relationship for her husband, should she ever have one. She was puzzled. Hadn't she just told Peg she was never getting married? Was she changing her mind? Or was Doug responsible for changing her opinion?

He nodded. "Now we're talking about intimacy. Who said anything about that? Not that I haven't been thinking about it-- a bit – a lot." He was breathing hard. "Why did you have to bring that into it?" He was scowling.

She shrugged. "I'm sorry. I just felt I had to let you know where I stand. I don't move in with a boyfriend. I reserve that stuff until my wedding night."

Stuff? He narrowed his eyes. "Are you proposing? I mean, I think it's a little too soon for that."

Her fist met with his arm. She realized then what she'd done. "I'm sorry."

"You keep saying that, Sam. There's nothing to feel sorry for. I just want you to know that I'm human and I do have feelings for you. I have to admit that some of those feelings are very strong feelings; but I respect your right to your opinions, and I would never do anything against your wishes. In fact, I agree with you."

"You mean you wouldn't do whatever you had to do so you could have your way with me? I read about things like that all the time."

"Sam, I don't even drink alcohol. Aside from my religious beliefs, I made up my mind a long time ago that if I was going to be a doctor, I would be responsible enough to stay away from alcohol."

"I'm glad."

"No. I have to be honest. It's more than that. It's necessity." He took a deep breath. He had to tell her, and now was as good a time as any. "My dad is a doctor, but he was an alcoholic. I can't tell you how many times I saw him take a chance and have a drink when he thought he wasn't on call. Then something happened and they needed him at the hospital. I worried what would happen to those patients. How he got by with it, I'll never know, but as far as I know, his patients never suffered for the fact."

She was appalled. "He's still practicing medicine?"

He nodded. "Mom insisted he go into treatment or give up his license to practice."

"And?"

"He went into treatment. He hasn't had a drink in ten years."

"What a wonderful story to tell your children."

He chuckled. "If I ever have any. At the rate I'm going, I won't even get to the *Will- you-go-out-with-me*-stage." He took her hand. "Sam, what I've been trying to say is I want to go out with you. I don't want to see anyone else. I want to have a meaningful relationship with you. I want us to be friends, and someday…"

"Don't say it, Doug. I told you I won't--"

He raised his eyebrows. "Even if we're married?" He raised his voice. "You mean *never*?"

She started to laugh, but she grabbed her side when it hurt. "Can we just not think about that part for a while?"

"Okay. Let's start over again. I want to get to know you better. Will you go out with me?"

She smiled. "Yes, Doug, I'll be happy to go out with you."

"And you'll put off any thought of working in the ER for a while?"

She frowned. "Why on earth would you ask me a question like that?"

"Because I'll be practicing in a small town when I finish my residency."

She nodded knowingly. "What does that have to do with where I work?" Suddenly, it hit her right smack in the face. "I get it. The woman gives up her dream of a career." Her whole body stiffened. "Why is it that you're not willing to stay in the city if you want to get to know me? Why do I have to be the one--"

The front door opened and Max leaned his head out. "Are you two coming in?" he yelled. "I want to get back to the hospital."

Sam already had her hand on the door and was out of the car before Doug could come around to help her. "We're coming," she told her dad.

"We'll talk later," said Doug softly enough so Max couldn't hear.

Her chin went up in the air. "And then again, maybe not." She went inside.

They both put aside their differences to make it a pleasant time for Katie. They played a game for a while and watched her favorite sitcom before it was her bedtime. She stalled, of course, but she knew she had to do as she was told.

When she was ready for bed, Sam took her into the bedroom and tucked her in and hugged her. "Sleep tight," she said.

"Sam?" She waited for Sam to give her permission to go ahead and say what was on her mind, which Sam did. "Do you think Max and Peggy like each other again?"

She nodded. "I think so, Katie. What made you ask?"

"Oh, I don't know. I guess I didn't like seeing them so sad."

"I agree, but you know, it's not our problem. As much as we care, we can't help them. If they're going to be a couple, they have to work at it together. There will always be differences in opinions, but they'll just have to work them through."

"Like Mom and Dad. Whenever they argue, they put me to bed and by morning, they love each other again."

Sam strained to hold back a chuckle. "Yeah. Adults are like that."

"Are you?"

Sam thought for a moment. "You know, I'm not sure. I never thought of myself as half of a couple."

Katie giggled. "That sounds funny."

"It does, doesn't it," she agreed. "Right now, young lady, it's time to go to sleep. See you in the morning."

"Goodnight, Sam. I love you."

Sam told her she loved her, too. She joined Doug in the living room and found him staring out the window into the blackness. She could tell he wasn't happy with her. She wasn't happy with him either, but she had to hold her ground. No way was a man going to tell her where she could work. Next thing you knew, he'd be telling her what she could or couldn't do or where she could go or what she could wear. She could see it now. She'd be shopping for groceries and he'd tell her she should shop at a different store. He'd probably tell her what to eat and drink.

She took a deep breath. She was really going off the deep end here. Why? Doug was a nice man, a man sensitive to the feelings of a little girl. Why couldn't he be sensitive to her feelings? Why did she care? It hit her suddenly that she *did* care, and it scared her. She and her dad had lived alone, having only each other for a long time now. Sure, they were involved with Gram, too, she thought, but she and her dad were pretty well set in their ways. Could that change now that Peggy was in the picture? Peg definitely seemed to be in her dad's life. She'd have to think about this.

Sam straightened up as she went into the room. "She's one tired little girl."

Doug turned around. "She's had a traumatic day. Do you think she's okay?"

"I think so. She still thinks it's her fault that Peg was hurt, but we'll have to reassure her from time to time. Poor thing. She must have flipped when she thought her dad had died."

Doug nodded. He sat down on the sofa. Instead of joining him, Sam chose the chair across from him.

"Sam, I'm sorry if I sounded domineering. I just want to give us a chance, and if I'm away from here, how does that give us a chance?"

"I think I've been honest about where I want to work."

Doug looked at her, his eyes sincere. "And I have no choice."

No choice? What was he talking about? We always have a choice. Life is full of choices from the time we know how to think for ourselves, and even before that. "What you're saying is that you refuse to practice in a city, and I should do what? Consider nursing in a small town hospital where the ER probably gets used once or twice a day?"

He sighed. "When you put it that way-- Forget it. I'd better get going."

She was stunned that he didn't say anything more, but she wasn't going to pursue it. If he wanted to leave, let him leave. Good riddance. "Thank you for the ride home," she said stiffly.

"You're welcome, Sam." He was ill at ease. "Katie will be okay. If you need anything..." He let his words trail off.

She nodded. "Thanks."

They were at the door. "I'm sorry, Sam." He was out the door before she could respond. When she closed the door, she was bewildered for a moment before she broke into tears. She didn't know why she was crying. She hadn't known Doug long enough to be emotionally involved, had she? He was some chauvinistic, big headed would-be doctor who-- That was unkind. She was angry and hurt, but why? She knew why. Because she really cared about him.

CHAPTER FOURTEEN

▼

Max sat beside Peg, watching her sleep. Did they have a future together? He hoped so. He loved her and he wanted to spend the rest of his life with her. He knew now that God did exist and that it was God who saved Peg's life. In fact, he'd been thinking about it. Katie was just one instrument in the orchestration of life. So was Bernice, Sam, Max and his mother. Really thinking about Bernice made him see for the first time that it was possible that her life hadn't been cut short. It was possible that she lived as long as she was supposed to live, that God had a plan for her and He allowed it to play out the way it had to. *How can we tell how and why God does what He does*?

Going deeper into the subject only convinced him that he and Peggy were destined be together all along, just not in the time frame that he had originally planned. His marriage to Bernice was only temporary according to God's plan, in spite of the fact that they had a wonderful marriage and produced a child. Could it be possible that God had this plan all along? As he said before, had he not married Bernice, if things had worked out with Peggy years ago, he wouldn't have had a daughter. Well, maybe he would have, but it wouldn't have been Sam. He didn't remember his beliefs being so confusing when he was younger.

Just when he was delving into his thought process a little deeper, Peg moaned.

"Hi," he said quietly, taking her hand in his.

She opened her eyes and squinted. "How long have you been here?"

"A while. How are you feeling?"

She sighed. "Tired. They keep waking me up."

"How thoughtless," he said with a grin.

"I thought so." She opened here eyes a little farther. "How is Katie?"

"She's fine. Doug and Sam are with her." He looked at his watch. "She should be fast asleep by now."

"What time is it?"

"Almost midnight."

She looked confused. "You shouldn't be here. Visiting hours--"

"I'm your fiancé, remember?'

"Hmmm. To be honest, I don't remember being asked."

He smiled. "Shhhh. Somebody might hear you and throw me out."

"Can't have that," she whispered.

"They decided that I could be the one to wake you every so often."

She frowned until she remembered. "The concussion."

"Peg," he said softly, "how would you feel about being engaged for real?"

She looked into his eyes. He sounded serious.

"I mean, I think we've waited long enough, don't you? We're old enough to know that we want out of life, and I know I want you in mine."

She remembered having told him she didn't want to see him anymore. "What about our differences? I thought we talked about this. Did they go away suddenly?"

"You know," he brushed a strand of hair out of her face, "I think they did."

There was hope in her voice. "What are you saying, Max?"

"I'm saying that I think God had a plan all along." He quickly silenced her by touching her lips. "Don't say anything. Let me explain."

She nodded, moving her head carefully, but it still hurt.

"When you were lying in the ER and I didn't know what was happening or how badly you were hurt, I just about went crazy." Her eyes were filled with sympathy. He went on. "I found myself praying to God that you would be all right. As I told you, I believed in God all along, but I just didn't trust Him. Suddenly, the whole thing made sense. You were right. God had a plan, and the way we lived our lives was part of the big picture." He held up his hands to stop her comment. "Okay, it might not be exactly the way you think of it, but can you live with the way I think of it?"

He took a deep breath before continuing. "I married Bernice. She was a good wife and mother, and I loved her, but she wasn't you, Peg. I didn't realize that until the last few days. My love for her was one that grew out of our friendship, and I do believe that there are different kinds of love, maybe love in different degrees. You don't need passion to have a good marriage; in fact, I didn't even realize that it was missing from my marriage until I saw you again. The point is that I think we were meant to be together."

Tears were in her eyes. "I guess I asked God for being here in this condition." She saw his puzzled expression. "I said that something would have to happen to restore your faith in God."

"I remember." He took her hand in his. "This may not be the best time to ask, but Peggy Swenson, would you do me the honor of being my wife? Will you marry me?"

The tears ran down her cheeks. "Yes. Oh, yes, Max."

He stood up so he could bend down and kiss her without making her move her head. "I love you, Peg."

"That's good," she whispered against his mouth, "because I love you, too. I always have."

"Since college?"

"Yes. I loved you so very much, and when you never called, I ran. I was heartbroken. I thought you didn't care. I worked hard at my studies, did everything I could to forget you, but I couldn't. I ended up meeting Dennis. He was attentive and kind, but he wasn't you. I settled for second best. I thought he was all I could hope for so I married him, but he was the wrong man and," she shrugged, "you know the rest."

"Right or wrong, I believe it's all part of the plan, Peg. I'm convinced it was the way it was meant to be." He kissed her on the lips. "I don't want to wait. I hope we can have a short engagement."

"You don't want to wait another twenty-some years?"

"I don't want to wait twenty days. Do you think we could plan a quick wedding when you're well enough? Maybe we could elope."

"I think your family will want to be there. Why don't we settle for a private ceremony in the church or the pastor's office, for family only?"

Max smiled. "I like the way you think, future Mrs. Madison."

"Ahem," was the comment that came from the nurse standing in the doorway. "I see the patient has a good reason for her elevated heart-rate."

"The best," said Peg with a smile.

The nurse turned to Max. "I suppose you'd consider me mean if I said you should go home."

He chuckled. "Yes, but I'd understand." He kissed Peg briefly and turned to leave. Before he had reached the door, he went back to her and kissed her more thoroughly. He sighed as he turned once again to leave and waved to her as he left. "I'll be floating home on cloud nine."

Peg was stunned. "Make room for me," she managed to say. "Maybe I can go home tomorrow."

He sighed. "We'll see. Sleep tight." He left.

Max watched Sam walk down the stairs and come into the kitchen listlessly. "You look like you lost your best friend." He would delay telling her his happy news until she could be more receptive.

"I think I did. Doug doesn't want to see me anymore."

Max frowned at the thought. "I can't believe that. Did he say so?"

"He didn't have to."

"That's it? That's all you're going to tell me?"

She sighed. "He wanted to get to know me better."

He frowned. "Yes, I can see that something like that would upset you."

She overlooked his teasing. "Well, it doesn't matter. He wants to set up practice in a small town."

"I know."

"And I want to work in the ER."

He nodded his head slowly. "You're not telling me anything new."

Sometimes fathers could be so aggravating. "Don't you see? If he moves to a small town, we won't be able to see each other anymore, not that it matters. He's pig-headed and stubborn and--"

"And you're not?" he said with a glint in his eye.

"You don't understand," she whined.

"I think I do. You want to work in an ER in a *city*, and he has to practice in North Branch or Wyoming. Someplace up north of here."

Anger took over. Her dad was as dense as Doug. "What do you mean he *has* to?"

Max was surprised. "He didn't tell you about his agreement?"

She put her hands on her hips. "Agreement? Dad, what are you talking about?"

Doug should have explained this to her, but Max would have to do it for him. She had to know the details. "Because of a disagreement, Doug refused his father's offer to put him through medical school. He needed to get his funding elsewhere, so he agreed to work in that town for at least three years, in exchange for their putting him through medical school. I know he'll keep his word. He's an honorable man."

Sam stood there as if in shock.

He waited for her to comment. "You have nothing to say?"

That had taken the wind out her sails. "Why didn't he tell me?"

"I don't know. Why didn't you ask him why he insisted on a small town?"

She shrugged. "I thought he just liked small towns."

Max shrugged. "Maybe he does, or maybe he'll learn to like them. Who knows?"

"Good morning." Katie yawned as she came into the kitchen.

"Good morning," they said at the same time.

"Did I hear some arguing last night?" She yawned again and turned to Max. "Don't you like Peggy anymore again?"

Max laughed. "I like her just fine, young lady. So much, in fact, that," he looked at Sam, "that I've asked her to marry me."

Stunned, Sam sat for a moment absorbing his words before she jumped up and threw herself into his arms and Katie clapped.

"I'm so happy, Dad."

"Me too," said Katie, smiling from ear to ear.

"That makes four of us."

Sam backed out of his hold. "What did Gram say?"

"I haven't told her yet. You're the first to know."

Katie beamed from ear to ear. "I can't wait to tell Mom and Dad." Her expression turned somber. "How long is it gonna be before I can talk to my mom?"

"You know," said Sam, "I'll bet when she can handle her emotions, they'll let you talk to her on the phone. Now, don't count on it, because it's just an idea I had, but we could ask."

Katie jumped up. "Let's call now."

"Later," said Sam. "Be patient."

"I have been," pouted Katie.

"I know. I want to ask Peggy what she thinks about it first."

"Maybe she could ask. She's there anyway."

Max poured coffee for Sam and milk for Katie. "I'll talk to her today."

Katie sipped her milk. "I bet she's happy."

"I hope so. I intend to do everything I can to make the rest of her life what it should have been in the first place."

Sam took out the cereal. "She had a bad marriage, didn't she?"

He nodded. "And that was probably my fault, but I'll explain that later."

Katie's eyes searched his. "But you're going to be a happy couple, aren't you?"

He tweaked her nose. "You bet we are."

Sam winked at him. "You'd better tell Gram, don't you think?"

"I'll call her right after breakfast."

Peg came home from the hospital three days later with strict instructions to take it easy and let others wait on her. Yeah, right, she thought. Maybe she should call her uncaring mother or maybe her dad would bring his latest girlfriend to help look after her. She kept her mouth shut, certain that the doctor wouldn't discharge her if he knew she'd be alone at home.

She was dressed, ready to go, just waiting for Max to drive her home.

He arrived behind the nurse pushing the wheelchair. "Your carriage awaits," she said, helping Peg into the wheelchair.

Peg grimaced as the nurse pushed her down the hall. "I suppose this is necessary."

"You've got it," she answered with a chuckle. "You know hospital rules."

When she was tucked safely into the car, they drove off.

"She pointed to the right as they passed the street which led to her house. "You forgot to turn."

"So I did," he said without emotion. "We might as well go to my place."

"But--"

"Shhhhh. I talked it over with your doctor and with Sam and Katie. You're staying with us."

"Is that proper?"

He laughed. "With two chaperones, not to mention Mom and Michael coming anytime of the day or night? Unless you'd rather stay in the hospital."

"I guess it's okay. Are you sure you want me?"

"Are you sure you want *me*?"

"That wasn't what I asked."

"I know, Peg. I'm teasing. I don't know what I'd do with myself if you weren't right here where I can see you and touch you."

"Are you sure there's room for me?"

"There are four bedrooms, one for each of us, if that's what you're worried about. It will all be very proper."

She smiled. "I suppose it's sort of silly, especially since we're getting married soon."

"*Soon* is the operative word. I'd say as soon as you can stand up under your own steam. What do you say?"

"You don't like wheelchairs?"

He laughed. "Don't tempt me, honey." He put his hand on hers. "Sit back and relax. We're going home."

Sam tried to be happy for Peg and her dad. She had to hide her depression from Katie, but she wasn't always sure she did it successfully. She had tried to call Doug, but he was never available. She assumed that he didn't want to talk to her, and she couldn't blame him. Why hadn't she asked him why he felt it necessary to practice in a small town?

"They're here," said Katie excitedly. She ran to the front door and held it open for Peg to come in.

Max guided her inside and led her to the sofa. "Sit for a while."

Peg thankfully sank into the sofa. "I can't believe how tired I am."

Sam and Katie said, "I do." They looked at each other and laughed.

"You are officially welcomed," said Sam, "to the home for disobedient patients."

Peg laughed. "Disobedient? I'm not sure I like that."

"She didn't mean it," said Katie. "We're always good and it's really fun here."

"I'm sure it is." Peg turned to Katie. "How are you feeling?"

"Except for my arm, there's nothing wrong with me. I don't know why I had to stay in the hospital so long."

They all looked at each other and laughed. The doorbell rang.

Max jumped up. "I'll get it."

Sam picked up the suitcase Max had brought in. "Let me take your bag upstairs."

Peg held up her hand. "Not on your life. You're still restricted."

"I forgot." She put the suitcase back down.

"And that's precisely why you can't go back to your clinicals."

Sam spun around to see Doug staring at her with a grin. He motioned to her. "Could I speak with you privately?"

Sam just nodded and led him into the kitchen. "Doug, I'm sorry I said what I did. Why didn't you tell me about your agreement with wherever it is you're going to set up your practice?"

"You were so angry."

"I'm sorry, Doug. I'm so sorry."

He had his arm across her shoulders. "Your dad told me I should have told you."

"When did he say that?"

"I ran into him at the hospital." He took her by the shoulders and turned her to face him. "Sam, does it make a difference?" He waited, hoping against hope that she'd softened.

"I don't know what to say."

"I'm not going to be that far away, but if you're determined to work in a city ER, our schedules are bound to be different. There's no way it'll work for us. Neither of us will have much time to ourselves. I don't think either one of us wants to invest a year, or even a few months in a relationship that's going to be nothing but trouble, not to mention the broken heart of a certain doctor."

She looked down. "I know."

The silence was painful while the thoughts Sam had been mulling over for the past week ran through her mind. Her career was important, but if the rest of her life was going to be anything like this past week, she'd have to opt for letting that dream fall by the wayside. She looked in to his eyes. "I want to get to know you, Doug. Six months from now, you might decide we weren't meant to be together, but at least we'll know."

"And what about your dream?"

"Hmmmm. Did I ever tell you about my other dream?"

He shook his head.

"I have to admit that it's a dream I very recently discovered myself, but I want to have a husband and a family."

He smiled. "Then my question is, am I a believable candidate for that position?"

She smiled. "What do you think?"

He wrapped his arms around her and kissed her. "Mmmmm. Maybe it's not going to take a year to see if we're compatible."

"We don't want to be hasty," she said lazily against his lips. "Maybe we could figure it out in say six months."

He kissed her again. "Or even three."

They laughed.

EPILOGUE

▼

Three weeks later, they were all present as Max and Peg stood in front of the minister at the church where Max had grown up. Max and Peg had written their own vows, promising to cherish each and every moment of every day that God graciously granted them. They thanked Him for their second chance at happiness.

Life was good. Max and Peg were starting the life they had wanted years ago.

Doug and Sam were enjoying each other while they were finding out if they were meant to be together. Sam learned there was give and take in a relationship, and that the give didn't hurt all that much. After all, they were working toward the same dream of a happy marriage. Michael and Edna were contemplating marriage. Edna realized that her family was right with the world and with God. That meant she had the freedom to make her decision without considering the opinions or consequences to the rest of her family.

As for Sheila, she had quite by accident met the man who could make her life complete. She and Jacob agreed to date for a period not less than six months to find out if at the end of that time, they were still interested in each other. Meanwhile, Jacob promised himself to take her to all the places she couldn't afford to go during the time she was supporting her sons. They both loved plays and musicals, and Orchestra Hall was a dream-come-true for her. If nothing else, he said she would get to do the things she had missed out on for so many years.

Katie's mother was being discharged from the hospital next week, and her dad wouldn't be too far behind. Their health insurance provided nurses to help them at home until they were able to take care of themselves. Katie would be going back to her school, but she knew she'd miss Sam and her family. They had all been so wonderful to her. They promised to visit Katie once in a while. Just the thought of going home with her mother made her happy.

Veronica Tillman had come into the store to see Max. "I know he's a busy man, but this *is* his store. You can't tell me that he's never here. I know better."

Sheila wasn't quite sure how she should break the news to her, but she knew she had to. Max wouldn't have a minute of peace if Veronica wasn't told. "I told you that he isn't here. I --"

"I don't believe you," her voice was cold and hard. "I demand to see him."

"I can't make him materialize, Mrs. Tillman."

"Then tell me where he is. I'll go to him."

"I somehow don't think he'd appreciate your doing that right now."

"Just tell me where he is," she demanded.

Sheila took a deep breath. "Max and Peggy Swenson are at the church--"

She'd lost her patience. "Which church?" she demanded.

"Grace Church on Spring Lane." Sheila watched as Veronica turned and started to leave. She raised her voice. "Max and Peggy are being married as we speak."

Veronica stopped in her tracks. "Married?" Veronica fell into a chair and for probably the first time in her life, was speechless. After she had recovered from the shock, she cried and said life wasn't fair.

Sheila almost felt sorry for the woman. "On the contrary," she said kindly. "God has a plan for everyone."

Veronica Tillman shook her head, unable to accept what she'd heard. She backed out of the store, vowing never to come back. It was then that George Collins, the salesman who had approached Max with an unacceptable offer, was coming in. Veronica bumped into him. She instantly recovered, smiled and introduced herself to him.

Sheila thought it looked like she gave him her phone number before she left. By the time George asked to see Max, Sheila noticed that there was something different about him. He carried himself proudly, unlike the last time she'd seen him.

"I came by to thank him," he said with a smile. "Your boss told me to come back when I was with a reputable company, and that's exactly what I did. Most guys threw me out of their stores, but Max Madison didn't. He took the time to point me in the right direction. When do you expect him?"

She shook her head. "He just got married."

George looked at the piece of paper Veronica had given him. "I think I'll stick around the area for a while. I just met the nicest lady."

Sheila almost choked trying to hold back the laughter that threatened to come out in a roar. Although she knew she was being less than charitable, she was sure that Mrs. Tillman's reaction was part of God's plan, for He had a plan for everyone. God was all-knowing. He was a wise God, a patient God, and a most merciful God.

ABOUT THE AUTHOR

▼

Margot always had a talent for creativity, if not writing a novel or poetry, she was composing music or creating dishes in the kitchen. Rarely did she sit idle, and when she did, her life felt out of kilter. She has composed and published many pieces of music for piano as well as voice. Many of her pieces, written under the name Margot Vesel, were presented at Schmidt's New Materials Music Clinics. She taught music in school as well as teaching piano, organ and voice privately. She later accepted the position as organist at a Federal Correctional Institution. Deciding which avenue of creativity is more important to her is almost too difficult to decide.

Margot Vesel Rising has published seven novels, each dealing with personalities she has found fascinating through the years. Along with working in the prison system and becoming acquainted with the inmates, living in apartments for the past thirty years has allowed her to become acquainted with many people, each unlike any other. That in itself is fascinating. She tries to bring personalities like those into her writing.